OF FIRE AND WATER

USA TODAY BESTSELLING AUTHOR

CAMEO RENAE

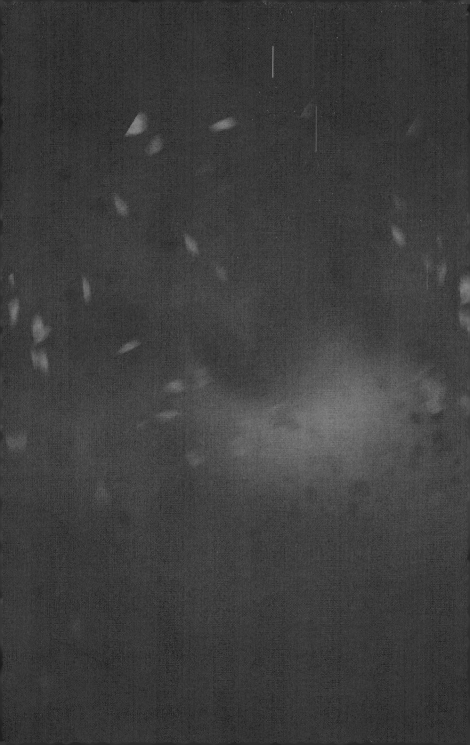

OF FIRE AND WATER

2

HEIR OF BLOOD AND FIRE

USA TODAY BESTSELLING AUTHOR

CAMEO RENAE

MORE BY CAMEO RENAE

In My Dreams
In My Reality

-

HIDDEN WINGS SERIES
Hidden Wings
Broken Wings
Tethered Wings
Gilded Wings
Wings of Vengeance

-

MIDWAY NOVELS
Guarding Eden
Saving Thomas
Dominating Dom

-

AFTER LIGHT SAGA
ARV-3
Sanctum
Intransigent
Hostile
Retribution

-

Misteria

This is dedicated to the readers.

Because you bring our stories to life.

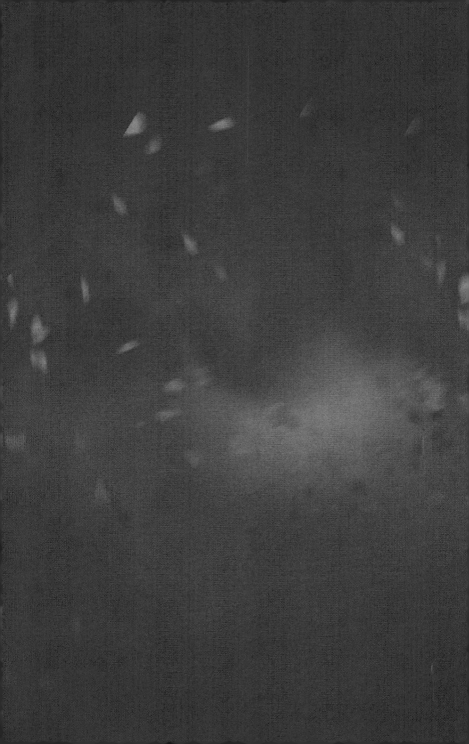

CHAPTER ONE
KINGDOM OF INCENDIA

A cool breeze tousled my hair as we anchored in an alcove just off the island of Incendia. I stood on the deck of *The Damned*—my unsteady home over the past few weeks—and breathed in the balmy, salt air. Directly in front of us was a small patch of beach with velvety white sand that stretched between rocky formations on either side. Beyond that, toward the center of the island, I could see a forest of lush trees which fronted a towering mountain that, to me, appeared like a tall palace.

Was that where the Fire Goddess lived?

My eyes scanned the empty shoreline, wondering if I'd see any sign of life. There were none that even my heightened eyesight could spot, aside from the birds and a few furry creatures scurrying about.

After barely surviving the rough weeks at sea, I'd never been happier to see solid ground. The daily seasickness made me never want to step foot on another ship again. If I could help it.

I was grateful for the escape Captain Sebastian Salloway had given us.

We hadn't seen Nyx since she'd left, but I swore I caught traces of Trystan's scent in the breezes. A scent which warmed my insides and made my blood stir, and I often found myself wandering alone on deck, craving to catch even the slightest hint of it.

A sense of peace eased and settled into my bones, knowing Trystan had seen me through Nyx's eyes. That he knew we were heading to Incendia.

I often wondered about my best friend, Brynna, who was now in Trystan's care. She was tangled in Roehl's deadly web because of me, and I had a constant ache in my gut, wondering if she'd finally found out her parents were dead. I knew she'd have questions, and Brynna would demand answers. I hoped they were strong enough to handle her.

The only thing holding my brokenness together was that I had seen my mother in the In Between. I'd had the chance to speak to her and say goodbye. I was also given the knowledge that even in the afterlife, she loved me and was still watching over me and my father.

Keeping my back to the deck, I wiped away the tears and gathered myself. I didn't want anyone else seeing me distraught.

From the ship, Incendia reminded me of a picture hanging on my parent's wall back in Sartha. My mother had brought it back from one of her trips to Merchant Port, and after she'd hung it, I often found myself standing in front of it, studying it, wanting to sink my toes in the golden sand, or swim in the crystal blue water, or lay under the beaming golden sun.

Deep inside, even as I looked at the tropical paradise before me, I knew I would never enjoy freedom. Not while Roehl was alive. By now, he must have known the bond between us had been broken, and once he found out I'd escaped his heavily warded cell, with help of his head guard, his rage would follow us to the ends of the world. He'd hunt me and Markus. We were both certain of it.

Roehl was an asshole with a power trip. A pompous prick who would easily sink his teeth into and rip out the throat of anyone who made him feel weak or question his authority. Now that the spell he'd placed over his father had been broken, there would be nothing to stop him from hunting us.

I could almost feel the thickness of his hatred roiling through the atmosphere, heading toward us like a dark, ominous cloud. Roehl's gift was powerful and extremely dangerous. His magic came easy. It was ancient and dark.

This made it vital for me to learn about my powers so I could fight back. Right now, he had the upper hand and was much stronger than me. We both knew that if he came right now, I wouldn't be strong enough to fight him. I had to find a way to survive and keep everyone I loved safe.

The fact we'd made it to Incendia was a dream and a nightmare.

I closed my eyes and envisioned the horrible events that took place on this beautiful island. The inhabitants of Incendia were said to have been destroyed by the Kingdom of Morbeth. The same wicked ruler who was also my ancestor.

The thought made my stomach roil and bile push up my throat. How could someone be so cold? How could a man attack a kingdom who'd borne his grandson?

Psychopathic, murderous prick.

I sucked in another deep breath, and in my bones, felt a stirring, knowing that there were answers here. Answers to help me understand who my ancestors were and the magic they possessed. Magic I now possessed.

We waited for the sun to set before we disembarked *The Damned,* knowing Markus wasn't immune to sunlight. Sabine had also been suffering a horrible bout of seasickness, so he remained inside the cabin with her while she rested.

Sebastian had been an entertaining, generous host, and I would be lying if I said I wouldn't miss his playful banter. He kept my whirlwind of a mind occupied and fed my thirst, and it was something I would never forget.

I felt terrible that he had lost a few of his crew members to the Sangerian sea serpent, but most had survived and managed to repair any damages to the ship. They celebrated the triumph and survival nightly, and I was shocked at the seemingly endless supply of alcohol *The Damned* possessed. Then again, they were pirates, known for their brew and unruly behaviors, and I'd grown accustomed to them all.

As the sun disappeared on the horizon, my heart thrummed loudly in my chest, knowing that once I stepped off this ship, I would be undertaking an entirely new adventure, and was glad I wasn't alone. I was thankful Markus and Sabine were with me. They had become my most trusted friends and allies.

As the last bits of light slipped beneath the horizon, Markus and Sabine exited the cabin and made their way toward me. Sebastian and his crew lined the deck to see us off.

The Captain of *The Damned* looked dashingly handsome, donned in his full captain garb. The wind tousled the stray locks of his hair, while the rest was tied behind his neck. When I reached him, he gave me a broad smile and took my hands in his.

"Twas nice to have met an incredible mystery as yourself, dearest Calla, and to have shared quite an adventure with you and your friends." Sebastian pressed his warm lips to my cheek. "You've kept my crew on their toes and gave us some much-needed excitement." The upturn of his lips and the sly gleam in his eyes spoke clearly.

I felt my cheeks heat, then smiled at him and bowed my head. "Captain Salloway, we are forever indebted to you and your crew for delivering us safely to our destination."

Sebastian smiled widely, his sea-blue eyes crinkling on

the sides. "My ship and my crew will be forever in your debt and will always be available should the need arise. If we are within the area."

Inside, I felt a small pang of sadness, wondering if I would ever run across this handsome pirate again. "Thank you, Sebastian."

He bowed at the waist, his soft lips touching the back of my hand. "If you happen to see King Romulus again, please give him my regards."

"I will." I said, watching him take a step and cringe in pain. I reached out and grabbed his arm, wishing there was a way I could help him since he was injured saving me. "Please be sure to rest, Sebastian. After all, you are mortal."

He let out a laugh. "That, I am. The crew and physician will make certain of my quick recovery. They know they won't last long under my father's supervision."

I smiled and nodded. "Then, it's good to know I'll be leaving you in good hands."

"Not as good as yours," he winked, "but at this point, I can't be picky."

After bidding our farewells to Sebastian and the crew, we disembarked his ship, and after days of celebration, it was hard to say goodbye.

However, I was thankful to finally be off the sea and so was Sabine, who hadn't been able to keep any food or water down from the seasickness. Because of it, I refused to take any blood from her, or Sebastian, who was also healing.

It had been a few days since I'd fed. I was feeling a little weak but would never admit it to anyone. This was my curse and my burden to bear.

As soon as my feet touched Incendian soil, my blood stirred, and bones hummed with warmth. I let my head fall back and inhaled the pure and unfamiliar scents of Incendia. Even the breeze felt different here, holding a current of energy that lightly brushed against my skin, welcoming me home.

We waited on the shore until *The Damned* disappeared and all that remained was the inky black water which reflected the sparkling moon and stars above.

Standing on a small sandy shoreline, I couldn't see or hear many signs of life, aside from crickets, a hooting owl, and the wind. Under Markus's guidance, we made our way toward the center of the island.

With every step, I could feel a part of the island seeping into the souls of my feet, tingling up my legs and throughout the rest of my body. I felt stronger here, like the magic of the island was healing me.

Once we made it past the sharp rocks, we encountered a large wall of trees that seemed to reach up and touch the sky. It was the first time I'd seen trees like these. They were like a wall, thin and tightly knit together, and I wondered if we would be able to make it through.

"It's a bamboo forest," Sabine said. "Bamboo is as strong as steel."

Markus grasped one of the younger trees in his hand and snapped it in half like it was a twig. Then, in a flash, he thrust the tree through the air like a spear. The twenty-foot tree sailed out of sight.

Markus turned, eyebrows raised, and gave Sabine a crooked smile. "So much for your steel tree."

"Show off," I growled.

Sabine crossed her arms over her chest and huffed. "For your information, bamboo is not a tree. It's grass."

"Grass?" Markus growled, his brow furrowed like she was crazy.

"Yes," Sabine noted. "So, you broke a blade of grass. That's not so badass, Captain."

Markus patted one of the bamboo stumps next to him and tilted his head at Sabine. "I'd like to see you break this blade of grass."

She stepped up to him, arms still crossed, eyes narrowed into slits. "I don't kill plants, Captain. They are living things." She then pushed past him and slid through a few of the trees before Markus caught her arm and pulled her back out. They locked eyes for a few moments, then Sabine shook free from his grip.

"What?" She huffed.

A soft rumble escaped from Markus's chest. "I'm the

leader here. I'll go first. You stay in the middle, mortal. Stay close and keep your eyes open," Markus warned.

Sabine glared at him.

"You two obviously have some pent-up issues you need to work out. I'll admit, I am partly to blame for having you two stuck together in the ship's cabin those awful weeks. Why don't you just kiss and make up?"

Both Markus and Sabine's heads snapped to me, jaws dropped open, eyes wide.

I shrugged. "What? I'm not blind."

"And you obviously don't know anything," Markus bit out. "There is nothing between us."

Sabine didn't say anything, but I could see the disappointment written all over her face. Then, she blinked, and it was gone.

"He's right, Calla," Sabine muttered, a tick in her jaw. "Markus and I tolerate each other."

I shrugged. "Yeah, you both can keep believing that, but everyone else sees something different."

I watched, and even in the darkness, both Sabine and Markus blushed. Markus immediately turned and plowed his massive frame through the bamboo trees before growling four words. "Move. And stay silent."

Grump. Someone desperately needed to feed. Or maybe he needed sex. In all honesty, he was probably lacking both.

Sabine followed his path as he easily pushed the bamboo trees aside, uprooting the long, stringy roots with ease. While

9

Markus and I could see without light, Sabine couldn't, so I held a flame in my palm, out in front of me, illuminating the surrounding area.

The flame I called seemed different. Felt different. It was almost an iridescent color. It felt like the magic used to produce the flame was coming from the earth itself. I could feel the power pulsing through me. It felt raw, like there was no end to its source.

The forest remained silent, except for Markus and his path of destruction, and it felt like hours had passed when we finally pushed out of the bamboo forest and into a wide, open field. Before us lay miles of green meadow and lush hillsides.

Even though the power inside me was strong, my thirst was growing even stronger. I hadn't fed in days, and after the endless hours of traversing this non-inviting terrain, my muscles were aching. I tried to fight the hunger, but knew if I didn't feed soon, I'd be too weak to move.

Blood. It both disgusted and pleased me. It was the bane of my existence. Yet, the mere thought of the rich, crimson nectar made my mouth water and incisors lengthen.

I flashed back to a time, only months ago, when I lived a simple, quiet life. But that life had shattered in an instant, and now, after sailing weeks across a ruthless and unforgiving sea, I'd finally made it to the home of my ancestors.

I could almost picture it filled with Incendians, who once lived and thrived here. A people who received their power from the Fire Goddess.

I prayed there were answers here. Answers about my origins and my powers. I wasn't even sure if there was anyone here. Yes, I came because Leora told me I'd find answers here, but also because I felt an overwhelming pull to the island. I knew I had to be here, but for what? I still didn't know.

I'd fallen behind Sabine and Markus, who were up ahead. Sabine had asked Markus a question, and he responded in a surprisingly friendly tone. Hearing their voices gave me a sense of peace, and I was so glad I wasn't alone. I was thankful for their companionship, because I knew without them, I wouldn't be here. I owed them my life.

Alone with my thoughts, I'd fallen even more behind. The pungent smell of wet grass and the sound of a restless murmur called to me. My lips were parched, and my throat felt arid like sandpaper, so I pushed on, reaching a small creek. It would have to do until I found the nourishment my body craved.

Bending, I scooped the water into my gaunt fingers and placed it to my lips. The cool drink was invigorating, but no matter how much I consumed, it still didn't appease the thirst.

I frowned, spotting my rippled reflection in the water. My auburn hair was matted, my golden eyes had become dull, enclosed within dark circles. I was a shell of the person I used to be.

Another reflection appeared in the water directly behind me. Spinning around, my eyes landed on a young woman standing behind me, an arrow nocked in her bow, aimed directly at my forehead.

"Don't move," she ordered.

I froze, slowly raising my hands in the air.

A cloth mask covered the bottom half of the girl's face, only revealing her eyes. She wore a long golden braid over her left shoulder and was wearing a brown tunic, knickers, and boots, with a belt slung around her waist lined with sharp knives.

"Move and you die," she spoke gruffly, her eyes narrowed.

I was suddenly surrounded by at least ten men who stepped out of the shadows. Gods, they were stealthy. I hadn't even heard them.

Where the hell was Markus?

Sabine screamed and my head whipped in their direction. She and Markus were hemmed in by a few dozen raiders with arrows and swords aimed at them.

The girl who had her arrow aimed at my head made a gesture to the others, and I was immediately seized. My hands were bound behind my back, and a dark hood was placed over my head.

I didn't struggle because I had recognized the girl. She was the one I saw in Melaina's magic bowl of water. The girl with golden hair and different colored eyes—one emerald, one sapphire. Melaina said she was related to me, someone in my bloodline, so I had to play cool until things settled down and had a chance to speak to her. Maybe I could figure out exactly who she was.

Lifted off the ground, I was thrown over a broad, bulky shoulder. No one in their party spoke a word, aside from the girl, and they remained silent for their entire trek, which seemed forever.

Finally, I was pulled from the man's shoulder and dropped to the ground. I groaned, knowing my backside would be bruised. My muscles ached like hell as I tried to sit up. Then someone ripped the hood off and walked away. As my eyes adjusted to the darkness, I realized I was in a cell. Another gods-damned cell. The door clanked shut, and I heard it lock.

This cell wasn't enclosed with thick rock, like Morbeth's was. These cells were open and barred all the way around, and mine had a cot with an actual blanket and pillow. This was luxury compared to Morbeth.

"Calla?" Sabine's voice whimpered.

I hopped to my feet and ran to the bars. "Sabine? Markus?"

"What?" Markus growled. He was in a foul mood, sitting on the cot with his face buried in his hands.

"Are you both okay?" I called fire to my palm and extended my arm between the bars, more worried about Sabine since she was mortal.

"I'm fine," Sabine replied. I watched her slowly stand to her feet. She was three cells down across the hall from me. Markus was in a cell directly across from her. "Who are they?" She asked, her voice trembling.

"I think they're Incendians," I said.

"Of course, they're Incendians," Markus grumbled, standing, and grasping a couple bars, trying to forcefully bend them . . . to no avail. A deep growl rumbled in his chest as he rattled them instead. "They're assholes. That's who they are."

Marcus was a well-trained Captain of the King's guard, and this was probably the first time he'd been captured or caught off guard and thrown into an enemy's cell. That had to be messing with his head.

"Can't say I blame them. We are trespassing on their island," Sabine noted. "They don't know who we are or why we're here. They're just taking precautions. At least we aren't dead."

"You're right, Sabine," I agreed. "After all, if this was Morbeth and someone tried to sneak over the Red Wall, you'd probably do the same, right Markus?"

Markus growled. "No, I wouldn't. Because no one can sneak over the Red Wall."

"When was the last time you've eaten?" Sabine asked him.

She knew his hunger was a huge issue to his mood.

"Last night," he hissed. "I don't want to be bothered. Get some sleep. It's been a long night." He headed back over to the cot and threw his body back on it and it sunk with his weight. Then he threw a muscled arm over his eyes.

I sighed, biting back a snarky remark. I didn't want to push it with Mr. Grump. Besides, I was too tired and weak to come up with anything witty.

"Sabine, are you going to be okay?" I called.

"Yes," she answered. "I have a bed and my room isn't moving. This is much better than being at sea. Especially knowing you both are here with me."

"You always find the light in the darkness." I smiled. "I'm glad you are with me too."

I kept my flame on high until Sabine was settled in bed.

"Do you think Roehl will come after us?" she questioned. I knew it was heavy on her mind. It was weighing heavy on all our minds.

"He will," Markus answered. "And he'll not grant us mercy."

Sabine sighed loudly and pulled the blanket over her. "Goodnight," she said softly.

I closed my fingers, killing the light. "Goodnight."

Markus didn't say a word after that. I just hoped the sourpuss would be nice tomorrow. Knowing he was a vampire and head guard in Morbeth wouldn't play well in his favor. He was connected to a place that destroyed Incendia. So, we would have to keep it secret.

Maybe that was one of the many things worrying him. I knew Markus was out of his comfort zone, and the only reason he was here was because the King of Morbeth had ordered him to follow and protect me. Yet here we were . . . captured. Even I hadn't heard them approach. Those sneaky devils.

I chose not to tell Markus or Sabine about the girl with the different colored eyes. Not yet. Not when I didn't know if there were ears outside, listening to our conversations. But still, the thought of her face kept me awake. How was she related to me?

She had to have been from Leora's bloodline. Was she royalty too? She seemed to oversee the men, and they obeyed to her orders.

I settled down and although the cot was stiff, it wasn't wooden planks, and the room wasn't rocking back and forth.

Smiling, I felt happy, knowing there were survivors of Incendia. Survivors who could help me find answers and tell me more about the island and the powers birthed here.

I was back on a ship in the middle of the sea. The ship wasn't familiar and there were no crew members on board. Then, above me, a black crow circled. Nyx.

I slowly made my way around the deck when a breeze picked up and I caught his scent. That perfect blend that sent tingles across my skin and warmth to my core. When I looked around, there still wasn't a soul aboard.

"Trystan?" I called out, but there was no answer.

I knew he was here. Somewhere. I could sense his presence, his scent lingered in the air.

"Trystan!"

The sky suddenly turned a dark gray, and the air became frigid. So cold I could see the breath exit from my lips in white puffs.

Trystan's scent was gone, and as I glanced into the sky, so was Nyx.

A wave of fear crashed over me. The boat tipped from side to side as large waves crashed against it. I was in the middle of a storm, and I was the only one on this gods-damned ship.

Then, above the howling wind, a dark and horrifying voice spoke. "I am the raging storm that will hunt you across the sea. You can never outrun the wind, pet. I will find you wherever you are."

Turning, a monstrous wave, nearly 100 feet high, crashed onto the deck, swallowing me whole.

"No!" I screamed, shooting up, tears streaming down my face.

"Calla, what's wrong?" Sabine's voice echoed in the darkness. My vampire eyes adjusted quickly, and I could see her standing against her cell, looking in my direction. Markus was also on his feet, his eyes sweeping the room.

"What happened?" he asked.

"I—" I sucked in a few deep breaths, trying to calm my trembling nerves. My skin was cold, like it was real. But it wasn't. "A nightmare," I panted. "I'm sorry I woke you up."

"Remember, it's just a nightmare." Markus's voice was calm. "He's not here. I won't let him hurt you."

"*We* won't let him hurt you," Sabine added.

"Thank you," I said, settling back down, turning my back to them.

A new set of tears trickled down my face. Tears of comfort, knowing that even if Roehl did find us, I wasn't alone.

CHAPTER TWO

The next morning, we were awoken by the sounds of voices. Two men had come in, obviously not caring if we were asleep. They were wearing black uniforms with red and gold embellishments. Each had a large sword sheathed on their sides, and on their chests was a crest in gold. A crest that looked exactly like the one on my right palm—the one representing fire. It must have been the mark of Incendia.

The two men carried three steaming bowls of food and set one in front of each of our cells.

The guard who set the bowl at my door paused and looked at me. He was good looking, tall, with sharp features, brown hair, and brown eyes. The other carried a stern look with a crease between his eyes. He had blonde hair and aqua colored eyes.

"Eat up," the brash soldier spoke. "We will take you to the queen when you're done."

The queen?

I was happy to hear that. She had to have known Princess Leora.

I glanced over at Markus and stifled a laugh. His cot was pushed up against the wall, opposite where the sun was shining in. His blanket was pulled up over his head, but he was so big, his legs were sticking out.

Sabine stood and took her bowl and thanked the guard. With no expression, he bowed his head and moved back toward the guard at my cell.

At least they weren't too rude. If they were guards from Morbeth, I'd end up with multiple lacerations and bruises.

The dark-haired guard pointed to the bowl he'd set on the ground in my cell. It was oats with fresh berries, and it smelled so good. I wished I could eat it, but I couldn't.

"Could you please take it to her?" I whispered, pointing at Sabine. "I'm not feeling well this morning, and I'd hate for it to go to waste."

After a brief pause, he nodded and carried my bowl to Sabine. When he reached her cell and handed it to her, she looked at me and smiled. "Thank you," she mouthed. I nodded, glad she was able to eat and keep it down.

My stomach growled. I was hungry, but there was only one thing that could satisfy that hunger. I wasn't sure how my Incendian relatives would take to me wanting to drink their blood.

Not only that . . . what would they think if they knew I

was an heir to Morbeth?

They must have known about Leora and Romulus's tragic love story.

All-in-all, these Incendians were survivors, just like me. I just hoped they would understand and accept me. I mean, why wouldn't they? I was a direct descendent of their princess. That had to count for something.

My stomach growled loudly and the thought of having to drink someone's blood still made me a little nauseous. Maybe, after I explained everything to them, they'd let me and Markus hunt for animals. That thought made me even more sick, and I highly doubted Incendia had a blood bank for hungry vampires like Carpathia did. After all, it was vampires who destroyed their home.

I suddenly wished my Incendian gift could cure my bloodthirst. It had protected my heart and allowed me to walk in the daylight, but I couldn't eat real food. I was still part vampire, and I would have to deal with surviving off blood for the rest of my immortal life.

The guards headed for the exit. "We'll be back soon," the one with the brown hair said. His eyes were kind. Not harsh like the other guard.

A few minutes after they were gone, Sabine spoke. "Why didn't you tell them who you are?" She had set down an empty bowl and picked up the other.

I glanced down at the tattoos on my palms. "Because I'm still not sure if they will accept me. I need to feel the situation out a bit before I reveal who I am."

"Smart girl," Markus said from his bed, his eyes still closed.

"What do you think they'll do with Markus?" Sabine asked again.

"We can't tell them about Morbeth," I whispered loudly, hoping no one could hear. If they were vampires, I would be concerned. "Morbeth destroyed Incendia, so we cannot expect them to welcome anyone associated with open arms. Especially not a Captain of the Guard."

"Don't worry about me," Markus grumbled, eyes still shut. "I'm fine until I decide to leave. I need sleep anyway."

Sabine pressed her face against her bars, looking into Markus's cell. "What do you mean . . . until you decide to leave?"

A grin lifted on his lips. "It means, I can leave if I want to."

"How?" Sabine asked.

"Yeah, how?" I parroted. Was I missing something?

His arm lifted from his eyes and his head twisted until his dark eyes met mine. "I'm Captain of the King's guard. I've learned how to get out of many dire situations. This cell is a temporary place to rest my head that keeps strangers away. It'll do for now." Markus smiled, flashing his lengthened incisors.

I shook my head, knowing there was a lot I still didn't know about Markus. At least I was hopeful that if we really needed to get out of here, he could make it happen.

We also had to remember we were on an island. An island we didn't know anything about, with people we thought were long gone. I still didn't have any idea how we were going to get off Incendia. Sebastian wouldn't be coming back this way for at least a few months, and there weren't any other sailing vessels on the side of the island we'd been dropped off on.

Perhaps they were hidden to keep prying eyes from realizing anyone was still alive on Incendia. From the look of those who captured us, along with the guards who brought us food, the islanders seemed to be thriving.

Inside, my stomach was twisting. I was anxious to see the queen. Maybe we were also related. It seemed too good to be true, but I'd survived the deadly journey to get here, knowing there was something here for me. There had to have been a reason.

"How will we keep Markus from being taken outside?" Sabine's voice held a deep concern. "He will turn to a lump of coal."

"Ash," Markus bit. "Not coal."

"Well, you're hardheaded and definitely not soft. I think you'll turn into a big old lump of coal," she bit back.

I barked out a laugh and immediately stopped when Markus growled.

"Don't worry about me." Markus turned his back to the wall, his large frame making the cot sag.

"I'll think of something," I sighed. "The last thing we need is two dead guards and for us to become Incendia's most wanted. There is nowhere to hide on an island they know every inch of."

"I agree with Calla," Sabine added. "Markus, just pretend like you're sleeping."

"I don't have to pretend," he grumbled. "Keep it down."

Sabine and I glanced at each other and shook our heads. My stomach rumbled and growled, demanding to be fed. I'd gone weeks without consuming anything but water in Morbeth's dungeon. Yet, I was still alive. A few days wasn't going to kill me.

The same guards returned a few hours later, and much to my surprise, I'd fallen back asleep. I was glad for the time I didn't have to worry about the hunger. But as soon as I opened my eyes, it was back with a vengeance.

"Fold your hands behind you and press your back against the bars," the blonde guard with aqua eyes ordered. I did as he said, wanting to keep this as civil as possible.

"My friend isn't feeling well," I lied. "He had a fever when we left the ship and now, he feels nauseous. He tried to get out of bed but was too weak."

Lies. All lies. Markus could stand just fine. He chose not to.

"I will call our healer," the dark-haired man replied.

"No, a few sailors had the same thing. The ship's doctor ordered bedrest and in a few days they were fine." More lies.

The two guards glanced at each other.

"Fine. We'll leave him here," the light-haired one spoke.

I let out a deep sigh of relief. It worked, and I knew they

were more than happy to leave him. Because even lying on his cot, presumably sleeping, Markus looked intimidating.

"Are you sure he won't require a healer?" the guard behind me asked.

"No," I replied. "Just a few days' rest."

I was a bit shocked the guard offered the help of a healer. It was never offered help in Morbeth—no matter how close to death I came. But that's how Roehl operated. He wanted me to suffer to the point I would give up.

Eventually, I did give in. When death lingered at the door, but never entered because of my immortality.

I hated myself for giving in, but I had no other choice. Giving up gave me freedom from the cell.

That series of unfortunate events led me here. I had to remember I was playing a dangerous game with the one who invented it.

Hopefully, with Romulus back on the throne, changes would be made. But one thing remained. Roehl was out there, alive, and that made me afraid. Not afraid that he could kill me, because I knew he could, but because he could hurt or kill the people I cared about. The people around me.

The bastard had taken my mother, without remorse, and I had every intention of repaying him for that. I still had a lot to learn. Roehl was powerful. He'd had years of practice, mastering his powers and the magic of the dark arts. I had just received mine. It was still raw and untamed and almost cost me my life. I did find that the more I used it, the weaker I became. It drained me, and I wasn't sure if exerting too much power could kill me.

Hopefully, after our meeting, I could get some answers.

After the guards bound our wrists behind our backs, they led Sabine and I to the exit.

Markus had stayed silent and still as we left but was listening to everything that was said. I knew he wanted to keep me protected, as his King had ordered him, but he would die if he stepped into the sunlight. Besides, this was something I had to do on my own. With what little I'd already learned, I could protect Sabine. I just hoped that the Incendians and their queen would hear me out. An Incendian vampire.

But I wouldn't get my hopes up. We were outsiders who would have to gain their trust.

As soon as we stepped outside, we were greeted with a stunning view. All around us was lush greenery, tall trees, and flowers blooming in hues my eyes had never seen before.

Fall hadn't touched Incendia yet. The air was warm, and the sun sat high in the sky. The heat on my skin was like a comforting hug. I hoped the reception with the queen was just as warm.

We were led down a dirt pathway, enclosed by trees, but soon came to a large stone wall. Two guards stood at the entrance, and through the gate I could see hundreds of rooftops of homes inside the wall. There was a cobbled path that led up to a huge dwelling built into the mountain. It was their palace. This must have been where the Incendian's lived, and it was beautiful.

I glanced behind, noticing their prison was outside the wall. That was strange, but also good for Markus. There would be fewer prying eyes.

"I thought Incendia was destroyed," Sabine exhaled.

The dark-haired guard glanced at me. "It was. This is the new Incendia."

"New Incendia?" I breathed. "How many Incendians survived the attack?"

"Don't answer them," the light-haired guard replied. "How do we know they aren't spies?"

"If we were spies, which we aren't, we will probably be executed anyway," Sabine huffed. "It wouldn't hurt to answer the questions. Where would we go with the answers, anyway?"

"Why did you come to Incendia?" the light-haired guard asked. "No one comes here. Not unless they want to die."

"Well, I don't want to die," Sabine rebutted. "I came here to find out for myself if the rumors were true. I wanted to see if Incendia was destroyed and its people extinct."

The dark-haired one spoke. He seemed to be the nicer of the two. "There were a few hundred who survived. They rebuilt and repopulated the Kingdom of Incendia. It's now even greater than before. Morbeth thought they defeated us, but Incendians don't easily die. We fight and we survive." His words were filled with pride.

I smiled and couldn't help but feel proud for them too. They were strong and resilient. They were survivors.

"Did someone send you here?" the dark-haired guard asked, keeping his stride. His eyes were kind, and it was hard not to tell him the truth. If I did, maybe he could help me.

"No," Sabine replied. She wasn't sent by anyone. She had traveled with me, so she wasn't lying.

Would they believe that the former Princess of Incendia sent me? That I was her heir and given her power and bore the marks of Incendian royalty?

Right now, I would stay quiet, and was thankful for the gloves covering my palms.

They led us past the guards onto a cobbled path that led through the center of the town. We passed dozens of homes where inquiring eyes watched our every move. Children playing on the streets stopped and there were whispers all around us.

I held my head high as we came upon a small marketplace filled with vendors selling fresh fruit, vegetables, and even clothing and shoes. As we were led down the center, everyone, adults, and children, stopped and stared. I could feel the weight of their stares. We were outsiders and by the scowled looks on their faces, they weren't happy to see us.

My enhanced vampire hearing let me eavesdrop on their whispers. They wondered who we were, and how we arrived on Incendia. Some were frightened, wanting to know if there were others like us. Most didn't like us being here.

They all stayed back as the guards continued to lead us up the winding cobbled path toward the palace. When we reached the palace entrance, six more guards, dressed exactly like ours, were stationed directly in front.

"Where's the third prisoner?" The largest guard asked.

"He's ill," the dark-haired guard answered. "Asleep in the cell."

"The queen won't be happy," the other guard growled.

The dark-haired guard stepped aside and motioned in the direction of the cells. "Well, if you want to go and fetch him, by all means."

Sabine and I glanced at each other, while inside, I said a silent prayer to the gods that they would leave Markus alone. If they went to retrieve him, things would end badly. For them. He was sleep deprived, grumpy, and hungry.

The large guard considered what my guard had said, then waved them through. "You explain it to the queen."

The dark-haired guard quickly grabbed my forearm and pulled me forward. I was glad he didn't want to linger.

"What's your name?" I asked him.

His eyes met mine before he softly spoke, "Everett."

I smiled at him. "It's nice to meet you, Everett. I'm Calla."

He didn't show much expression, but there was a slight upturn on his lips. I didn't expect him to smile back. He was a guard, so I understood his position.

We entered a large circular courtyard. White marbled stones on the ground spiraled from the center outward, creating a beautiful pattern. Around the courtyard were manicured hedges and more wildflowers. We walked through the courtyard and came to large wooden doors that opened into the palace.

Two more guards were stationed outside the doors and greeted Everett and the other guard as they swung the doors open. The inside of the palace was magnificent. All the floors were made of white marble, as were the stairs leading to the upper floors. Beyond the white marble, the walls were gray stone. It must have been where they carved through the mountain.

"This way," Everett said, taking us to the right. We wove through a few corridors before coming to another room with large wooden doors. As we entered, six more guards were stationed at the back of the room. There were a dozen others, without uniforms, standing in front of them. At the front of the room, sitting on a large white throne was a woman dressed in a red gown. Atop her head was a golden crown inset with red gems. She had long dark-brown hair and dark eyes that almost appeared black.

"Bring them," she said, her voice low and harsh.

As we walked forward, one of the people standing at the front turned to me. It was the girl with the different colored eyes whose eyes were glaring, as were all the others in the room.

The guards brought us before the queen and then stepped to the side. Sabine and I both bowed our heads.

The queen glanced between the two of us. "Wasn't there three of them?" she asked in a loud, clipped tone.

"Yes, my queen," Everett answered. "But the male is ill with fever. He's asleep in the cell."

The queen's eyes narrowed. "Next time I give an order, you obey it. I don't care if someone is dying. If I tell you to bring them, you drag their body to me."

Everett and the other guard bowed. "Yes, my queen," they both replied.

The queen's dark eyes fell on me. "I think the one question on all of our minds is . . . why are you on our island?"

Sabine looked at me and then at my hands, her eyes telling me to show them, but I wasn't about to blurt out that I was Incendian royalty. I needed to feel them out first. I didn't know them, and they didn't know me.

The queen's eyes bounced from me to Sabine, but Sabine kept her head down and her mouth closed.

I straightened my back and looked directly at her. The queen was pretty, but there was a sternness in her eyes.

"Well? Is someone going to answer me?" Her brow was crumpled now, eyes narrowed.

My heart hammered against my chest wondering what I should do. There was only one thing for me to do. I had to tell the truth, whether they believed it or not.

CHAPTER THREE

"We aren't here to cause any trouble, and we definitely aren't spies," I began. "We're here because we escaped from Morbeth and are seeking refuge."

Gasps and whispers erupted around the room.

"Morbeth?" the queen spat. "Those wicked blood sucking bastards?" Her icy glare landed on me. "Why would you seek refuge here? What have you done?"

I stood tall, unwavering. "The Prince wants to kill me because I am of Incendian blood."

The room burst with gasps and whispers again.

"Quiet!" the queen yelled, and everyone fell silent. "And how do we know this is true? I know every Incendian who survived the attack from Morbeth. They and their descendants reside within these walls. None have left."

"Two left," I said softly. "A handmaiden and an infant boy." I then paused, knowing that my next words would rock their world. "The child was Princess Leora's son, Nicolae."

Something in the queen's demeanor changed. It was hardly noticeable, but I saw the slight widening of her eyes, the furrow in her brow, the arch in her back, and the way her grip tightened on the sides of her throne.

There was no way I was going to tell her I was part vampire. Not now. Not while the vein in the middle of her forehead still throbbed after the mention of them. There would come a time when she would find out the truth. If she knew that I was related to Leora's son, she would also know that I had King Romulus's blood as well.

"How would she know about Princess Leora?" one of the males standing behind me asked.

"She's lying," a woman shouted. "She's never been to Incendia. No one has ever seen her. How could she know this?"

My insides heated, but I knew this outcome could have been a possibility. I was an outsider. Leora would've wanted me to be strong. I was her heir. I was the one she bestowed her power to. I couldn't be afraid of them or what they could do to me.

I straightened my back and held my head up high. "Unbind me, and I'll show you."

The room hushed as the queen's eyes moved to one of the guards. After offering him an approving nod, he instantly stomped toward me and unbound my wrists.

Sabine offered me a comforting smile. Having her with

me helped a great deal. I gently tugged off my gloves and tucked them into my belt.

Turning my palms upright, I called to the magic inside me, and instantaneously, fire appeared and danced in both my palms. I lifted them up for everyone to see.

Eyes flew wide. But not as wide as the queen's, so I fisted my hands and snuffed out the flames. Then I held out my palms to reveal the tattoos.

"She's Incendian royalty," one of the women proclaimed. "How is this possible?"

"Witch!" another called out.

Every eye turned to the queen, but her eyes were on me, her expression unreadable.

"How is this possible?" the queen added, almost in a breathless whisper.

I placed my palms down to my sides. I just needed to prove I wasn't a liar. I didn't want to rub the fact I was royalty in the queen's face. She didn't know who I was, and if she didn't trust me, or if I got on her bad side, it could lead to a lot of troubles for me and my friends.

"Who are you?" the queen spoke again in a thundering voice, her fists slamming down on the sides of her throne. I had to give her an answer.

"I am a descendant of Princess Leora. Her son Nicolae, is my grandfather."

Gasps and chatter erupted around the room. "Leora and her son died," a female voice declared.

"Yes, they did die," a rough voice exclaimed. "Morbeth slaughtered all the royals."

"Nicolae didn't die," I replied. "He was sent away with Leora's handmaiden before Morbeth attacked Incendia."

"Lies!" a few members of the crowd roared. The queen allowed their voices to be heard.

A burly man strode forward and glared at me. "If you are Nicolae's granddaughter, you are likewise an heir of Morbeth. You are one of those demons," he spat.

The room went dead silent again, all eyes on me.

"I am a descendant of Morbeth, just as much as I am from Incendia. But my mother was mortal." I stared at all the confused and bitter faces around me. "Trust me when I say I don't want anything to do with Morbeth, where I was tortured and starved in a cell. I never want to step foot in their country again." Tears welled in my eyes reliving memories of what I had suffered. "I would be dead if it weren't for my friends. They rescued me and helped me escape to Crimson Cove. We boarded a ship that carried us here."

"Why would you come here?" A woman screeched from the crowd. "Why Incendia, when you know what they did to us?"

"Princess Leora said this would be a safe place to come and learn about my gifts. I won't stay long and put your island at risk. I just need to get some answers, and then we'll go."

"She does bear the marks of Incendian royalty. She is Princess Leora's heir," another female voice declared.

I turned to the queen, but her face remained impassive.

The queen slowly rose to her feet, and the room fell silent once again. She motioned to the guard Everett. "Take them to the guest rooms and see to it that the handmaidens draw them baths and give them clean clothes."

Everett bowed at the waist. "Yes, my queen."

The queen then looked at me and smiled. It was a sweet smile. Also, a smile that sent a shiver down my spine. "You and your friends will dine with me tonight. Then, I will see if I can answer any of your questions."

I suddenly felt as if a huge weight had lifted off my shoulders. The queen was allowing us freedom. We weren't going to rot in a cell or be executed, and she was going to help me. Or so it seemed.

"Thank you," I said, and really meant it. This could have gone entirely wrong, but things seemed like they were taking a turn for the better.

Everett came and stood next to me. "Please, follow me."

I bowed to the queen before we left, and Sabine did the same. The queen gave a serious nod, and as we left, voices began murmuring. They were talking about us. About me and my marks and the fact I was still one of Morbeth's creatures.

Everett stayed quiet as he led us back toward the large staircase. There were so many questions twisting in my mind. I wanted to know if the queen bore the same marks of royalty on her palms. I couldn't tell because she also wore gloves and kept her palms face down.

Everett led Sabine and I up the marbled stairs. On the way, he stopped one of the servants and told her what the queen had ordered before he continued up another flight of stairs. When we reached the third floor, Everett took a left, and walked down another hallway. As soon as we came to the first door, he stopped.

"This room is yours," he said looking at Sabine.

Her eyes went wide. "I have my own room?"

"Yes," he replied. "The servants will be up shortly to run your bathwater."

Her hands shot up in front of her. "No, it's okay. I can run my own bath."

I grasped her wrists and shook my head. "You're free, Sabine. Let them do this for you. You deserve it."

She slowly nodded her head as tears filled her eyes. "Thank you, Calla. I don't know if I could ever get used to being served."

This was probably the first time she had someone catering to her. She'd been a servant most of her life.

The smile on her lips and the tears falling from her eyes, spoke a thousand words. She was free. Free, and I was going to make sure she'd never be enslaved again.

"This way, Calla," Everett said.

"I'll see you later." I gave Sabine a smile as she wiped the tears on her cheeks. At least she was smiling, and they were happy tears.

Everett took me to a room a few doors down from

Sabine's and stopped before stepping to the side. "If you need anything, just ask one of the servants." He was about to turn around and walk away but paused and looked directly at me. "Are you truly Incendian royalty?" he asked in a soft whisper.

I nodded and showed him the tattoos on my palms. His eyes studied each one. Then, he placed his fist over his heart and took a knee. "You are the rightful heir to Incendia. You are the true queen," he said.

I was stupefied and quickly grabbed his arms and pulled him back up. "No. No," I said, shaking my head. "I'm not. You already have a queen."

Everett stood to his feet, brow furrowed. "Not our true queen. She's—" he paused as footsteps came up behind us.

A servant girl wearing a white smock came down the hall, holding a set of towels in one arm and a basket of toiletries in the other.

Everett bowed his head. "If you are ever in need of anything, please let me know." He then pivoted and walked away.

I stood there wondering what the hell he was going to say. What did he mean when he said she was not their true queen? I hoped he didn't mean that because I bore the marks of Incendian Royalty, that I would become their queen. Because that wasn't going to happen. I didn't want the burden or responsibility of ruling any kingdom.

Besides, I was having a hell of a time trying to keep myself alive.

The servant girl walked up to me and curtseyed. She appeared around the same age as me, maybe a year or two younger, with strawberry-blonde hair that was tied up into a bun, and bright green eyes. I could tell she was nervous, or shy, because her eyes never really met mine.

"I'm here to draw your bath, miss," she said, her eyes glancing toward the bedroom door.

"Oh, I'm sorry." I quickly turned the knob and swung the door open.

She smiled and made her way inside and I followed.

The room was huge and open. Light poured in from the two large windows that overlooked the town below.

The bed was much larger than the one I had in Morbeth. The furnishings, bedding, and drapery were all color coordinated in deep reds and golds. The walls were painted in light cream.

This room was luxurious. My heart ached knowing my mother would have died to have a room decorated like this.

In the corner of the room was a small sitting area with plush chairs and a dresser with a large round mirror hanging above it.

This was a room fit for a queen, and it made me wonder if all the guest rooms were decorated this way. By the look on Sabine's face, it must have been equally wonderful, and that made me happy.

How did they get all these expensive furnishings? Did they also travel to Merchant Port to barter?

I heard water running inside the room the girl had disappeared into. Walking toward the sound, I stepped into the bathing room. It was half the size of my cottage back home. A large, clawfoot tub sat in the center, and against another wall was a table where the girl was arranging all the shampoo and soap bottles from her basket. I couldn't wait to use them, because right now, I smelled horrendous. Which was probably why the queen requested we bathe before dinner.

After the tub was filled, I told the servant girl she could leave.

At first, she stood there, brow crumpled, like she was planning on staying to help me. I assured her I could bathe myself and that I preferred to be alone. She was satisfied with my request and said that she'd be back later with a new change of clothes.

"What's your name?" I asked before she left.

"Fern," she replied.

"Thank you, Fern." Her eyes widened, like she was surprised. "It's nice to meet you."

She smiled and bowed her head, her eyes averting me. "It's nice to meet you too, miss," she said softly before shuffling out the door.

Sloughing off my dirty clothes, I wondered about Sabine and how she was faring with her servant. I had a feeling she'd probably sent hers away as soon as she set up her bathing soaps. Sabine was strong willed and liked to do things on her own, but I wanted her to experience a better life. A life where she was pampered for a change. Sabine had been there for me from the moment I met her. I vowed to make it up to her, even if it took the rest of my life.

Sinking deep into the steamy water, it felt amazing. Its warmth hugged my tired achy body, letting me finally relax. I laid my head back and closed my eyes. Then I remembered — Markus.

Was he still in their cell? I hoped Everett would let him sleep—or pretend to sleep—until after dark. I knew it would only be a matter of time before they found out what Markus was. The massive guy that slept during the day.

I took my time scrubbing my hair and body, and when I was done, smelled like a bouquet of flowers.

As I finished my bath and wrapped a clean towel around me, there was a knock at the door.

"Come in," I hollered.

Fern entered with a bundle of clothes in her arms. She laid out a gold dress on the bed and set a pair of sandals on the ground, which was probably for my dinner with the queen. She then placed another set of folded clothes in the dresser.

"Someone will deliver lunch to your room soon, and I'll come back for you when dinner is ready," she said, then turned to leave.

"Wait." I quickly gathered my dirty clothes and wrapped them in the cloak Sabine had given me. "I know these look and smell like they should be thrown away, but I'd really like to get them washed and have them back."

She strode over and took the bundle from me. "I will immediately take them to the launderer, and have them back to you by morning, cleaned and pressed." She strode over and took them from me.

"Thank you, Fern."

"Don't thank me, miss. It's my duty." She smiled, bowed, and before I could say anything, she exited the room.

I walked over to the bed and lifted the dress. It was beautiful. A sleeveless, double layered, floor-length gown. The first layer was a muted gold, and over it was a translucent fabric that had gold glitter over it in shapes of flames.

I wondered what kind of dinners they had around here. I wasn't going to complain. I was a guest here and would now have to play by their rules.

And I still couldn't believe that I was here, in Incendia, and that maybe, some people here could be related to me.

Was I related to the queen? Maybe I'd find out the answer to that question at dinner.

My stomach growled loudly. I was hungry and knew I wouldn't be able to eat any food they served for dinner. Because no matter how wonderful it would taste or smell, I would be sick if I took a bite.

The plus was that Sabine would get to eat, but Markus and I had to find a way to get blood. Maybe he could find a safe and discreet way for the both of us to feed. It would be hard. We were amongst people who hated vampires, especially ones connected to Morbeth.

There were so many questions stirring in my mind. I had to relax and remember to breathe and figure out a way to deal with things as they presented themselves. Because maybe, just maybe, nothing would go wrong, and I was worrying for nothing.

Everett didn't seem to mind, and he was in the room when it was revealed I was part vampire. Besides, I knew I could take care of myself if I had to. And between Markus and me, we would be able to keep Sabine safe.

I looked at the cozy bed filled with pillows that looked as soft as clouds. They were beckoning me to come. I was tired and hadn't had a decent night's sleep in weeks, so I ambled over to the bed and sat on the edge. It was soft. So incredibly soft.

Maybe if I took a nap, the thirst would disappear for a little while.

Pulling back the covers, I slipped under the blanket and laid my head on the billowy pillow. This bed was even more comfortable than the one I had back in Sartha.

And before I knew it, I fell fast asleep.

CHAPTER FOUR

A rapping on the door woke me.

The world outside had darkened, but my room was dimly lit from a few lanterns placed on the nightstand and desk. There was a fire cracking in the fireplace.

I'd fallen asleep. A sleep so deep that I didn't hear whoever had come in and set the lanterns there.

Did I miss dinner?

Another soft knock snapped me from my thoughts. "Come in," I said, my voice weak and crackly.

The door opened and Fern stepped in. "I'm sorry to wake you, Miss, but dinner will be served in an hour."

"Thank you, Fern," I said, stretching my arms over my head. At least I didn't miss it.

Fern paused at the threshold. "If you don't mind, I've brought someone to help get you ready for dinner."

I threw my legs over the edge of the bed and stood. "Of

course, come inside."

Fern motioned to someone outside the door, and another servant girl stepped inside with a basket full of things. I slipped out from under the blankets and carried the gown into the large washroom and laid it on one of the counters.

She pulled out a chair from a small table that had a large round mirror in front of it and motioned for me to sit. I did as they said, and the two of them worked on me. They used powders on my face and kohl on my eyes and pulled my hair up into a bun with intricate braids. I had no doubt they'd done this many times before.

When they were done, they helped me put on the gown, and it fit like a glove.

"You look beautiful, Miss," Fern said, bowing again.

"Please, call me Calla."

"Yes, Miss." She bowed her head and then her eyes went wide, looking at me. "I'm sorry," she paused.

"Don't be sorry. I prefer Calla. It's what my friends call me." She and the other girl glanced at each other with widened eyes. "That goes for both of you."

A grin grew on Fern's lips. "Thank you. We'll leave you now, but Everett will be up shortly to escort you to dinner." With that, they both bowed and hurried out the door.

I stood in front of the mirror and looked at myself. Aside from the growling in my stomach, I was no longer the corpse girl I was in Morbeth. My skin was a little tan from being on the sea and the gown shimmered as I twisted. It almost looked like a dancing fire.

Another knock rapped at the door, and it had my stomach churning. It must have been Everett coming to collect me. I walked over to the door and opened it, seeing Sabine with a broad smile on her face. She looked beautiful. Her long, raven hair was braided down over her right shoulder, and she was wearing a floor-length, rust colored dress that was cinched at the waist.

"Don't we clean up nicely," she said, and gave a low curtsey. "Your highness."

I grabbed her arm and yanked her into the room, then pushed the door shut.

"Don't call me that," I scolded.

"Why not?" She shrugged with a smirk on her face. "It's the truth."

"No, it's not. Not while they have a queen on the throne. We just got here, and I don't want to make any trouble. I'm just a girl who wants to find out more about the markings on her palms, and how to control the power that came with them. Then, we'll be on our way."

"Those aren't just any markings," Sabine sighed, her eyes glancing down at my palms, which started to feel sweaty. "They are marks of royalty, passed down from your *royal* kin." She shook her head before heading over to the large windows and peered outside into the torch-lit streets below. "Did you see their faces?"

I made my way over and stood next to her. "Who's faces?"

"The faces of everyone in the throne room." She gave me a side-eyed glance. "They were shocked. Like, truly shocked. I mean, think about it. They just witnessed an outsider coming in with the marks of Incendian royalty on her palms, wielding fire magic. Their minds are spinning right now, and I can only imagine how many people are whispering your name throughout those streets." Her finger pointed out the window to the town inside the wall, and all the homes lit from within.

Sabine took in a deep breath and exhaled slowly. "There is something about the queen that rubs me the wrong way. I can't put my finger on it. It's just an uneasy feeling." Her eyes met mine, brow crumpled. "Just be careful what you say around her tonight. Around anyone."

I nodded, not saying a word because I felt the same thing. The last thing I wanted was to become an enemy of Incendia, or their queen. I didn't travel all this way to take her throne, or to make her feel threatened. I just needed someone to show me how I could defend myself. Because Roehl would come for me.

Another knock at the door had both Sabine and I twisting back.

"Come in," Sabine hollered. The knob turned, and the door swung open, revealing a huge dark figure standing in the doorway. "Get in and close the door," Sabine scolded.

"It's nice to see you too," Markus growled.

"Who let you out of the cage?" I asked as he made his way over to us.

Markus was dressed in long black slacks and a black tunic which was tied at his waist. He was still huge, but he didn't look like a vampire or Captain of the King's guard. He looked . . . normal. If that was even possible.

"My, my," Sabine said, her eyes skirting down his length. "You look very handsome, Captain." The Captain smiled at her, a sweet, non-scary smile that made Sabine blush.

"Where are you staying?" I asked him.

He angled his head. "Directly across the hall from you." He snickered. "I told the guard I am your guardian."

"My guardian?"

"It sounded better than your keeper."

"Maybe it's good you're across from her," Sabine muttered. "You might need to be saved."

Markus stepped directly in front of her, his dark eyes frozen on hers. "You're lucky I'm close by. These Incendians have no loyalty to you . . .to one who grew up in Morbeth."

Sabine growled and threw her arms over her chest. "And you think you can stop elementals?"

Markus chuckled. "Not all Incendian's have elemental power. Just their royals and those blood related. And to answer your question, I could take out more than my fair share."

Sabine stepped closer to me and locked her arm with mine. "I'd rather stay with Calla."

"Stubborn mortal," he growled.

I gave Markus a big toothy grin, right before another knock came to the door.

Sabine dragged me past Markus and swung open the door. Everett stood there in his full guard costume, but he smelled nice, and his hair was brushed back. He bowed at the waist and rose. "I'm here to escort you to dinner."

"Thank you," I replied.

Everett's eyes lifted, and I turned to see Markus standing right behind us.

Everett smiled and tipped his head. "Shall we?"

"We shall." Sabine replied and yanked me out the door.

We followed Everett back down the stairs, but this time took a right, heading in the opposite direction of the throne room. The wonderful aromas of meats and spices and baked goods were wafting in the air making my mouth water.

Gods, I missed the taste of food, and wondered if there would ever be a cure that would allow a vampire to consume anything besides blood. They'd been around for countless centuries, so I doubted it would happen anytime soon. But there was hope. I was living proof that miracles could happen. I was a vampire who still had a beating heart and could walk in the daylight.

"You must be hungry," Everett stated, and he was right.

"Starving, actually," I replied.

He paused his steps and waited until I was standing next to him. Markus came up right behind me, so close I could feel his body heat on my back.

"I'll make sure you get what you need for dinner," he whispered, then continued to walk.

"Thank you," I said, following him. I liked Everett and wondered if he had a family. Was he married? Did he have a wife and children? He wasn't old. Maybe late twenties, early thirties.

I picked up one thing about him. He was loyal, and loyalty was one of the greatest assets to a kingdom. Or person.

We took a turn down a hallway and came to the Great Hall. A long, polished wooden table was elegantly decorated with place settings fit for royalty. Above it was a cut-glass chandelier, and around the room, sconces were lit. It was a table fit for a queen.

Servers from the kitchen carried out roasted and salted meat—beef, pork, mutton, and foul—along with large platters filled with freshly baked bread, cheese, fruit, and vegetables. It was a magnificent feast. One Markus and I were unable to eat.

The queen stood from her seat at the far end of the table, dressed in another beautiful red gown, her lips painted the same color. Atop her head was her gold crown inset with rubies. I guess red was her thing.

"Welcome. Please have a seat," she spoke loudly, a smile on her lips that didn't seem to reflect in her eyes. "We will dine shortly."

"Thank you," I said, walking to a seat that was being held out by a tall, thin man with disheveled red hair and freckled skin. I took a seat, and he pushed me in. Sabine sat on my left and Markus on my right.

Around the table were a bunch of new faces I hadn't seen before, and a few faces I recognized from the throne room . . . one being the girl with the colorful eyes. She was sitting on the right side of the queen, staring at me.

In fact, all eyes around the table seemed to be pinned on us, and it was unnerving. I hated being the center of attention, and I was glad Sabine and Markus were with me to share some stares.

Markus cleared his throat and shifted in his seat. I could tell he was uncomfortable, and I could only imagine what he was thinking. He was a vampire guard from Morbeth, surrounded by a race his kingdom had once destroyed, and he wasn't a small man. He was tall and muscular and very menacing. I just hoped he didn't do anything rash because he was grossly outnumbered, and I didn't want to start a war with my own people.

The thought made me wonder if Markus had been alive and a part of Incendia's *almost* annihilation. That would be enough to make anyone nervous. Hell, it was making me nervous thinking he might have been part of it. Gods, why hadn't I asked him about it before?

It was obvious many Incendian's had survived, and I would love to hear that story someday. Especially knowing I was connected to them. Leora's people.

After the servers had filled the table from end to end, they stepped back against the walls, hands folded behind their backs. I counted six guards posted around the Great

Hall, including Everett, who seemed to have momentarily disappeared.

The queen rose from her chair, her hands gloved, which sucked. I wanted to know if she bore the marks.

She gave another smile that didn't seem to reach her eyes and clasped her hands in front of her.

"Tonight, friends," she began in a regal voice . . . loud and deep. "We welcome one of our own. An Incendian that has never, until recent, stepped foot on our soil. One that is not accustomed to our ways. So, we must be tolerant as we teach her *and* her friends."

I sensed something—possibly jealousy, but something not kind—seeping from her unsaid words and unsmiling eyes. Eyes that seemed to be boring into mine. Her creepy smile sent a cold chill down my spine.

I may be young, but I'm not stupid. I knew she was making sure everyone in this room knew I was an outsider, despite the marks on my palms.

All eyes were fixed on me.

I took in a deep breath and exhaled slowly, trying to soothe the growing heat beneath my skin. I wished Leora was here. Or that she could give me a sign. Any sign. Maybe say something in my head like she'd done before or let me know what I should do. Because right now, I was at their mercy.

I slid my seat back and stood. Sabine's head snapped to me, her eyes wide, probably wondering what the hell I was going to do.

I smiled and slowly bowed my head to the queen. "Thank you for accepting us and taking us in. We appreciate your hospitality and hope to learn more about Incendia and your ways." I bowed again and took my seat as the tall, freckled man appeared behind me, pushing me back in.

"Thank you." I turned and smiled at him, but he backed up to his place against the wall.

The queen raised her head and closed her eyes, and everyone at the table did the same.

"We give thanks, Goddess of Fire, for the abundance you provide."

"We give thanks," the room echoed.

And then, they all started digging in.

Short and sweet. I liked those kinds of prayers, and apparently, so did the people. I took a forkful of meat and placed it on Sabine's plate, since she seemed frozen in place. What I really wanted to do, was shove a little of everything on the table in my mouth, because, good gods, this was torture.

"Eat well," I said, giving Sabine a wink. She smiled and scooped some potatoes onto her plate, along with some bread and cheese and a ripe red apple.

"Care for a drink?" a woman asked, appearing between me and Markus holding a carafe. "It's from a friend." Her eyes darted to the far wall, and when mine followed, I noticed Everett taking a position against the wall, a smile on his face.

"Sure," I said.

She set a large, dark mug down in front of me, and began

to pour. As soon as I caught a whiff of the liquid, my incisors lengthened.

Shit! No.

I could feel my cheeks heat and ripped the napkin off the table and held it over my mouth, dabbing it ever so lightly so it didn't appear like I was trying to hide my sharp freaking teeth.

The woman then turned and casually poured, before setting a mug in front of Markus. I eyed him as he picked it up and sipped like it was a cup of coffee, all while managing to keep his incisors in place. How the hell did he do it?

"It's okay, Calla," the queen announced from her spot, nonchalantly popping a grape into her mouth. "Drink. We all know what you are."

A monster. A monster connected to the country who once destroyed them. She didn't need to say it. Everyone knew what she was referring to.

The room fell deathly silent. All eyes aimed back on me.

Heat warmed my palms and my cheeks, but I think I was more embarrassed than anything. I wasn't going to give her the satisfaction of having the upper hand on me. Queen of Incendia or not, she was being rude.

Sabine's hand gently lay over mine, like she knew I was battling some inner demons. Her touch worked. I closed my eyes and took in a deep breath, willing my incisors to retract, and gods above, they did.

I slowly opened my eyes and lowered the napkin from

my mouth, my gaze meeting the queen's. I bit my tongue, bit so hard I could almost taste blood. Then, I felt Markus's boot kick the side of my shin.

I turned to him with a wicked glare. "What?" I whispered, completely agitated.

"Have a drink, princess," he said casually. "It'll lighten your foul mood."

I growled at him, not caring who was staring. Then, I lifted the glass to my mouth and in one long pull, emptied it entirely. It was warm and sweet and holy hell, the buzz hit me hard. I steadied my shaking body, set the glass back on the table, dabbed my mouth, and then turned my attention to Markus—the only one who understood this bloodthirst—as the buzz coursed through my veins.

The challenging look in his eyes made me hold my shit together, making it easy to ride the high. As I did, his brow raised, a sly grin curled on his lips. "Feeling better?"

Closing my eyes for a moment, I gathered my trembling self together and answered. "Much."

"Good. Because everyone is watching you," he said quietly.

The room had gone unnervingly still, so I slowly turned, not surprised to see everyone staring.

"Miss Caldwell," a man sitting directly across from me addressed, breaking the awkward silence. He was older, with thinning white hair, dressed in an expensive suit. "Where are you from?"

I cleared my throat and straightened my back. "I was born and raised in Sartha."

He nodded slowly, taking a bite of meat. "Sartha is a nice country," he said. "I've been there several times myself."

"Really? For what?" I asked, the bloodgasm slowly releasing its grip on my senses.

"For business, of course," he chuckled, matter-of-factly. Others joined in.

An older woman, with whitish hair pulled up into a bun, asked, "Where are your parents, dear?"

For a moment, I swallowed the pain of that question, my eyes meeting hers.

"My mother was murdered, and my father is somewhere in Talbrinth, running for his life."

"Oh, dear. I'm so sorry." The old woman's hand clutched her heart, her eyes looked genuinely concerned.

"You've put us all in danger coming here." A burly gentleman with long blond hair and a beard stood from across the table, furthest away from the queen. The room erupted in agreement, their eyes looking to their queen, who seemed to have no readable expression on her face.

Markus flinched, but I put my hand on his thigh and patted, trying to keep the situation calm.

I hated the interrogations, but they needed to know why I was here and that I wasn't a threat. I hadn't seen most of these people in the throne room when I showed them the tattoos, so I pushed my seat back and stood. "The reason I am here is that I was recently given this gift." Despite if they thought they were real or not, I showed them my palms. Gasps erupted around the table. "I don't know much about this aside from the fact, it was born from Incendia and the Fire Goddess." I took in a deep breath. "Leora came to me during the Shadow Fest and told me I should come here to find answers. I won't stay long. The last thing I want to do is put all of you in danger. As soon as I find out how to control this power, we will leave."

I turned to the queen and thought I saw a wave of relief wash over her. "I'm sure you've heard the stories. You should know why we are fiercely protective of our land and our people. Morbeth destroyed us once, and we will not allow that to happen again," she said. "You, stepping foot on this island, has already put every citizen at risk."

Everyone agreed, except Everett, who stood still against the wall.

My heart was crushed. The Incendian's didn't care who I was. They wanted me gone.

But the queen was right. Roehl would come for me, and the longer I lingered here, they *were* in danger.

Markus stood before I could stop him. "We'll leave your walls tonight, if we must, but all we ask is for someone to teach her how to control her gift."

"I will!" The voice came from the girl who sat next to the queen. The girl with the different colored eyes. She also stood and looked at me. "I will, and I'll tell you what you need to know about Incendia."

The queen's eyes narrowed, her jaw set. "You will not, foolish girl," she scolded quietly.

The girl placed her hands on the table and leaned in toward the queen, her eyes hard. "She's here because she needs our help. She is Incendian Royalty, and I will offer her whatever she needs."

The queen's body tensed. Oh, she was pissed, especially being defied by the girl with the colored eyes, and it made me wonder how they were connected. "Fine," the queen said through gritted teeth, but the look in her eyes said something completely different. "Tomorrow you will take her to the Crag."

The girl nodded and sat back in her seat, satisfied with the queen's answer.

The Crag. That sounded ominous.

No one else asked any more questions for the remainder of the evening. Thank the gods. I sat and chatted with Sabine, living my eating fantasies vicariously through her. She moaned in delight with each bite, licked her fingers and lips, and I enjoyed every second of it. It made my heart swell to see her fed and happy.

After dinner, the queen dismissed everyone and left. She was obviously bothered and made no attempt to stay. That made my stomach turn. Why wouldn't the queen accept me?

Everett strode over to the three of us and escorted us out and that's when I noticed a small reddish stain on his inner arm.

Blood.

That's why he'd disappeared.

"Thank you, Everett," I said as we made our way out of the Great Hall.

"For what?" His brow crumpled.

"For dinner. You didn't have to."

Markus turned to him, eyes narrowed. Everett seemed unaffected by the big guy and shot me a knowing smile. "I am loyal to my queen."

I swallowed the lump in my throat and continued walking, despite whatever look I knew Markus was giving me. A look I knew would warrant questions I didn't want to answer right now.

With Sabine delivered safely to her room, Everett stood between Markus and me.

"I will be posted down the hall tonight if you need any assistance," Everett bowed to me, and as he turned to Markus and acknowledged him, I slipped inside my room and closed the door.

I was expecting a knock on my door from Markus, but his door creaked open and clicked shut. Letting out a loud and long breath, I was glad the night was finally over.

Gods, what had become of my life. I stepped up to the large window overlooking the town below. There were people down there. Hundreds and hundreds of Incendian's, that were at risk because of me.

Closing my eyes, I thought back to my small, cozy cabin in

Sartha. It was safe and comfortable and filled with everything I possessed. I missed my bed and blankets and books, but most of all, I missed my horse Shadow. He was one of the few loyal companions I'd had, and I vowed that one day I would return to claim him.

Without pause, my thoughts then shifted to Trystan, and then to my best friend Brynna.

Kylan, Brone, Feng, Andrés . . . and even Melaina. My heart swelled at the thought of them. They risked everything to come into Morbeth to save me. Risked their very lives, and that was a debt I would never be able to repay.

There was a knock at the door, so I shuffled over and twisted the knob. Markus was there. Shocking. "I can't handle any more questions tonight," I moaned.

"I can't be with you tomorrow," he said, his jaw tense. "Keep Everett close and take Sabine with you."

"Okay."

"And don't trust anyone." He leaned in close. "Especially the queen."

My eyes froze on his. "You felt it too?"

"We shouldn't stay in Incendia longer than a few days. Roehl must know there is trouble by now. It's only a matter of time before he calls on his dark mages and finds us. His fury will be unrelenting when he comes for us."

I saw a darkness in his eyes. Not of fear, but knowing that we would soon have to run or fight.

"I know." My chest and stomach tightened.

"Talk to your guard tomorrow. Ask him if there is any way we can leave this island. We have no more than a few days, Calla. And that's pushing it."

"Everett is not my guard."

"He will be when I cannot be around." Markus took a step closer. "Just be careful. Keep your eyes and ears open at all times."

I let out a deep sigh as Markus stepped back. He paused at his door. "Please make sure Sabine is safe."

"I will," I promised, giving him a knowing smile. Markus dipped his head before retreating into his room.

I had no doubt I could take care of Sabine, but the mere thought of Roehl coming to Incendia and harming, possibly killing, any of these people was —

No. I wasn't going to let that happen. There wouldn't be another attempt to destroy Incendia. Tomorrow, I would let the girl with the colored eyes take me to the Crag, wherever that was, and I'd ask her the questions battering my mind. If she could give me any tips or tricks on how my gift worked— something I could use or practice with—then we could leave.

Maybe Leora simply wanted me to come to see that Incendia was still alive and thriving. That her people weren't dead, and maybe, if I learned how to harness and use my gift, I could help protect them. Not that they needed it. They seemed to be doing fine without me.

Stripping off my gown, I laid it on the dresser before rummaging through the drawer to find a bedgown. Finding one, I slipped it over my head and headed for the bed. Even after getting nourishment from Everett, my mind was tired. I needed to sleep. I needed to shut off my mind and make this evening disappear.

Incendia wasn't what I thought it would be. They didn't welcome me with open arms. A few did, but I guess I didn't blame them. They were Leora's people. Not mine. I was just an outsider who happened to be related to their former Princess.

There had to be others with the same power as me, right? Leora had said that everyone who had royal blood, even the males, had power. Did the queen have the same markings and power as I did? Maybe she did and didn't want to share that with me.

BUT . . . if she didn't have the markings, well, that could pose an even greater problem for me. It would give her reason to worry or be jealous, even though she had no reason to be. I wouldn't be staying in Incendia, and hopefully, within the next few days, we would find a way off this island. They had to have transportation.

Until Roehl was incapacitated, Sabine, and Markus and I would be forced to live a life on the run. I wondered if there would ever come a time when Sabine would find a place to stay and live out the rest of her mortal life without worry. She'd paid her dues in Morbeth and I wanted to see her settled and happy.

Even Markus knew that standing and fighting against Roehl was inevitable. I could see it in his eyes. He knew how

CAMEO RENAE

powerful Roehl was. He'd witnessed his power firsthand, and even though he wouldn't admit it, it frightened him.

Roehl was a pureblood vampire with the gift of magic. Powerful magic that he sharply honed throughout his life, but because he felt his magic wasn't enough, he sought out that dark and forbidden magic which made him nearly indestructible.

I just wanted it all to go away for a while. I didn't want to constantly have him in the back of my mind.

I lay my head on the soft pillow and closed my eyes.

I saw a lake of water, calm and clear. The ripples across its surface were fluid, serene. Above it, a fire grew roaring and bright, its light refracting off the surface of the water. Together, they danced—fire and water—twining and swirling together. The water never quenched the fire, and somehow, each seemed to compliment the other. So different, yet so in sync. Yin and yang.

Together, flame and water lulled me to sleep. I knew it was my gift, and in my mind, thanked the Fire Goddess for them.

CHAPTER FIVE

At first light, I sat up and stretched, watching the rays of light pour in through the window. Fern, silent and stealthy, must have come in before sunrise and placed my clothes on top of the dresser, along with a canteen. My pants, tunic, cloak, and even my boots were clean and polished, so I slipped them on and quickly braided my hair.

The amulet was still affixed to my neck and Trystan's dagger, I strapped to my side, and somehow, I felt safer with them on.

I took the canteen in my hand and turned the lid. The scent of the blood hit me hard. It was the same scent as the blood I was given last night. Everett. I would have to thank him when I saw him. Hopefully, he'd be escorting us.

I quickly downed the blood and clutched the dresser as it coursed through my veins. I felt my muscles, ligaments, mind, strengthen. Blood wasn't only food for the vampires, it was magic. It healed us and kept us strong.

As the buzz settled, I walked over to the door, opened it, and peeked down the hall. It was empty, and the hallway was quiet. There were no voices, and no one seemed to be stirring. Which was odd. This was a palace filled with dozens of slaves.

Would the girl with the different colored eyes come as she said she would? Maybe the queen forbade her to help me. I wouldn't doubt it. Maybe she pulled Everett from my watch too.

I waited, watching the sleeping town below, until the sun broke the horizon and enveloped it. Then, it greeted me at my window and kissed my face with its warmth. That wondrous, magical warmth.

I stood there basking in its glory until there was a knock at the door, and before I could answer, it opened. I knew it was Sabine because I could smell her. I was still getting accustomed to my heightened vampire senses.

"Are you ready for today?" I finally asked, pulling away from the window and opening my eyes to look at her. She was dressed in long pants with knee-high boots and a long-sleeved, olive colored tunic, tied at the waist. Her hair was pulled back behind her neck and she looked rested.

"As ready as I'll ever be," she said. "Last night was the best night's sleep I've had in years. The bed was so incredibly soft, and when I woke up, there was coffee and a tray of fruit, cheese, and bread on the dresser.

I smiled. "I'm glad." I stepped up to her and took her

hands. "You deserve this, Sabine, more than anyone."

"I still think about all of those slaves trapped in Morbeth and often think . . . why me?"

I squeezed her hands and gazed deep into her dark-chocolate eyes. "Because despite the dangers, despite the repercussions, despite your own life . . . you chose to help me. It is a debt I will never be able to repay."

Sabine shook her head. "It's not a debt. It's called human decency, something Roehl knows nothing about. Besides, you took me out of Morbeth. I would have died in that miserable place if Roehl didn't kill me first. So, I say we're even."

Heavy footfalls pounding outside the door alerted me that one of the guards was near. Before they knocked, I opened the door. Everett was there with his fist ready to knock, and as soon as he saw me, he smiled and lowered his hand.

"It looks like you're both ready. I'll escort you to the stable."

"Stable?" Sabine asked, her eyes widened.

"Yes," Everett answered. "It's a few hours ride to the Crag."

"I've never ridden a horse," Sabine admitted, her eyes shifting to me.

I smiled and patted her back. "Riding a horse really isn't that hard, and we can give you some tips before we go. Right, Everett?"

"Yes, our horses are well-trained. I'll make sure you get a mellow one."

She nodded, and we both followed him out.

I could smell horse manure before we saw the stable. Five horses were saddled just outside. The girl with the different colored eyes was brushing a dappled white mare. Another guard—the one who was with Everett the first day in the cells—was sitting on top of a chestnut stallion. Next to it was a similar horse that had the guard emblem imprinted on its saddle. The two remaining were a black stallion and a palomino mare.

"This is the tamest mare in Incendia," Everett said, patting the palomino. "Her name is Amara."

"She's mine," Sabine said, claiming her. She ran a gentle hand down the mare's muscular neck. "You're a beauty, aren't you, Amara," she said softly.

As if answering, Amara nodded her head, making Sabine laugh.

While Everett helped her on her horse, he gave her a few riding tips. I took the reins of the stallion.

"That's Thunder," the girl with the colored eyes said. She was dressed in black pants and boots with a brown tunic, a bow and quiver of arrows strapped over her shoulder. Her blonde hair was tied behind her neck, and she wore brown leather cuffs on her wrists that were stamped with the same seal as the guards. The one tattooed on my right palm.

I ran a hand along the side of Thunder. "I have a black Frisian back home in Sartha named Shadow," I said.

"I know," she replied. "I've seen him in my dreams." My head snapped to her. When my brow crumpled, she added.

"You were both in my dreams."

"You dreamed about me?"

"Yes," she replied. "More than once, but it only started a few months ago."

I mounted Thunder, my mind spinning by her words. "What's your name?" I asked. I didn't want to keep referring to her in my mind as the girl with the different colored eyes.

"Thalia," she replied, heeling her stallion. "We should leave."

So much for pleasantries.

The five of us set out with Thalia leading the way. I followed her, with Sabine sandwiched between the two guards. Every now and again I'd twist back to see how she was doing, and it seemed as if Everett's instructions worked. She seemed comfortable on her horse, her eyes soaking up the landscape.

We headed west toward the mountains. The ride was long and arduous, through meadows, forests, over hills, across rivers, and finally up the rocky mountain edge.

As we started our ascent, I felt a buzz in my blood and a tingling in my palms and wondered if the Crag was a sacred place to worship their Fire Goddess.

"Don't look down," I heard Everett say, breaking my thoughts.

"What if I fall?" Sabine's voice was shaky.

"Your horse doesn't want to fall, just as badly as you," he added. "Just hold on tight and she'll carry you safely. Close your eyes if you must."

I twisted my head back and saw Sabine white-knuckle the horn of the saddle, her eyes tightly closed.

"Tell me when we're almost there," she said.

"It won't be much longer," Everett replied.

I was thankful for his answer because my ass was aching. Meanwhile, Thalia still hadn't said a word, and I wondered if I'd said or did something wrong. Maybe her dream about me and Shadow was more of a nightmare. I'd have to ask her about it later when we were alone. If we ever had the chance.

I wasn't going to worry about things I didn't know about until we got to the Crag.

As we reached the top of the mountain, I spotted a large opening in the tallest formation. Thalia led us closer, then dismounted her horse.

We all did the same, and good gods, my body was as stiff as a board. I didn't feel too bad when Sabine slipped off her horse and let out a loud moan.

"Goddess. I think my tailbone is broken," she muttered.

"Just stretch a bit," Everett suggested, dismounting his horse like a champ.

"I'm worried about the ride back," she whined. "My entire ass aches."

"When we return, soak in a hot tub with our red salts," Thalia said. "You'll feel fine the next morning."

"You don't happen to have any of those red salts with you now, do you?" Sabine asked.

"No," Thalia bit, heading toward the cave opening. "We should get going."

As we got closer, I spotted carvings embedded into the rock around the entrance. Symbols of the zodiac and of the elements along with other ones I didn't recognize. Symbols that looked ancient.

But sitting at the very top of the entrance was one symbol I did recognize. The tattoo on my right palm.

"Looks like you're meant to be here, Calla," Sabine whispered from behind.

I turned back to her and smiled. "Let's hope there are answers in there."

"Yes," she breathed. "Answers would be great."

I felt for her. Her life was in limbo because of me. I was kidnapped and literally thrown into her world and life, and now, here we were, running for our lives in a land that was supposed to have been long destroyed.

Thalia and the two guards lit some torches at the entrance, then we set off into the dark and dank cave. It smelled like stale air and earth with hints of sulfur. Beneath my feet, the ground was alive, like the earth itself was shifting. Unbalanced, I reached out to steady myself against the cavern wall, but a firm hand grasped my arms from behind.

Turning, I gasped, looking into familiar, dark eyes.

"Markus?" I gasped. "Where did you? How did you?"

His eyes shifted toward Everett. "He told me where you'd be. I left hours before dawn." He steadied me and then let go of my arms and stepped back. "Something this big, I couldn't miss. Besides, I want to see this Fire Goddess myself."

I'd never been so happy to see him. I wanted to throw my arms around his thick neck and give him a squeeze. But I'd never let him know that, and he probably wouldn't appreciate it.

"No one has ever seen the Fire Goddess except the chosen. Those who are marked with the signs of royalty," Thalia said with a little bite to her words. "The goddess never shows herself to any other."

Markus shrugged. "Well then, I guess our *Chosen One* will give us the details."

I smiled at him. "You know I will."

Thalia rolled her eyes and continued down the corridor. Gods, she was in a foul mood this morning.

Markus glanced at me then quickly placed a fist over his heart before falling in line directly behind me. I felt a lot safer with him here, but now he'd be stuck in the cave until nightfall because he wanted to make sure I was safe. I guess that's what made his arrival even more special.

I whispered, ever so quietly, so that only vampire ears could hear. "Thank you, Markus."

Markus grunted behind me, making me smile.

Soft-hearted brute.

It seemed like we'd traversed for nearly an hour, through the rocky tunnels that seemed to lead deep into the mountain until we finally reached a large open area. As soon as I stepped inside, carvings of runes along the cave walls illuminated in a glittery gold, illuminating the room.

"Well, this confirms you are Incendian Royalty," Thalia noted, turning in a circle, admiring the carvings.

"Did you doubt her, princess?" Everett asked.

Princess?

Thalia glanced at him but didn't speak. I knew she had doubted. I mean, who wouldn't? They'd never seen or heard of me before. I was a stranger to them.

"What is this place?" I asked no one in particular.

"This is the mortal residence of the Fire Goddess," Thalia replied, setting her bow and quiver of arrows on the ground. "She does not live here, but she comes when an Incendian Royal passes through the entrance. The runes call to her."

My heart was racing, wondering if I was, in fact, going to meet the Fire Goddess. "Have you ever seen her?" I asked Thalia.

Thalia gave me a smirk, then showed me her palms. She had twin tattoos on her palms, but they didn't look like mine. Hers were of a triangle with a tree in the center. "I have not. I have not been chosen, but I am of the royal bloodline."

I shook my head, confused. "How do you know who gets chosen?"

"We have to stop here," Thalia said, her colorful eyes meeting mine. "Calla, you have to go the rest of the way alone. No one, but the chosen are allowed beyond this point." She pointed to an opening in the wall that led into another dark corridor.

Great. I would be alone again, and I hated being alone, especially in dark places that I'd never been before. At least I was able to summon fire. That would help.

"I'll go with you," Markus said, stepping beside me.

Thalia growled and glared at him. "Do you have a death wish, blood demon?"

Markus growled back. "Maybe. How do we know this isn't a trap?"

"Then, by all means, go ahead," Thalia said, gesturing toward the entrance. "But know this . . . all those who have entered without the mark, have never returned."

I put a hand on Markus's chest. "Hey, I killed the Sangerian Sea Serpent. I think I can handle this alone." I hoped he didn't hear the racing of my heart because it proved I was afraid.

After a long, loud exhale, Markus stepped closer to me. "Keep your eyes and ears open. Be aware of everything around you. Always know where your next step will land."

I nodded, thankful he cared enough to give me instructions.

"Calla," Sabine ran up and wrapped her arms around me. "Please be safe."

Thalia huffed a laugh and shook her head. "Goddess. She'll be back soon."

"She better," Markus said in a low and serious tone.

I glanced over at Thalia and smiled. "They're my friends. I would do the same for them." I turned my attention to Sabine and Markus. "I'll be back soon. I promise."

And I hoped I could keep that promise. I don't know

why my insides were filled with nerves. Probably because I thought Incendians had been wiped out. And I sure as hell never believed there was a Fire Goddess, and now, the thought of meeting that Fire Goddess, the one who gave the Incendian royals their power, was more frightening than anything.

Would she find me worthy? Or would she turn me into a pile of ash?

I guess I was about to find out. Gathering my courage, I stepped toward the entrance. The cavern behind me was silent, and I knew my companions were watching. I could feel the weight of their stares on my back. My heart thundered against my chest and in my ears, and I was sure Markus could hear it, but I pressed on.

As soon as I stepped through the next cavern, a blast of hot wind slammed into me. The walls and floor began to quake, and my palms heated. When I lifted them, the tattoos on my palms were glowing bright blue.

"The Goddess knows she is here," Thalia said behind me.

Like that was comforting.

CHAPTER SIX

I proceeded down the darkened passageway, and just before I called my flame, a great, blue ball of fire suddenly appeared, hovering before me. It slowly bobbed up and down, and I was utterly fascinated.

I raised my hand to touch it, but the freaking fire let out a piercing scream, startling the shit out of me.

The flame suddenly burst into a bird with a long tail and wings. I knew this bird. I'd seen it drawn on the pages of a few of my fantasy novels. It was a firebird. A phoenix. An elemental bird able to create, shape, and manipulate fire. It was likewise known to heal, or even resurrect itself using the element of fire.

It let out another high-pitched shriek, which echoed off the cavern walls. Gods be damned, I was going to murder that bird.

The fiery bird waited until I moved toward it and then,

it flapped its wings and shot off, flying down the shadowy, rocky passage. I ran, following it, and noticed a glittering, bright trail left in its wake. A trail that illuminated a path down the corridor.

The glittery specks led me down another dark passageway, and I spotted a light at the end. A mesmerizing blue light that attracted me.

My feet were on autopilot, my entire body humming with an intensity I couldn't describe. My heart was pounding, my pulse was galloping. There was no turning back. Whatever was drawing me in, was driving me toward something I had no control over.

It was then, I understood my life was no longer my own. It was now subject to the gift and its power of Incendia. No matter how hard I tried to fight it, I was chosen, and every cruel thing that happened to me over the past months had led me to this very moment. A moment I was certain would define and write my future. My destiny.

The quiet girl that used to hide behind her best friend and her books was gone. Forever. The new girl was . . . well, she was terrified. Terrified of the power flowing through her veins and what it could do. Terrified of her past and her future. Terrified that she wasn't worthy and would die before she even had a chance to figure out what the hell she was doing.

Maybe the answer was close.

With all the questions whirling in my mind, I hadn't noticed that I was at the threshold of another entrance lined with more runes that were glowing an even brighter blue.

And without another thought, and before I could change my mind, I stepped through.

I entered an open cavern, and at the center was a gaping hole from which the source of the blue light flowed. I inched my way closer, my body thrumming with power. A power that nearly drove me to my knees.

My limbs were trembling, my palms heating to the point of searing pain.

A few feet from the edge of the hole, I glanced down and gasped. The veins in my arms were also glowing bright blue. The same color as the tattoos on my palms. What the hell was happening to me?

My eyes were heavy. Darkness threatened to shut them, but it was fear of the unknown that held them open.

"Calla," a voice spoke. A voice that seemed to come from every direction, making every cell in my body hum in response.

"I'm here," I answered in a shaky voice, searching for the source.

"Come forward," the voice commanded. It was female. Soft, yet powerful.

I paused, noting that forward was toward the gaping hole that lay before me, two feet away. A pit engulfed in blue flames, that burned warmth instead of heat.

My shaky legs took a step forward. One step away, I peered over the edge, into an endless blue abyss.

The blue flames danced and twirled and leaped with reckless abandon, and I became entranced with its rhythmic patterns. So fluid. So beautiful.

"Come to me, Calla," the voice echoed, reverberating through my chest.

"I don't know how," I replied, completely enthralled by the flames.

"Jump into the fires to find me."

My feet moved, taking a half a step closer. Then reality slammed me.

Hell no. What was I doing? There was no way I was going to jump into that pit. I mean, what if this goddess was sadistic and there was a hazing involved?

I shuffled back a few feet, struggling to pull myself together, trying to resist the heaviness that was steadily slithering into my mind.

Pivoting to run away, my entire body warred against me. Resisting what my mind demanded to do. To leave. I didn't choose this. I never asked for this, and now, a mysterious voice was advising me to jump into a pit of blue flames with no end in sight?

I knew a guy who jumped off a cliff into a pool of water, but there were rocks in the shallow where he landed. One decision, carried on a whim, without thought, caused him to become crippled. His entire life was destroyed because of it.

"Come to me," the voice rumbled again.

I swallowed the lump in my throat. "I can't." *I'm too*

afraid, I wanted to add.

"You must if you are to find your destiny and the answers you desperately seek."

Gods be damned.

Her words had me considering. But they were just words. However, words were powerful.

Words could enlighten. Words could be used as swords to slice or mutilate. But words could also bring healing, like a glass of cool water poured on a parched, thirsty soul, giving it new life.

I needed more proof that her words wouldn't have me jumping toward my death.

"Show yourself to me. Show me you are real," I said, turning back toward the pit.

"I reveal myself only to those who are worthy."

Really? *I wasn't going to win this match.*

Closing my eyes, I listened to my heart. It, along with everything else inside of me—except my brain that tried to rationalize everything—told me to jump.

I stepped closer to the edge, the blue flames flowed over the edge and licked my boots, sending a calming warmth throughout me, beckoning me to jump. Before my mind could talk me out of it. I sucked in a deep breath, closed my eyes, and jumped.

I was weightless, screaming, as I free-fell through the endless blue flame. My stomach tightened in knots with that sickening feeling of not knowing if there was an end.

Seconds? Minutes? I couldn't tell how long or far I had fallen.

And then . . . I stopped.

I was hovering in the middle of the blue-flamed gorge, my hair floating around me like I was underwater.

I watched as a figure rose from the bottom of the abyss. A figure encased in fire. My breath seized as her eyes finally met mine. There were no earthly words to describe the goddess before me.

Ethereal? Beautiful? These words couldn't even measure. She had an otherworldly charm. Her skin was bronze and her hair fiery red, but the ends were blazing with that blue fire. Her features were soft and perfect, her skin flawless. She was tall and slender and toned, her eyes the color of molten lava.

I could feel her energy. It swirled all around her.

Her arm raised, and long, flaming tipped fingers lightly caressed my cheek, but her blazes didn't burn. They felt warm and soothing.

"Fire Goddess?" I whispered. My voice was hoarse from screaming on the way down.

A single nod and a smile adorned her full, crimson lips. "I am Helia," she spoke, her molten eyes examined my face. "Welcome, Calla. You have overcome your fear."

I nodded, finding it hard to speak in her presence. One so beautiful who bore exceptional power. This was no simple immortal. She was a goddess. The deity who gave the Incendians their gifts.

CAMEO RENAE

"Come, Calla." Helia extended her hand to me, and as soon as I took it, we were no longer hovering in the blue fire pit, but standing on solid ground.

We were in a place, a magnificent and bright place that seemed to glow. The floors were a pristine white marble, with golden veins throughout them. In large gold vases throughout the area were deep red roses, all fully bloomed and the edges, if my eyes weren't playing tricks, were flickering with red flames. Gods, that was a wondrous sight.

Around the room were tall white columns that reached upward toward the sky. Good gods. The ceiling was the sky. A brilliant blue sky with billowy clouds and birds flying by. The air was the perfect climate, and at our feet was a shimmering mist.

Along the outside of the columns were white marbled walls with wide open windows. Beyond the windows was the most remarkable view. A view of vivid green fields and blossoms of every shade. It was . . . heaven.

"I bet you didn't think a Fire Goddess would live in such a place, did you?" Helia turned and grinned.

"Truthfully, I was thinking fire and brimstone. Maybe lava flowing in moats around your dwelling."

Helia laughed and her countenance illuminated like the sun. "Yes, I suppose most would think a volcano is a fitting residence for a Fire Goddess. The Crag, as my people call it, is merely a portal to," her arms spread out to her sides, "my true home here, in Celestial Realm."

80

She slowly strode—more like glided—up to a grand dais which held the most beautiful throne I'd ever seen. It was made with a variety of materials—wood and gold and onyx. Set on either side were golden pedestals that carried twin flames that appeared to burn without timber or fuel. Fires that danced and shifted colors from red to orange to yellow to blue.

On her left, was a staff and atop the staff perched the fowl made of fire. It thrashed its wings and settled, its fiery eyes scrutinizing me.

Helia went up and sat upon her throne, and as she did a crown of fire encircled her head. The firebird flew down and perched next to her.

"Come," she said.

I walked to the foot of the dais and paused. Should I stand, kneel, bow? I felt like a fool for not knowing the *How to Meet the Fire Goddess protocol*. Was there an Incendian Royalty handbook? A secret handshake? Was there anything I should or shouldn't say that would upset her?

The firebird let out an ear-splitting screech, but Helia pet its head, "Quiet. She's a guest here."

Helia then snapped her fingers and two golden chalices inset with glowing rubies appeared in her hands. "Have a drink," she said, holding out a chalice to me. I stepped up and took it from her hand. She raised hers up and took a sip, and I did the same.

Whatever touched my lips and tongue was the most delightful drink I'd ever tasted. It was a sweet liquor with hints of citrus and something else I couldn't place. It immediately warmed my insides and caused me to feel as light as a feather.

With another snap of her fingers, a white chair with fluffy cushions appeared in front of Helia's throne.

"Sit, Calla. Let's talk," she said, and I obeyed. Her molten eyes studied me as she swirled the drink in her goblet. "So many questions lay within those lovely bright eyes. I realize you have much on your mind, but do not worry. The gift embraces the one deserving of my marks and worthy of the tasks that come with them."

I glanced down at the tattoos on my palms. "I don't feel like I'm worthy . . . of any of this." She tilted her head, molten eyes narrowed. "I don't know anything about these gifts. I don't even know the Incendian people or their ways, and they obviously don't know me. Their queen should be the chosen one. She's ruled them until now. They trust and respect her."

A slight smile rose on her fiery lips. "They neither trust, nor respect her," she replied. "They fear her."

Her response shook me. "Why?"

Helia snickered, and I saw flames and embers in her eyes. "Because she is a fraud. She is a descendant of Incendia, but not from the chosen bloodline. She is related to your line only through marriage, but she does not bear the true marks. Nor is she the chosen one."

I shook my head. "But how did she become queen without the marks?"

"She has marks, but they are not true marks. She does

not hold the power you do. She has limited power, as most descendants of the royal line do. She rules because she believes she is worthy. However, I have seen the darkness hiding in her heart. I have witnessed the things she does away from the eyes of the people. Incendia is not hers to rule. Neither are the Incendian people. They are mine. I created them, and I choose who is worthy to rule them." Flames blazed in her narrowed eyes. "And I tell you now, that false queen is *not* worthy."

I swallowed the huge lump in my throat. Well, that was terrifying news. Especially coming directly from the Fire Goddess, herself. It was no wonder the queen didn't greet me warmly. I *was* her greatest threat. I could see it in her eyes. She did not want to give up her position of power. The queen would not bow silently. She would fight.

But I didn't want to rule Incendia. I had no idea how to run an entire kingdom.

"If the queen is fake," I asked carefully, "Then why can't you do something?"

I thought it was a good question.

Helia exhaled loudly and took another sip of her drink. "Because even the gods are governed and it is law that we cannot interfere in any affairs, mortal or immortal." She turned her molten eyes to me. "I have been waiting for you. I watched your mother give birth and have kept an eye on you ever since. Although Leora put her spell on you, I knew you would grow up to be just like her. Strong. Resilient. Able to conquer anything thrown at you." She raised her glass. "I saw how you defied the evil Prince of Morbeth and even killed the sea serpent."

I gasped, in complete awe. "You saw that?"

"I am a goddess. We see all . . . when we want to." A sly grin rose on her perfect lips. "It showed me what you are capable of, Calla."

I let out a sigh, swirled, and gulped down whatever was left in my goblet. "Is there any way I can learn about my gifts? Is there a book or a person who can tell me how to use them?"

"There is not a book. Nor is there anyone alive in Incendia who can tell you how to use them. For there is no other true female royal who lives, but you."

"Then, how will I learn?"

She shook her head and stood from her throne, then glided over to me. "Everything you need to know is right here." She placed her hand on the center of my chest. "And . . . here." She laid her other hand on top of my head.

"But…"

She tsked me. "So many doubts for someone who has escaped the inescapable and fled to a land you thought was destroyed to find answers. Yet, everything you need is already within you."

"How do I find what I need if I don't know where to look?"

"Stand, child." My body instantly obeyed her order. Helia stood at least two feet taller than me. She was long and lean and toned and curved in all the right places. She was perfect.

"Because Leora placed the binding curse on you, keeping you in the dark, I will awaken your mind."

Helia placed both of her palms on the sides of my face. They were warm and tingling with energy. Then, she came so close, I could feel her soft lips on my forehead, uttering a few words that my mind instantly translated.

"Et omnes intellegunt." *You will understand all.*

My body suddenly jolted as if it were slammed with an electrical current. My knees gave, but Helia grabbed hold of my arms and set me down on my chair.

I caught my breath and looked into her smiling eyes. "Is—is that it?"

She nodded and strode off the dais toward a table set with the most glorious array of fruit and cheese and wine that hadn't been there when we arrived. She plucked a red grape, double the size I was used to, and popped it in her mouth, eyes closing, moaning as she chewed.

Then, her eyes popped open and found mine. "Do not fret, Calla. From this day forward, you will fully understand your gifts, because they are part of you. You are one, connected through word and thought. Your gifts will be your greatest ally and will help protect you from harm." She then gave me a serious look. "Do not be afraid to use them. The elements are yours to command."

"You mean both elements, right? Fire and water." I just had to make sure because those were the two elements tattooed on my palms.

"You are of fire, however you are also Incendian Royalty. Because you are the only female left of royal blood, your power is not shared amongst those in your bloodline. Thus, you have access to *all* the elements."

All? Did I hear that right?

"You mean I can manipulate earth and air too?"

"Yes."

"How? I've only been able to call fire and manipulate water. The two elements on my palms."

"Although I am the Goddess of Fire, the other elements are shared with my sisters—Water, Earth, and Air. Before Incendia's destruction, there lived more than one marked royal and they shared the elements. Every Incendian royal could wield fire, but they also had a secondary element. Like yours is water. Leora's was earth, and her mother, air. Because you are the only female Incendian royal, you can wield all elements. However, fire is your greatest power."

I was utterly dumbstruck and couldn't wait to test it out.

Helia held out her hands and a ball of fire, buzzing with energy, formed within them, her eyes mimicking the flames. "Fire nourishes and protects, but it is also the cause of much death and destruction." She slapped her palms together, and the flames burst into tiny fire butterflies that flitted away. "Remember that."

I felt something happening inside me. My blood was stirring and an energy that wasn't there before seemed to be humming through my bones. Overwhelmed and emotional, tears fell down my face.

I was standing in front of the Fire Goddess, the one who created the Incendian race and gave them their power. A race known to be one of the most powerful on any continent. Until Morbeth caught them off guard and came in and slaughtered them.

Yet here I was. A simple girl from Sartha, who never knew or experienced the real horrors of the immortal world until a few months ago. Then, one night and one handsome prince upended my safe life with a single bite, sending me on a dangerous and downward spiral.

From that night, every anguished and terrifying moment led me to this moment. This pivotal moment that would shape my future and the future of those around me. I knew my life would never be the same. Gods, it was so far from normal that I wasn't even sure what the definition of normal was anymore.

The firebird behind me squawked again. When I turned to look at him, he had one wing over his beak, and it looked like he was — "Are you laughing at me?" I whispered, glaring at it.

It squawked again, as if mocking me.

What was with these higher-ups having birds as pets? This one seemed like it was a handful, but I guess having a bird was useful. They could fly over great distances and relay information to their owners. That's what Nyx did for Trystan.

Trystan.

"Does your mind often wander?" Helia asked. She was

back on the podium, petting her firebird. How awkward was that? It wasn't even a real bird.

The bird screeched and burst into a brighter red flame, his blazing eyes set on me.

Good. Gods.

Helia laughed and patted the bird on the head. "Easy, easy. Remember, she doesn't know any better, and you must mind your temper."

That sealed it. They *did* hear my thoughts.

I tried to clear my mind, my eyes averting from the still, brightly burning bird to my goblet which was again full. *Heavens.* I had to remember I was in the house of a Goddess. Things would happen here that weren't normal. I took another long pull.

"The bird is yours," Helia spoke.

Whatever drink was in my mouth spewed from my lips, but it disintegrated before it hit the Goddess's pristine floor.

"I—I thought you couldn't interfere?" I stuttered, wiping my lips dry. "Wouldn't a flaming bird be an interference?" Besides, it was obvious the bird didn't like me.

"No." She held out her arm and the bird, now burning bright blue, hopped onto it. "I'm not interfering. Consider him a gift."

A gift?

Um… *Think happy and nice thoughts. Nice and happy.*

"I can't possibly take him," I blurted. "He's—well, he's your pet."

"Oh, but you can." She started walking toward me, the bird still glaring at me. "I created him this morning. Just for you."

I swallowed the huge lump in my throat, taking a few steps back. "Created? For me?" My words came out in a squeak.

Helia burst into laughter. "It's been quite some time since I've had a visitor from the mortal realm. I've forgotten how entertaining you are." She held out her arm toward me. "Here, take him."

I folded my hands behind my back and took another step backward, stepping right off the dais. I fell, but Helia held out her hand. Before my body slammed into the ground, it halted, hovering midair. Helia slowly raised her hand, and with the movement, I lifted right back to a standing position in front of her.

"Watch your step," she said with a cock to her head, holding out her arm to offer me the bird again.

This time I froze. "I can't. He'll burn me."

She shook her head, a smirk on her lips. "You are the only one in the mortal realm who cannot be harmed by his fire."

"But—" Okay, I was grasping for an excuse. "I can't take a bird made of fire back to my realm. That would cause a lot of trouble."

"Fire is his true form, but in the mortal realm, he will have a disguise."

My brow furrowed. "You mean, he'll turn into a real bird?"

The bird let out another shriek that pierced my ears and dropped me to my knees. Gods, he was a pain in the ass.

"Yes," Helia spoke, her smile widening. "He'll be a real bird, but first things first. You must give him a name."

I slowly stood back on my feet and stared at the bird. The first name that popped into my mind was . . .

"Flint."

The bird and the Fire Goddess looked at each other.

"I like it." Helia nodded. "Flint it is." She patted the bird's head, and their eyes locked again, both sets burning with golden flames. "Flint, I am placing Calla in your care. She is the last true royal of Incendia, and no harm must come to her. I give you permission to do whatever, by any means necessary, to keep her safe. Do you understand?"

The bird closed its eyes and bowed its head. It understood her.

"Good." Helia nodded then raised her arm, and the bird took flight. We watched it circle high above us, three times, before it spiraled downward. In a ball of flame and smoke, Flint morphed, and out of the smoke, a bird flew and spread its silky black wings.

A crow? Seriously? Out of all the birds in the world, it morphed into a crow? What about a bluebird? Or cardinal? Maybe I should have named it coal.

Flint came and landed on my shoulder and I stood deathly still as it adjusted itself.

"Relax, Calla. Flint won't bite," Helia said, sitting back

down on her throne.

I then realized my body was stiff as a board, and I couldn't make myself relax. Not with a morphing fire crow on my shoulder. Especially, when it had been glaring at me, the entire time I was here.

"Do you have any other questions for me, or are you ready to return?"

"You said I'll know how to use my powers. I won't need practice?"

"Practice makes your powers stronger. The more you use your power, the more connected it will become."

"When I do use my power, it drains me, and I can barely move afterward."

Helia smiled. "Yes. The power within you is great, and because you were born half-mortal, your body will weaken. With time and practice, as you exercise those powers, they will bind to the fibers of your being, making you stronger. You are connected to your power, and it to you. When the time comes for you to call upon it, it will answer."

"If I use too much power, could I die?"

"No, but you can be left vulnerable. Someone like the wicked Prince of Morbeth could take advantage of that. So be careful. Have trusted allies with you." She looked at the bird on my shoulder. "This is why I am sending Flint. He will aid you."

Flint danced on my shoulder, his talons piercing through my shirt and into my skin. "Ouch," I huffed. "Can you please stop moving?"

Helia grinned from ear to ear. "Oh, I can't wait to see how this relationship blossoms. You two are perfect for each other."

Perfect? This bird was getting on my gods-damned nerves. I would have no problem roasting it.

"Ouch!" I hissed as Flint dug his talons into my flesh, paying me back for obviously reading my mind.

Helia placed her empty goblet on the arm of her throne before standing. She paused inches away, sighing and brushing her fingers down the sides of my cheek.

"The path ahead of you is rocky and treacherous with many twists and turns. You must be strong and brave, Calla. I have faith in you. I have watched and have witnessed you disregard your own safety to protect the lives of others. That alone, my dear, makes you worthy."

I still didn't feel worthy. "Do you think I can survive Prince Roehl?"

She gave a fiery smile. "I think you can do whatever you put your mind to."

That wasn't really the answer I wanted, but I wasn't about to argue with her.

"It's time for you to return to the mortal world," she said. "You will not see me again."

"Never?" I suddenly felt a coldness, because she was the only one who understood me and could give me answers.

Helia gave a sweet smile and shook her head. "Flint will

be with you. Take care of him. He is yours now, and a part of you."

I guess roasting the bird was out. Flint squeezed his talons again, and I growled at him.

"Remember, Calla. The elements are yours and are always ready to serve those who are worthy."

Helia was now glowing with blue fire, right in front of me. "Be brave, Calla."

I nodded, a tear escaping my eye. Helia smiled then caressed my face in her hands, pressing a warm kiss to my forehead.

In an instant, I was standing back in the dark, cold cavern. Flint took flight, but he was so dark now, I couldn't see where he was going. This time, there was no golden trail to lead me.

That good for nothing — At least Nyx had a purpose.

I held out my hand and called fire. A large flame burst in my palm, bigger and brighter and a much clearer blue than ever before. I could feel the great power coursing through me. For a moment, I was afraid. Afraid I wouldn't be able to handle whatever the Fire Goddess had unleashed inside me.

Not wanting to be here alone, I ran down the corridor and finally saw a flickering light at the end. It must have been the room where I'd left Markus and Sabine.

Just before I reached it, a black mass flew at me. I screamed and threw my flame at it, but it swallowed it whole, turning back into a firebird, its narrowed eyes set aflame.

"Flint! You scared the hell out of me."

The bird squawked, so I held out my arm and it landed on it. "Do I seriously have to keep you?"

The bird cocked its head and let out a caw. Ruffling its wings, Flint returned to the simple black winged crow. Gods, that was going to take some getting used to.

Walking to the end of the corridor, I paused and looked at Flint. "I hope you're good with people. No biting, and behave."

The bird squawked, so I took that as an okay.

CHAPTER SEVEN

Everyone was asleep, except Markus.

Markus was leaned back against a large rock with Sabine curled up next to him. As soon as his eyes met mine, he jumped up from the ground and was in front of me in a flash. His eyes searching my face, making sure I was okay.

Flint, however, didn't like the sudden movement and lurched forward to try to nip him. Markus's quick reflexes missed his beak. Markus raised his hand, but I caught his wrist.

"Whoa, big guy. No injuring the bird. He's mine."

Markus narrowed his eyes on Flint. "Is that the Carpathian Prince's bird?"

"No," I exhaled. "The Fire goddess gave him to me as a gift."

His narrowed glare met mine. "She gave you a crow?"

"Yes, and no. He's—" I glanced at Flint and his little

black head cocked to the side like he was waiting for my reply. "He's complicated."

Flint cawed loudly then took off toward the cave's exit.

"Your bird's gone," Markus noted with a smirk.

"Yeah, but I'm okay with it," I smirked back. Flint was created by magic, so I wasn't worried about him. Besides, I wasn't going to attempt to tame a sassy, newborn firebird-slash-crow.

"Calla!" Sabine popped up from her sleep and ran toward me, her eyes heavy with sleep. "You're back. I was getting worried."

Behind her, Thalia, Everett, and the other guard had woken. Everett bowed his head to me.

"She lives." Thalia said, then stood to her feet.

I wrapped my arms around Sabine's neck. "Why would you be worried? I wasn't gone that long." I had two glasses of wine with the goddess. That couldn't have been more than a few hours.

"You've been gone for nearly two days," Sabine said, her brow furrowed.

I shook my head. "It couldn't have been two days. I was with the Fire Goddess for two hours, tops."

Sabine grabbed hold of my hands. "The Fire Goddess," Sabine breathed. "What was she like? What happened? What did she say?"

"Whoa. One question at a time," Thalia blurted, dusting herself off. She threw her quiver of arrows over her shoulder and picked up her bow. "I'd like to get back to the town and take a bath." She and the guards began walking back down the tunnel toward the exit.

"Come," I whispered to Sabine. "I'll tell you about it on our way back." I linked my arm in hers and followed Thalia and the guards out of the cave. Markus walked behind us.

"Was she in the caves?" Sabine asked.

I sucked in a deep breath. "I came into this large room, and at the center was a huge pit filled with blue fire. I was terrified at first, but then, I heard a voice that told me to jump."

Sabine stopped, yanking me to a stop, her eyes wide. "Did you jump?"

I smiled and noticed that everyone had stopped, and all eyes were turned on me. "I did."

Sabine gasped, throwing a hand over her mouth. "I was terrified at first. Then, before I could talk myself out of it, I jumped, and the flames didn't burn me." I shook my head and chuckled. "I fell so long, and screamed so bloody loud, my throat was raw. Then, I stopped midair." I grabbed hold of Sabine's arms. "I was floating in the middle of the fire pit, and that's where I met her."

"The Fire Goddess?" Sabine exhaled.

"Yes." I tugged her back into a walk. I didn't want to stay here and was in desperate need of fresh air. "Her name is Helia."

"Helia," Sabine whispered with such reverence. "What does she look like?"

I smiled, shaking my head. "She's hard to describe, but she was . . . well, she was the most beautiful being I have ever laid eyes on. She is tall and slender, and she was glowing. Her hair was the color of fire and her eyes like molten lava. She is . . . flawless. Otherworldly perfection. There are no other words to describe her."

"So, you both stayed hovering in the pit?" Thalia asked from the front.

"No," I replied. "She took me to her throne room in the Celestial Realm."

Another gasp. "Is there really such a place?" Sabine questioned.

"Yes, and it is even harder to describe. The air there is different. It's the perfect temperature and smells sweet and fresh. The entire atmosphere was buzzing with energy. An energy that seemed to wipe out every doubt and fear and replace it with a calm I can't express. It was beyond breathtaking. Everything was pristine. White marbled floors inlaid with gold. The landscape was even more glorious. I mean, I thought I've seen some of the most beautiful places in Talbrinth, and even here in Incendia, but there is no place that can compare to the Celestial Realm."

"Of course, nothing will compare. It's made of magic," Thalia huffed.

Sabine scowled at her, making me smile, then turned her attention back to me. "What did she say?"

"She said a lot of things. It was mostly a reminder to

embrace who I am and not to be afraid."

Sabine nodded as my eyes moved to the front. I didn't want to say too much around Thalia. She was connected to the queen, and I knew her kind all too well. She would be interrogated when she returned, so I kept most of what was said to myself. Especially that I had learned I was able to wield all the elements.

"Well, she's right. Did she give you any tips on how you can use your powers?" Sabine was talking quietly now, but I knew Markus could hear, and who knew if the others could too?

"She said when the time came, I will know how to use my gift." I shrugged. "I guess there is no manual for these things."

Thalia let out another huff but didn't turn back.

"Do you have power, Thalia?" Sabine asked. I nudged her in the side, and she batted my arm away.

Thalia paused and pivoted, her blue and green eyes glowing in the firelight of Everett's torch. "I have some, but it's not as powerful as one who is chosen."

"On our journey here, we were attacked by the Sangerian Sea Serpent. It killed some of the ship's crew, but Calla single-handedly defeated it with her powers." Sabine was obviously boasting, and it raised Thalia's brow.

I inwardly moaned.

Thalia pivoted and began walking again. "That must have been a sight."

"I have seen many things in my long life, and that was a

moment I will never forget," Markus added. My head snapped behind us to look at him. He smiled and tipped his head before whispering. "I was impressed."

The Captain of the King's guard was impressed? With me? The thought made my heart grow a little more for the old brute.

"We've yet to see this great power you speak of," Thalia uttered. "I've seen her hold a flame in her palm, which is something even the queen can do, but I haven't seen any other power. Until such a time, please don't resent my . . . disbelief."

"There is no resentment from us," I said, speaking on behalf of my friends . . . hopefully. "I know how hard it is for anyone to believe a girl outside Incendia could be royalty. I was born in Sartha and didn't know much about Incendia other than it was destroyed. But through Leora, I learned that before Morbeth's army came, she sent her newborn son, Nicolae, away with her handmaiden. Everyone thought he had died, so no one questioned it, but Nicolae is very much alive and has remained in hiding all these years. He is very powerful."

Everett's pace slowed. "I heard stories about the prince who was connected to Morbeth, but the stories told were just . . . stories. Most assumed he died that night." Everett's voice seemed sad. "What is he like? The prince?"

Prince. I never considered Nicolae a prince, but he was born as Incendian royalty. He should've been king.

"I never met him," I breathed. When he turned back with

a puzzled look I added, "Growing up, I thought he was dead, but then I met Trystan and—" My insides heated at the thought of him. "Trystan came to warn me that Morbeth had sent out a death decree to execute Nicolae and his entire bloodline. They said that Nicolae murdered Morbeth's prince, but that was a lie."

"How do you know it was a lie if you've never met him?" Everett asked.

"Leora told me," I said. "I met her in the In Between during Morbeth's Shadow Fest. She told me everything that happened and what led to Incendia's destruction. She also told me about Nicolae, and how she had put a spell on his magic and the magic of anyone in his bloodline. That's why no one knew about us. That's why I never showed any power."

"How do you know the Carpathian Prince? Are you that close that he should come and warn you?" Thalia asked.

Of course, she would ask about Trystan. It seemed everyone in the immortal world knew about the handsome Carpathian prince, but I still didn't know why he chose to save me. He said it was because he felt a connection to a picture. Actually, it was a portrait, painted by one of my father's friends, and I still was baffled how they got it because there was only one copy.

But the immortal world was completely different from what I had grown up in, and everyone seemed to know everyone else. I only knew a handful of people in my family's circle in Sartha.

"When Trystan arrived at my birthday party, it was the first time I'd ever seen or met him." I smiled at the memory of seeing him across the pool and all the girls literally tripping over their own feet to get his attention.

"Birthday party?" Thalia turned with a crumpled brow. "I've heard of mortals celebrating the day of their birth, every year."

"Don't you?" I questioned.

"No," she replied in a snippy tone. "We live much longer lives than mortals, so why should we celebrate the day of birth? Instead, we have festivals to celebrate all life—the earth, sun, moon, creatures. Everything that surrounds us, that has nurtured and cared for us."

"I like that," I said honestly.

This new world had opened to me, and I hoped to experience all that it offered. Including their celebrations.

Thalia didn't have anything else to say after that and even picked up pace. I was glad because I really wanted to get out of and off this mountain.

Everett half glanced back at me. "We are honored you came back to Incendia, Princess Calla."

I cringed. "Please, just call me Calla."

He bowed his head and smiled, and that was it. No one said anything else until we stepped out of the dark, dank tunnel, and into the cool, dark night.

I was happy nightfall had come, so Markus could accompany us back to Incendia. I knew Sabine was happy too.

She even offered him a ride on her horse, and to my surprise, Markus accepted.

Saddled, we began our journey back down the rocky mountain trail. The moon and stars were bright in the clear sky, illuminating our path. Not that Markus or I needed it. We could see everything clearly, as if it were dusk, and it was such a beautiful night. The temperature was cool, and the landscape below looked as if it were painted in watercolor in a dreamy blue.

"Did the Goddess say anything about our queen?" Thalia asked. I had no doubt she was fishing for information.

"No," I replied. "She didn't mention the queen." That was a lie, but a safe answer, especially not knowing what the queen would do if she found out what the Fire Goddess thought of her. Calling her a fake. *Gods.* That would put me on a hate list I didn't want to be on. I already had Roehl on my back, and that was enough hate for a lifetime.

"Has your queen visited the Fire Goddess?" Markus asked. I twisted my head back, narrowing my eyes at him. He shrugged it off like it was nothing.

"She hasn't," Thalia replied flatly. "She is not one of the chosen, but she is a descendant."

"That's too bad," Markus rubbed in.

My face burned hot with embarrassment. What was he doing? Was he trying to ruin whatever friendship we'd built between these people? Goddess above.

Talia tilted her head to the side but didn't look back.

"Chosen or not, she is still our queen. She has been, since Incendia was rebuilt."

"She seems to be a good queen," I added, but no one responded. Not even a nod or a grunt of approval. And that was awkward.

It made me wonder what kind of queen she really was. Was she good to her people? I knew she had to be a strong woman to rule a kingdom, and to keep the people in line. But to what lengths did she go to make that happen?

I'd seen how Roehl used fear to acquire his people's submission. Was their queen the same way? I guess time would tell, but I had a feeling we were in Incendia for more than one reason.

Thinking back, my body shuddered, recalling that I'd jumped into a flaming pit and was taken to the Celestial Realm where the gods and goddesses lived. I had spoken to the Fire Goddess. The *freaking* Fire goddess. Someone I thought never existed and was a myth. It all felt like some sort of weird dream I still hadn't woken up from.

"Will we be able to see any new powers?" Markus asked.

I shrugged, knowing he could see me from behind. "Maybe we can train together tomorrow evening. You promised to show me some of your defensive moves. I'd love to learn from the best."

I heard Markus chuckle. "Well, you better rest up, Princess. You'll need it for my training."

"Just remember, Captain . . ." I held out my hand, and a small flame danced within it. "I play with fire."

Sabine and Everett laughed, and then, I heard a soft growl from behind. Markus didn't like my response.

"Oh, stop. You know it's true," Sabine blurted. "Our girl is transforming into something we cannot even fathom."

I let out a long breath. Was she right? Did the Fire Goddess really grant me what I needed . . . to use my powers without practice?

My insides twisted with excitement. I didn't think I'd be able to sleep. I wanted . . . no, I *needed* to test them, especially the newly given earth and air. But not around anyone who would judge me. I wanted to find someplace secluded. Some place where I could be alone, like on Sebastian's ship when I learned I could manipulate water. Although, the crew paid dearly for that test.

Truly, I didn't care if people ever saw my powers. I wasn't here to impress anyone. I came here for answers, and hopefully, Helia had already given them to me.

The rest of the ride back to the town was solemn. Every now and again I would hear Sabine and Markus mumble or laugh, and the sounds of their voices were comforting.

Everyone was tired, but I felt drained. Like the adrenaline I'd had since arriving, finally ran out, and everything that had transpired over the past few days, had finally caught up to me.

I couldn't wait to get back to my room, soak in a hot bath, and slip into a comfortable bed. Above us, I heard a crow caw, and as I glanced up, saw a dark bird circling above us, and I caught a flame in its eye, and it made me smile.

Flint. I guess the bird didn't ditch me after all.

"The wall," the guard, who'd been silent until now, spoke.

I had never been happier to see it. Bath. Bed. They both beckoned me.

CHAPTER EIGHT

As we made our way to the wall and through the gates, the only ones stirring were the guards. The cobbled streets were empty and most of the house lights were out, and it made me wonder what time it was. It must have been late. Or maybe they had a curfew.

I still needed to learn the rules of Incendia, especially since I was officially welcomed by the Fire Goddess. I knew we wouldn't be here for long. Not while Roehl was still out there with his army of followers.

I hoped that if Roehl returned to Morbeth, King Romulus would be able to stand against him. His only defense were the guards loyal to him, and the witches. I also had a sinking feeling Roehl wouldn't give up the throne without a fight, especially now that his mother and brother were gone. He'd had a small taste of what it felt like to rule, and from what I witnessed the night of the

Shadow Fest, he craved it, and the people seemed to admire him, even if it was a forced admiration created from fear.

"Princess," Everett said. I hadn't even noticed that we were already at the stables. He had already dismounted his horse and was standing on the side of my horse, arms up, ready to help me down.

I threw my leg over the saddle and slid off the horse, into Everett's arms. I moaned as he steadied me.

"Goddess. Everything aches," I moaned.

Markus had already hopped off their horse and was helping Sabine down.

"It feels like someone took a club to my ass," Sabine grumbled. "I don't think I'll be able to walk, let alone sit. Those red salts better work or I'll be out of commission for a while."

"They'll work. You'll feel better after a soak and a long rest," Thalia said walking away from the stables like she hadn't been on a horse for hours. We all followed, Sabine and I dragging behind making painful noises. My tailbone felt like it was broken.

I glanced at Sabine. "At least you won't have to get up early anymore. You can sleep in as long as you like, but if you do get up early, don't come visit me. Because I'll definitely be sleeping in."

"Deal," Sabine replied with a pained smile.

I woke in a dark forest, thick with decrepit trees that had twisted and charred branches. The earth was black with no signs of life, and above me, in a gray sky, vultures circled.

A black mist slithered along the ground, heading toward me. I turned and ran as fast as my legs could carry me, but the trees were like limbs, reaching out, tangling me in their rough branches, tearing at my skin.

I pushed and shoved, my skin burning, blood dripping.

At my back I felt a coldness sweep around me. Turning, I witnessed the dark mist had caught up to me. It slithered around me, around my ankles, legs, waist, chest and up my neck. And then . . . it whispered in my ear.

"You can't run from me, pet. I will always find you. And when I do, you will regret the day you left me."

My bones froze with fear. The mist coiled tighter around me, constricting the air from entering my lungs.

"I will find you, Calla," the mist hissed into my ear. "I will find you, and I will show you how powerful I really am. You will watch your loved ones suffer, and then, you will die."

I shot up from the nightmare, my entire body trembling. Freaking Roehl. How the hell was he entering my dreams?

Taking in long, deep breaths, I tried to settle myself. The bond had been broken between me and Roehl, but the thought it might not have been had me panic-stricken. Or he was using dark magic.

Fact was, he was still out there, hunting for Nicolae, and I knew he had men chasing my father too. The thought sent a dagger of ice into my chest.

I closed my eyes and tried to settle my nerves. *It was a dream. It was just a dream. The bond with Roehl was broken. He has no hold on me.*

The next time I opened my eyes, the sun was bright, peeking in through cracks in the draperies. Slipping out of bed, my bare feet padded across the warmed floor toward the windows. Tugging the draperies open, I closed my eyes as the heat of the sun enveloped me. I soaked it in until it reached my bones, taking away the aching darkness that had crept into my dreams.

My body wasn't sore like it had been last night. Maybe those bath salts did have magic. Or maybe, it was the vampire part of me that helped heal me faster. Or maybe, it was because I had been touched by the Fire Goddess.

After a few minutes of basking in the sunshine, I made my way to the small table that held a tray of fruit, cheese, biscuits, and even some warm tea steaming in a pot. I poured some tea into the cup and took a sip. I'd found that drinking liquids were fine. I never felt sick whenever I drank anything.

The hot tea tasted like summer, with hints of floral and citrus. Next, I picked up a biscuit and slathered some butter and honey on it. Holding it up to my nose, I sucked in a deep breath. Gods, I wanted to sink my teeth into it, but knew this *would* make me sick.

Or would it?

I was a vampire, yet my heart still beat, and I could walk in the sun.

What if I could eat regular food?

One small bite wouldn't hurt. A small bite to confirm my suspicions.

I brought the biscuit up to my mouth and took a small bite. My eyes closed, and I moaned out loud. Gods. This was freaking amazing. I savored the buttery, sweet taste in my mouth and then . . . I swallowed.

I stood there like a statue, waiting for a minute to pass.

Nothing happened.

I waited a minute more.

Still nothing.

Goddess. What if . . .

Oh shit. My stomach.

The nausea slammed me like a brick.

I heaved while sprinting to the bathroom and made it to the toilet just in time.

After ten minutes of heaving, I was spent.

That was it. Food was off the miracle table and would remain my curse.

My thoughts swung to Sabine and how she was doing. Hopefully, she'd slept in, and her bath salts worked. But, if I knew her, she was probably up at the crack of dawn, showered, with her bed and room made up before the servants arrived.

I was itching to get out of this palace and find a secluded place to see what my powers could do. If what the goddess said was true, and I could call the elements with a thought, I had to get out of this place and test it out for myself.

Cracking the door open, I saw a guard standing outside. He was new. A tall, broad man with sandy blonde hair and light brown eyes. As soon as he saw me, he turned and placed a fist to his heart, bowing his head.

"Can I get you something, princess?"

My internal self groaned. "Please, just call me Calla. By the way, do you know where Everett is?"

"He's off today, but asked me to post here."

"Oh, okay. Thank you."

I didn't sense anything negative about this guard, and if Everett trusted him to watch over us, then I guess I could trust him too.

"Do you know of any places I could go to be alone for a while? I'd like to be out in nature and . . . meditate." That wasn't a full lie.

"There are many places," he said, then a smile widened on his face. "But there is one place I like to take my wife and son. Not many know about it, and hardly anyone goes because you must travel into a dark cave to get there. Once you exit the cave on the other side, there is a place like nothing else on the island. A clearing with flowers and trees and even a small lake and waterfall. I happened upon it one day while hunting."

Water, trees, sunshine... that was perfect.

"Could you take me? I promise I won't tell a soul about your place."

He paused for a moment and glanced down the hallway. "Yes, when would you like to leave?"

I knew Markus wouldn't be able to come. Maybe one day I'd find a way for him to walk in the daylight. For now, he had to live in the dark, so I had to drag Sabine along.

"I'd like to go as soon as possible, and since this place is private, is there a way we can avoid being seen?" I whispered.

"Yes. There is a secret room with a tunnel that leads out to the stable." He pointed down the hall. "But that is another thing you cannot speak of. Only the queen and the guards know of this door. It was created in case we were ever attacked."

I placed a finger over my lips. "I promise I won't tell a soul, and neither will my friend."

"Good," he said, his face relaxing with relief.

"By the way, what's your name?" I thought it would be rude if I didn't ask. He had been nice to me.

He again placed his fist over his heart and bowed his head. "Callum."

"It's nice to meet you, Callum." I thumbed down the way. "I'm going to go check on my friend. I have a feeling she's already up."

He gave a nod, so I ambled over to Sabine's door and knocked. Almost instantly, the door flew open.

Sabine was dressed in black pants and a maroon tunic that was tied at the waist. Her hair was in a braid over her right shoulder, and she looked very . . . awake.

"I've been waiting for you to arrive," she said, popping a slice of orange into her mouth.

Laughing, I shook my head. "Yeah, I figured you were." Stepping inside her room had confirmed my assumption. It was clean and tidied up. "Hey, do you want to come with me to a private spot to *meditate*?" I asked and gave her a wink.

Her eyes narrowed. "Sure?"

"Good. I'll come get you in ten minutes. I just need to get ready."

"Okay. I'll be here. Waiting."

After throwing on the outfit Trystan had left me—black pants, tunic, belt, and boots—and braiding my hair, I opened the door to see Callum and Sabine standing there.

"I knew you'd be out soon, so I decided to meet you," she said with a wide, toothy grin.

Fern rounded the corner holding a bunch of bed linen and towels. She bowed and raised her eyes, only to my chin. "Are you going somewhere, miss?" she asked.

"Yes," I said. "My friend and I are going somewhere to meditate. It's somewhat of a ritual and I need to be outdoors. Maybe a garden or something."

"There is a beautiful garden at the back of the palace," she stated with a closed-lipped smile.

"Thank you, Fern," I said. "Oh, and you left me a tray of biscuits and fruit, but I can't have that."

Her eyes widened, and she bowed her head. "I'm sorry,

miss. I wasn't the one who brought it up. I'll be sure to tell the kitchen."

"Don't be sorry," I said, waving it off.

"They can always bring the extra food to my room." Sabine chuckled. "Those biscuits are to die for."

Fern's gaze never lifted from the floor, but another smile raised on her lips. "I will." She curtseyed again. "I'm going to change your linen, if that's okay."

"Yes, go ahead." I opened the door to let her in.

Fern nodded and made a beeline through the door. Poor girl. She must not have been comfortable around strangers. Then again, there was a time when I wasn't either. Hell, I still wasn't. It was just that this new life had pushed it right out of me.

As soon as Fern disappeared into the room and closed the door, Callum waved us over.

"Follow me." He quickly led us down to the end of the hall and turned to face the right wall. Callum grabbed the sconce and yanked it down. The wall cracked open, and Sabine and I glanced at each other, wide-eyed.

Giving a quick glance down the hall, to make sure no one was coming, Callum quickly pushed against the wall and it opened. "Quickly," he said. "Inside." There was an urgency to his voice. Like he knew he was doing something he shouldn't, and I didn't want to get him in trouble. Sabine and I quickly followed, and he shut the door behind us, leaving us in complete darkness.

I called a flame into my palm and the small tunnel illuminated.

"I'm sorry," Callum said. "I should have been more prepared."

"Don't be sorry. When I'm around, no one needs a light. Fire is at my beck and call."

"You're so convenient," Sabine chuckled, nudging my side.

Callum squeezed past us and headed down the stairwell. "Come, we must hurry. The stable hands will be changing soon. That's our only chance of taking the horses without being seen."

"What if we are seen?" I asked.

He shrugged. "I'll tell them you wanted to go for a ride."

"It's not a lie. By the way, what time is it?" I asked.

"Nearly noon. They will be heading to the kitchen for their midday meal."

Midday meal. That was a cool way of saying lunch. I'd use it in the future.

The tunnel smelled old and musty and there were cobwebs clinging to the walls. Thank the goddess there were no spiders attached to them because I'd incinerate this tunnel.

"How do you know Everett?" I asked, on our way down.

"He is my brother-in-law. His wife is my sister."

"And he sent you to watch over us?"

"Yes. There have been rumors going around that you are a witch who came to Incendia with marks that were created by mortals on your palms. They are also saying you plan to take over the throne."

I closed my gaping mouth. "Are you serious?" I growled, my flame growing larger.

"Whoa," Sabine squealed, jumping down a few stairs. "I don't want to burn in a hidden passageway."

"I'm sorry," I said taming my flame. "But that rumor is the furthest thing from the truth."

Callum nodded. "There are some who are loyal to the queen and would go to any length to make sure she stays on the throne."

"Does the queen know you are guarding us?" I questioned.

"No."

Sabine and I shot each other a worried look. He was doing this behind the queen's back, and so was Everett, for asking him to do such a favor.

"Well, Calla is not a witch, and those marks are real. I was there when the spell that bound her powers was released," Sabine huffed.

"I'm not saying that I don't believe. I do. And so does Everett. I'm just telling you what we heard. The rumors started from someone who doesn't want you here."

"It probably came from your queen. She's jealous of Calla." Sabine had her finger pointed at Callum.

Callum had an expression on his face that made me wonder if he didn't like the queen. She'd been queen for a long time, and they were still alive and seemed to be thriving.

"Look, I didn't come here to steal any throne, nor do I want to rule any kingdom. I came here for answers, and to learn about this land that was ruled by my ancestors. Although I've met the Fire Goddess and received her blessing, I have every intention of leaving Incendia soon."

Callum stopped and looked up at me with a worried look. "Why would you leave?"

I returned a sad smile. "I don't belong here right now. There may come a time in the future when I'll return to Incendia, but there are some things I have to do first," *and an individual I'll have to kill.* I was glad that there were at least two people who wanted me here. "Look, we really don't have time for this. I would really like to get out of this stairwell and to the secret place."

We all hurried down to the bottom and reached another door. Callum held his pointer finger up to his lips. I quenched the light and both Sabine and I stood like statues.

Callum cracked open the door and peeked out, then quickly shut it.

I called a small flame, the size of a candle into my palm, just so we could see each other's faces.

"They're feeding the horses. They should be done shortly," Callum whispered.

After a few more minutes, he peeked out the door again, then swung the door wide open. "Quickly. We don't have much time," he said rushing out.

He went to the stalls and grabbed a saddle and started

saddling the horse I rode the other night. Sabine grabbed a saddle and threw it onto her horse, Amara, and began to fasten it.

"I thought you never rode a horse before last night," I said.

Sabine shrugged. "There was a short time in Morbeth when I worked in the stables. My daddy was sick, so I took his place and saddled many horses for Morbeth's army. But I never rode one." Her expression turned sad. "Not long after, they both passed from the Black Death. It killed many of the mortal slaves. I was lucky to have survived."

"I'm sorry, Sabine," I breathed.

"Don't be. They're in a better place now, and that makes me happy."

I nodded, smiling at her.

With all three horses saddled, Callum quickly helped us mount ours before leading us out. Loud laughs echoed in the area behind the stable.

"They're coming," Callum said. "Hurry." He kicked his horse, and we did the same. Our horses took off galloping from the stables, into a small thicket of trees off to the side. When we were safely hidden, Callum slowed his horse.

"We'll have to go out the front gate. I'll tell the guards I'm taking you for a ride. You don't have to say anything."

In other words, he wanted us to keep quiet.

"We won't," Sabine and I answered together.

I started to feel a little uneasy, like we were going to pay for breaking a rule. But hey, I was a guest here. I wasn't a resident and should be able to see the place. I'd never explored Incendia during the day, except on our way to the mountain, and the entire time I was thinking about meeting the Fire Goddess. I didn't notice any of the scenery except the steep, rocky cliffs I was hoping I wouldn't fall off.

I wondered what Markus would think of us leaving the wall without him. I knew he wouldn't be happy, and we'd hear an earful—if, and when—he ever found out. He traveled to the Crag before the sun rose, so he could be there to protect us.

As we rode down the side streets, eyes seemed to stop and stare. Not one smile raised on their lips, which made me feel a bit uncomfortable.

"Witch!" voices spat. "Leave our island. You don't belong here!"

I turned and saw a gaggle of women, their judging eyes narrowed at me. "Imposter!"

Gods. So much hate for someone they didn't even know.

"She's not a witch, you bitter bitches!" Sabine hollered. I looked at her face which was twisted with fury.

"Sabine, it's not worth it," I said.

She turned to me and growled. "I'm beginning to hate this place."

"They don't know any better. They're protecting their queen."

"You are their queen," she murmured through narrowed

teeth.

"I'm not. Nor do I want to be."

"I wouldn't want to either."

As we neared the wall, Callum steered us back onto the main road. My stomach knotted, spotting six guards standing in front of the gate. When we first arrived, there had been only two.

When we reached the gate, two guards stepped forward, their long spears crisscrossing, stopping us from going further.

"No one leaves the town," one of them said, stepping forward with his hand on the hilt of his sword. He was short and stocky with black hair and dark-brown beady eyes, wearing a scowl on his face.

I could feel my skin heat and closed my eyes, telling myself to relax, or I'd burn his smug ass face off.

Whoa. Where did that thought come from? I'd never had thoughts of hurting anyone. Except Roehl. He was the only one who brought feelings of rage out of me and I hated it. I was the girl who had a hard time stepping on bugs.

I once found a nest on the ground after a storm. One of the baby birds was dead a few feet away, but I found one, barely alive. I cared for it and fed it until it was strong enough to fly on its own. The bird made its nest on my porch and would visit me regularly when I would sit outside to read.

But things were different now. This other life, this immortal world, wasn't simple or sympathetic. It was dark and dangerous with individuals who wanted me dead.

"Our guests would like to take a ride outside the wall," Callum explained, breaking me from my thoughts. "They want to experience the landscape."

The other four guards moved in front of the gate, weapons drawn.

"The queen has ordered that everyone stay inside, as a precautionary measure," the stocky man stated.

I moved my horse next to Callum's. "What precautionary matter? We are guests here, not residents."

"These are the queen's orders," His snarky attitude was heating me up. "If you have questions, I suggest you take that up with her."

These people didn't care who I was, or that I was Incendian royalty. And now, the queen was deliberately keeping me, and my friends caged behind these walls. She had no idea what I could do. But, on the other hand, neither did I. Not since my meeting with the Fire Goddess. The magic inside was itching to test its limits.

"They won't be alone. I will be escorting them," Callum said in a calm voice. "There is no reason she should be held here. She is Incendian royalty."

The guards laughed. "Incendian royalty? Just because she says she is, doesn't mean she is. Anyone can put tattoos on their palms and claim royalty. I've seen witches who can cast magic to make fire." The other guards murmured their agreement, nodding their heads.

"How dare you!" Sabine yelled, hopping down from her

horse, but her foot caught in the stirrup and she almost fell. The guards snickered, but she somehow managed to unhook her foot and stomp over to the stocky guard, her finger inches from his face. "She *is* Incendian royalty. She defeated the Sangerian Sea serpent, by herself, on our way here. Yesterday, we traveled to the Crag where she met with the Fire Goddess. Tell me anyone else here who has done that."

The guard smirked again. "Like I said, just because you say it's true doesn't make it so. None of us saw her defeat a sea serpent, nor did we see her enter the Crag. It's all hearsay."

Sabine turned to me, her face red, brow furrowed, and eyes narrowed. "Calla show them! Let them see how powerful you are."

Goddess above, she was a spark today.

I sighed and looked at Callum, whose brow was furrowed and dotted with sweat. There was one thing my dad taught me. *People will believe what they want to believe, so don't ever feel like you have to prove yourself. As long as you know who you are, that's all that matters.*

He was right. I didn't have to prove myself to these guys. Yes, I could probably rain down hellfire and burn the assholes to ash, but that wasn't me.

"Let's go, Sabine," I said, turning my horse around.

"Calla! Are you serious? Did you hear what they said?" Sabine was furious and stomped her foot on the ground.

"I did," I said over my shoulder, tugging on the reins. "And I won't lower myself. I am who I am, and nothing will change that. It's up to them to choose whether they believe or not."

Callum turned his horse and followed me. Sabine blurted a bunch of curse words as she mounted her horse. In less than a minute, she caught up to me.

"Why didn't you show them?" she huffed, riding alongside my horse. "It makes me so angry they don't believe you're the true heir to Incendia."

"I really don't care," I sighed, turning to her with a sad smile. "I'm the new girl here and still young. They think I'm lying because they thought all the royals had died when Morbeth came. I don't blame them for disbelieving, but I also won't use my power to prove myself. Besides, I won't be here long, anyway."

"You mean, *we* won't be here long." Sabine glanced at me and frowned.

"Of course, I want you to come with me. I also want you to find someplace to settle down and be happy. You shouldn't be running for your life across the continent with me."

"Look," she said pointedly. "I have no family and no friends besides those in Morbeth, and I will let you burn me alive before I go back there. And I sure as hell am not staying here without you." Her face was crumpled and so angry. "Besides, you and Markus are my family now. We're in this together and wherever you go, I go."

I reached over and grabbed hold of her hand, giving it a squeeze.

"Princess," Callum interrupted. "I don't know if I'll be able to stay with you for the remainder of the day. Please, be safe."

"Are you going to get into trouble because of me?" I asked.

"No," he said, but his eyes didn't meet mine.

I shook my head and heeled my horse, and it galloped toward the palace.

"Princess, wait!" Callum's voice called out behind me.

"Calla! Where are you going?" Sabine hollered.

"To talk to the queen!"

There was no way in hell I'd let Callum take the blame for taking me out of the palace. It was my idea. I wanted to go out to test my power. He just obeyed and I was going to make sure he didn't get punished for it.

CHAPTER NINE

I knew Callum and Sabine were following behind, but I didn't want them to stop me. As soon as I reached the stable, I dismounted my horse and handed the reins to the first stable hand I saw. Then, I headed back inside. I marched toward the entrance of the palace where two guards were stationed on either side. They didn't stop me from entering so I stomped right past them.

I watched Thalia exit from one of the back rooms, wearing a long, blue cotton dress that was cinched at the waist. Her golden hair was half-up, half-down, and from afar, she looked like a goddess.

"Thalia," I called, and she glanced up at me. "I need to speak to the queen."

She gave me an eye sweep and raised her brow. "Where have you been?"

"Riding," I exhaled. "I wanted to go outside of the wall

and see the island, but six guards stopped us at the gate and said we couldn't leave. It appears the queen has ordered everyone to stay inside because of *precautionary matters*."

"Precautionary matters?" Thalia's brow furrowed. It was obvious she didn't know about it. "Follow me." She led me down the same corridor we went the night before when we had dinner. "She's having lunch."

Figures.

As soon as we stepped inside the room, the queen's eyes met mine, and a scowl came and quickly disappeared on her face. She had a spread in front of her that she would never be able to finish. Meats, cheeses, fruit, bread. Gods, her leftovers alone could feed a third of the people outside.

"Calla," she said, trying to sound friendly, but failing. "Come, sit. Is there anything I can help you with?"

"Yes, actually," I said, walking up to one of the chairs. I placed my hands on the back of it but didn't sit down. "I asked one of the guards to take me outside the wall so I could explore the island. When we got to the exit, we were stopped. The guards there said we weren't allowed to leave. They had no reason, so I thought I'd come ask you."

The queen slowly placed her fork down, picked up her napkin, and gently dabbed her lips. "Yes. Well, there have been some rumors going around of a possible attack. I'm taking every necessary precaution to keep my people safe. I will not let them suffer and die like the others did." She was referring to Leora. "I will make sure no one behind these walls is injured."

A possible attack.

I suddenly found it hard to breathe. My heart jack hammered against my chest and in my ears. What if Roehl had found me? I knew it would be a matter of time, but this was only my third day here.

"What did you hear?" I questioned. "Who is coming?"

"I am uncertain," she said, slicing a piece of juicy meat and lifting it to her lips. We waited until she was done chewing, and gods, it was so annoying. "I have guards on our shores and some scouring the terrain. Until they return with news, everyone will stay inside the wall."

I guess that was a reasonable explanation. She was trying to protect her people and I couldn't get mad at her for doing that.

"I understand and respect your decision," I said, bowing my head. "I also want you to know that I will leave before any trouble comes to Incendian shores."

"For the next few days, you are safe here. Please stay." Her smile turned warm, and it sent a shiver down my spine. How could her attitude change so quickly? "Tomorrow, the guards will return with news. If there is no threat, you will be free to explore the island."

"Thank you," I said, and turned to leave.

"Calla, please stay and dine with me." The queen placed her fork and knife down on her plate and lifted her wine glass. She motioned for one of the servant girls and when she came, the queen whispered in her ear.

Thalia and I glanced at each other. She had an unreadable expression on her face.

The servant bowed to the queen then left the room.

"I don't think I've properly introduced myself," the queen said. She set down her wine glass and leaned forward. "My name is Garinda."

I smiled and bowed my head in respect, but Garinda seemed like a harsh name.

A few minutes later, the servant girl returned with a tall glass filled with crimson liquid and set it down on the table in front of me.

"Come now, don't be shy," the queen said. "Thalia, sit and join us." That was an order.

Thalia pulled out the seat next to me and plopped down, then began piling food onto the plate in front of her. I took my seat and instantly smelled the coppery liquid in the glass. I felt my incisors lengthen but closed my eyes and begged them to recede. When they did, I relaxed and took the glass in my hands. It was so warm. I placed it up to my nose and sniffed.

"I assure you, it's safe," the queen said. "I would take a sip to prove it to you, but blood disgusts me."

I sighed and placed the glass to my lips. It was sweet and warm and didn't have any bitter aftertaste. The servant who brought the glass, peeked out from the kitchen door, which was situated behind the queen. She smiled and raised her arm, which had a small towel pressed against it.

I gave a nod and smile, and the queen immediately picked up on it. She followed my eyes, but the servant quickly ducked back into the kitchen, avoiding her.

The servant girl had assured me the blood was safe, and I was grateful for that.

I promptly finished the liquid in the glass and kept my eyes closed as its magic coursed through my veins. I could feel the energy of the blood, restoring me, giving my cells what they required to regenerate. It was the sole thing I despised about being part monster—consuming blood. But, it wasn't as dreadful as most people assumed it was. I healed much faster than normal, and my senses were highly acute.

The queen cleared her throat, her fingers dancing over her lips.

"Don't you have those things? What are they? Fangs?"

Thalia began choking on something she'd just placed in her mouth. Really choking. So, I slapped a hand on her back and offered her water.

"I'm so sorry," Thalia wheezed, pushing her chair back. "I'll be back."

The queen rolled her eyes. "That girl has never had proper manners. She comes and goes as she pleases. She's lucky we have relations, or she'd be a servant."

"How are you related?" I asked.

"Her mother was my sister-in-law. She was murdered by those bloodsuckers, so I took her in and raised her."

"That was very kind of you."

She motioned for one of the servants to come and fill up her wine glass. "Yes. It was."

There was a moment of awkward silence, and I struggled with what to say. I felt like one wrong word, and those eye daggers would fly.

My eyes swept over all the food on the table. Where did it all go? Did the servants get to eat it?

"How have your accommodations been?" the queen finally asked, pushing her plate to the side. She then made another hand motion, and the servants cleared her dish.

"Wonderful," I replied as another servant came and cleared my glass. "The room is very spacious and comfortable, and everyone here has been so kind. My friends and I cannot thank you enough for your generous hospitality. Incendia is a beautiful place."

"It is beautiful. It took a lot of effort to rebuild after those monsters came. It took many years of struggling and finding the perfect place for a new town, but we finally created a haven for the people. We will never be attacked again. Not without us knowing."

Thalia stepped back into the room. "Sorry. I must have bit off more than I could chew." She gave a quick and short curtsey to the queen who returned a displeasing look.

"I have to attend a meeting, so I'll leave you two to finish." The queen stood from her seat and walked out of the room, without casting a glance our way. The pair of servants standing against the back wall followed her out. They must have been her handmaidens.

One thing the queen had said, had my mind churning. They had to find a place for their new town. That meant that there were ruins of the old Incendia. I wanted to go there. I wanted to see it.

I made sure the queen was gone before I asked Thalia. "Do you know where the old ruins of Incendia are?"

She broke off a piece of bread and shoved it in her mouth. "Everyone does. It's on the other side of the Crag."

It had taken us hours to get to the Crag, but I really wanted to see the place Leora, and her predecessors ruled.

I leaned in closer. "Do you think you could take me there?"

She dabbed her lips with her napkin and placed it on the table. "I don't know." She glanced around the room. "Once this town was rebuilt, the queen made it forbidden for anyone to visit the ruins."

"Why?"

"She claims she doesn't want us to look at our past failures. She said we should look forward to the new and brighter future we built together." Thalia shrugged, her facial expression was not showing me that she believed the words she'd just spoken but was merely repeating them.

"How did you know we arrived on the island?" I asked. "That night you found us?"

"There are guards stationed on every shore. As soon as they saw the ship arrive, they sent word."

"Are you part of the guard?"

"I am not. I am an Incendian female. We are supposed to be warriors." Her lips frowned and I could see the frustration in her narrowed eyes and crumpled brow. "We used to be, but since the queen created the wall, she only trains and sends the males out. The females were born to lead. We were born to fight, and she won't allow us to." Frustration laced her words and floated in those green and blue eyes.

I remembered what Leora had told me in the In Between. That Incendian females were the guardians of Incendia. They were the protectors, and the men fought alongside them.

"I'm sorry," I murmured.

"Don't be. It's not your fault," she grumbled. "And she probably won't allow you to go outside of the wall until you leave Incendia."

I shook my head. "I don't understand. Why wouldn't she?"

"Come," she said standing and heading out of the dining room. "Not here."

A servant bowed to me before I left. "Can I get you anything, miss?"

"Yes," I said. "I would be eternally grateful if you would pile a bunch of that food onto a plate and take it up to my female companion."

"Of course, miss," she said with a wide smile.

I quickly chased after Thalia who went down another hallway I hadn't been before. Almost at the end, she opened another door. "This is my room," she said. "No one will bother us here."

Thalia closed and locked the door behind us and went to sit on a lounging chair. Her room was larger than mine and had plush carpets and a large poster bed with lots of pillows. All her furnishings were made of dark wood, and her draperies and linen were done in purples and gold.

I faced her, crossing my arms over my chest. "Now, why won't she allow me out of the wall?"

Thalia gave her signature smirk. "You don't get it, do you?"

I had no idea what she was talking about. "Get what?"

"She said you couldn't leave because there is a threat. Well, *you* are that threat. She wants to keep you where there are eyes on you at all times."

Was she kidding me? "I'm not a threat." Good. Gods. I was getting tired of trying to prove I wasn't a threat. "I'm not here to take her throne."

"You say that, but she thinks otherwise. You sailed all the way here, out of the blue, and showed her your marks. Doing that, was like a slap in her face. I mean, what else is she to think?"

I blew out a harsh breath. "I don't know. It seems like no matter what I say, or do, she won't believe me."

Thalia shook her head. "Probably not, but just so you know, she's the one who started the rumor that you were a witch, and had the tattoos fabricated. She told those around her that you came to destroy Incendia. That's why you brought the others from Morbeth with you."

Shaking my head, my heart ached that she would think such a thing. "If I must, I'll leave tomorrow. I just need a way off the island."

"There will be a merchant ship arriving in three days. I'm sure they'll allow you to ride back with them to Talbrinth."

"I'll let my friends know." I walked over and gazed out Thalia's window, which overlooked a lush garden. Blooming flowers and trees and pathways led around a large courtyard. "Do you think the queen will approve of us leaving?"

This time she nodded. "She will. It'll probably be best for you too. I wouldn't want you or your friends to get hurt."

My spirit was crushed. "Speaking of friends, I have to go. I left my friend outside with the guard and she's probably wondering where the hell I went."

Thalia smiled, then walked to the door and swung it open. "If I were you, I'd lie low these next few days. If you have any questions about Incendia, send one of the servants to find me. I'll try to answer what I can."

"Thank you. I might just take you up on that offer."

Her smile widened and her blue and green eyes sparkled. "Well, you are Incendian royalty. I saw it firsthand at the Crag. And I guess we are related."

"Yes, how are we related?"

"My mother was Leora's first cousin. So, I may not be chosen, but I am of the royal bloodline."

"I guess that makes us cousins too."

"I guess it does." Thalia's smile grew, and for the first time I saw a dimple in her cheek. "Just remember this. There are things you shouldn't say out loud, even in your rooms."

"Well, that's not creepy," I groaned, and she laughed.

"Just remember. She doesn't want to hear—"

"I know," I sighed. "She doesn't want to hear that I saw the Fire Goddess, nor does she want to hear that I am heir to the Incendian throne. Even though that is the furthest thing from my mind."

Thalia nodded. "Just watch what you say and tell your friends to stay close to you. The queen has loyal followers who have nothing better to do than cause trouble."

"I will. Thank you." Thalia bowed her head as I left the room.

Easily finding the marbled stairs that led up to our rooms, I hurried up them, taking two at a time, thinking about leaving.

If the merchant ship took us back to Talbrinth, where would we go?

There was no place that was safe. Not when Roehl had magic and dark mages to help him. Not to mention he used a Wanderer who found me in the middle of the gods-damned forest while we were cloaked by a witch.

As I reached the top of the stairs, I noticed Sabine sitting in the hallway.

"Calla!" She puffed, standing, and marching to me. "Where were you?"

"I'm sorry I left you behind. I went to talk to the queen

because I needed to make sure Callum didn't get into any trouble for taking us out on the horses." I peeked down the hallway but didn't see him.

"He left," she said sadly. "He said he couldn't stay and told me to apologize to you that he wasn't able to take you out today."

"It wasn't his fault." I grabbed her hand and led her into my room, shutting the door behind us.

"What is it?" Sabine's brow scrunched.

"We're leaving Incendia in three days."

"What? How?"

"Thalia said there is a merchant ship coming. They can give us a ride back to Talbrinth."

Sabine shifted, hands on hips, eyes boring into mine. "What did the queen have to say?"

I sighed and proceeded to a chair. I needed to sit. "The queen said she closed the gate as a precautionary measure because she'd heard that there might be a threat to Incendia."

"Roehl?" Sabine gasped, and panic filled her eyes.

"No." I crossed my arms over my chest. "According to Thalia, *I'm* the threat. She thinks I am here to take over her throne, and you and Markus are here to help me."

"Is she mad?" Sabine growled. "Incendia is not what I thought it would be. They're all stuck up bitches here. It doesn't seem so great."

"I bet it used to be great, when the real royals ruled."

"Wait." Sabine held up a hand. "The queen isn't a royal?"

I placed a finger to my lips then went over and whispered softly in her ear, so no spying ears could hear. "The Fire Goddess herself told me she is false. She doesn't bear the marks."

"Goddess above," Sabine mouthed. "No wonder she's jealous."

Nodding, I got up and walked over to the bed, and fell backward, my arms above my head. "We have to lie low the next few days. Just until the ship comes."

"Okay, but I'm packing all the bath salts and taking extra biscuits."

I laughed at her. "Do it, and you can take mine too."

"I wonder what Markus will think about what happened today," she whispered.

"I'll talk to Markus," I said. "It's best if one of us stays quiet. Besides, I'm the one who dragged you along. You were an innocent bystander."

"What do you think he'll say about us leaving?"

"Honestly, I think he'll be thrilled to leave this place. I know he's uncomfortable here. Especially being locked up all day."

Sabine moaned. "I'm really not looking forward to being on the ocean again. I'm just starting to feel better. Except for my ass after riding that horse. It's still bruised."

I flung a pillow at her and she caught it. "That's for your sore ass."

Both of us burst into laughter as she stood and placed the

pillow on her seat and sat down.

"My ass is thankful."

"Good. Now, what are we going to do for the next three days?"

Sabine stood and ambled to the opposite side of my bed and dropped backward, right next to me. "Since we have all this time, and you couldn't talk to me in private until now, I want you to spill. I want to know what the Fire Goddess said to you," she whispered.

I rolled to my side and propped my head up on my arm, while Sabine stared at me.

"I have to be careful of what I say around here, but I know I can trust you. We must keep our voices down to a whisper."

Sabine nodded so I moved closer to her.

"Well, she confirmed I am the chosen one, and that I shouldn't be afraid of my power. And get this. She also said that I have the gift to control not only fire and water, but earth and air."

Sabine popped straight up. "What? Are you kidding me?"

I shook my head. "That's why I wanted Callum to take us to some place secluded. I wanted to test out this power she said I have."

"Did she tell you how to use it?"

I shook my head again. "She said that my gifts are connected to me, and I should already know how to use them. They'll come to me when I need them."

"Okay," Sabine's eyes were wide, and I could almost see the cogs in her mind turning. "Wait here. I'll be right back." She hopped off the bed and ran out of the room. A few minutes later she returned with a small, potted plant.

"What's that for?"

"It's earth," she chimed. "It's dying, so I thought maybe you could try to fix it."

"Um. I don't think I can fix a dying baby plant. Besides, I don't even know what I can do."

Sabine grabbed my hand and shoved the small pot into it. "Try it. Let's see."

Rolling my eyes, I held the small terracotta pot between my palms. I wasn't even sure what kind of plant this was, but it looked sickly and yellowish. "What this plant needs is water."

Sabine's eyes glistened. "Then, give it some. There's a cup over there."

I offered her an exasperated look. "Fine, but you do realize this will be me manipulating water. Not earth. And if it makes a mess, you're cleaning it up."

She gave a sly grin. "You know it's what I do best."

With the plant in between my palm, I looked at the cup of water and in my mind, asked it to come and water the plant. Slowly, the water began to rise until it was hovering above the cup. It looked like a see-through blob.

Sabine gasped as the water blob slowly made its way across the room.

"Goddess above, that is amazing," she said walking close to it. Her finger reached out to poke it, and as she did, my concentration broke. Sabine jumped back as the blob of water crashed to the ground, making a puddle on the floor.

Sabine squealed, jumping up and down, clapping her hands. "You did it! Goddess above, you did it!"

"Do you *not* see the puddle on the floor?"

Her hands shot to her hips, head tilted. "Then finish what you started," she said gesturing to the floor.

"Are you serious?"

"Dead," she said.

It was then, I realized Sabine hadn't seen me defeat the Sea Serpent. She was in the room when it happened. So, this was the first time she'd seen me manipulate water.

I blew out a breath and concentrated on the puddle. The water rose from the floor in droplets that glopped together to form the water blob. In my mind, I told it to go faster. Suddenly, the blob shot straight to the pot, slamming into it. Sabine squealed and clapped, then laughed and pointed at the muddy water dripping down my face. "You did it, Calla. You did it!"

I growled and headed to the washroom.

At least I had water and fire in my arsenal. The water was messy, but it worked. Now, I just needed to figure out how to tame it.

CHAPTER TEN

I couldn't help but feel satisfaction as I carried the newly watered plant into the washroom and set it on the counter. Grabbing a washcloth, I wiped the muck off my face.

Sabine peeked in the washroom. "Hey, I'm going to find my lady." She meant servant. "And ask her when she'll be bringing lunch."

"I asked them to bring you some food. Go check, and if they didn't, I'll take you down to the kitchen and we can scrounge something up."

"Sounds good," she replied. Not long after I heard the door open and shut.

My eyes moved to the plant.

Yes, I had manipulated the water, but the plant didn't do a thing. I mean, plants were part of the earth, right? And the goddess said I was able to manipulate all elements, including earth.

I picked up the plant and observed it.

"Do something," I ordered.

But nothing happened.

I focused on it, like I had with the water, but still . . . nothing. The only movement was from me rattling the damn thing. Maybe that part of my gift was still dormant. Or maybe, like Helia said, it would show when I needed it.

Sabine returned a few minutes later with a tray in her hands and a plate with a mound of food on it. "Do they think I can eat all this?"

"Obviously," I answered. It had a little of everything that was on the dining table.

She paused. "Whatever. You don't mind if I eat in your room, do you?"

"Go for it. They fed me while I was speaking to the queen."

Her eyes expanded. "They did? Who *fed* you?"

"One of the kitchen servants. But she secretly showed me it was safe."

"That's good." Sabine plopped her tray down on a table and pulled up a chair. She had baked bread with roasted meat and mixed vegetables, fruit, and more.

My mouth was watering, so I wandered toward the window and stared out. The sun was bright and there wasn't a cloud in the baby blue sky. I decided to open the window, and as soon as I did, a black mass flew at me.

I shrieked as Flint settled on the window sill.

"Where have you been?" I scolded, upset that he'd startled the crap out of me.

"That's the bird the Fire Goddess gave you?" Sabine questioned.

"It is."

"It looks just like Prince Trystan's bird."

"It does. But Nyx is helpful."

Flint let out one of his shrill screeches, making Sabine curse. Then, the bird started dancing on the sill, thrashing his wings. "I think he's trying to tell you something," Sabine noted, aiming her fork at him. "Or maybe it has to pee."

"Birds don't pee. They just poop that white pasty shit."

Flint glared at me, his wings flapped. Maybe he *was* trying to say something. "What is it?" I asked, holding a palm out to him. He hopped closer and touched his beak to my tattoo. A fire kindled in my palm, and my tattoo warmed.

Then, Flint turned and flew away.

"What was that about?" Sabine asked.

"I have no idea," I said, making a fist and stifling the flame. "That bird is so strange."

Sabine went back to eating while I shut the window, afraid of what else could fly in.

"I feel sad for Markus," Sabine sighed. "I bet he'd be a much more pleasant man if he had some sunshine."

I smiled, shutting my eyes to let the sunshine kiss my eyelids. "He definitely would."

I turned back to Sabine and leaned against the sill. "If you could travel anywhere in Talbrinth, where would you want to go? Once the ship takes us out of here, we will be free to go wherever we choose."

Sabine placed her fork down and tapped a finger to her chin. "I've always wanted to visit Carpathia." A broad grin spread on her face. "I've heard an extremely handsome and eligible prince lives there."

My heart ached at the mention of Trystan and Carpathia. "I don't think we should go there."

Sabine's lip pouted. "Why not? Isn't your best friend there?"

"Yes, but Roehl is still out there too. Right now, I am a walking curse. Wherever I go, he will eventually follow, destroying everyone and everything around me."

"But the Carpathian Prince is strong, and he has his cadre. I'm sure Carpathia has an army of their own."

"I know. There is no telling what Roehl would do. Trystan has my best friend in Carpathia. Her parents are dead because of Roehl, and the last thing I want to do is lead him there. She was taken, right out from under his nose, so I know he won't let that pass either. For now, I need to stay as far away from her as I can."

Sabine sighed and rose from her chair. "Calla, I know you don't want anybody around you to get hurt, but you can't do this alone. There are people who want to help you, like Markus and me. Prince Trystan traveled all the way from Carpathia to locate you in Sartha . . . to save you. He also came into Morbeth, for goddess sake, and tried to get Roehl to set you free. Maybe you shouldn't run from him, but toward him. Because I know he's already proven, more than once, that he wants to keep you safe."

I sighed and plopped back down on the bed. I knew she was right, but if anyone got hurt because Roehl was after me . . . it would be a burden on my shoulders that I couldn't bear. I had always been one to do things on my own. But I also realized that I wouldn't be able to defeat Roehl on my own. Even Helia said to keep my allies close.

"We'll see," I replied, and Sabine grunted.

I closed my eyes as she finished her midday meal.

"What about Aquaris? You mentioned your grandparents lived there."

"They did, but they've both passed on."

Sabine walked up to the window and peered out, her eyes intently staring out into the distance. "That's an unusual cloud formation," she said, her finger aiming in the distance.

I sat up on the bed and saw a heavy patch of ominous clouds coming. "It looks like a storm is brewing."

"Yeah, a bad one, but it's strange. It only seems to be in that one area."

A heavy pound on the door made us both jump and before I could open it, it swung open.

Thalia stormed in with an expression of terror in her eyes. She was clad in the garb she wore the night she caught us. A quiver of arrows strapped to her shoulder and bow in hand.

"You have to leave. Now!" she implored.

I was still trying to process her outfit. "What's going on?"

"The queen," she exhaled, trying to catch her breath. "The queen used her mages to contact the Prince of Morbeth. Roehl is on his way here. He's coming for you."

Panic. Dread. Complete and unmitigated terror gripped every part of me. The ominous cloud wasn't a storm. It was much worse. It was Roehl.

The world around me began to spin and go hazy and the sounds dampened.

"Calla!" I could hear Sabine calling me, but I couldn't breathe. My chest was tight. I couldn't suck in adequate air.

Hands gripped my shoulders and shook. Shook me until I met Thalia's widened eyes. "Calla! We have to leave *now!*"

I pulled myself from the fear that tried to take me captive and spoke one word. "Markus."

Markus couldn't be out in the daytime. There was no way for him to escape Roehl. He was stuck here in that gods awful room until nightfall, and by then, it would be too late.

Roehl would not go easy on him. Markus outrightly defied him. He took me from my cell, released the King, executed guards, and brought me out of Morbeth. He would be mercilessly tortured and executed for what he'd done.

"The guards will be arriving shortly. They'll lock you in the cell," Thalia cried.

I shoved her away and rushed to Markus's door and banged loudly.

"Markus! Markus, open the door! Markus! Now!"

The door opened, and a hand reached out and tugged me in. I stumbled into the pitch-black room and slammed into a broad, solid frame. "What the hell is all that gods-damned commotion?"

"Roehl is coming," I wailed, clutching onto his arms. "The queen told him I was here. He's on his way."

Markus cursed, a deep growl rumbled in his chest. "Calla, you have to leave. You have to get as far away from here as you can."

"I'm not leaving without you!"

Markus grabbed my shoulders. "Yes, you are. I am perfectly capable of taking care of myself. I haven't lived this long not to have a few tricks up my sleeve. Besides, I'm not easy to capture."

Tears spilled down my cheeks, my heart bursting. "Promise me, Markus. Promise me you'll get away. Promise me he won't find you."

Markus wrapped his arms around me in a tight embrace. "I cannot promise you anything, but I will give you my word. I will do whatever it takes to stay alive." His arms released me, but his hands cradled my face. "Now, you have to make me a promise."

Tears fell in torrents down my face. "What?"

"That you'll do whatever it takes to stay alive. Even if it means leaving me here."

A heavy sob burst from my chest.

"Princess," he said sharply, shaking my shoulders.

"I promise," I cried, hugging him again.

Sabine and Thalia were pounding on the door. Markus pried me off him and kissed my forehead. "Now run, Princess. Save yourself and take care of Sabine. I'll catch up to you both later."

I nodded, then he brought me to the door and opened it, remaining behind it in the dark. Sabine grabbed my arm and yanked me out and down the corridor toward the hidden room. Thalia was ahead of us, already tugging the sconce, revealing the secret passage.

We all rushed inside and leaned back against the door as I called fire to my palm, lighting up the room.

"Markus?" Sabine asked me, tears spilling down her face.

"He promised he'd catch up to us," I replied, wiping the tears from my face. She nodded, but her face told me she didn't believe me.

"How will we get out of the wall with the guards there?" Sabine's eyes were wide with fright.

Thalia gave me a look. A look of someone who was ready to fight. "Now is the moment to use your gift, Calla. Because you are on Incedian soil, your gifts are amplified. Your power is greatest here. You are the only one who can get us past those guards."

This was it. Now or never.

The sole reason I wasn't buckling with fear was because Sabine was here. The urgency to preserve her life gave me the courage I needed, knowing my greatest adversary, and greatest fear, was heading toward us.

My power had better come to me like the Fire Goddess had said it would, or we would be another tragic ending. I was the last Incendian royal, and I would make sure I gave a hell of a battle, even if it was my last.

"Where will we go once we're out?" I asked. "You said there is no ship for three days."

"We'll head to the shore. You'll have access to both fire and water there to fight. It's our best chance." Thalia ran down the stairwell. "They'll find us soon. We won't have time to saddle the horses. We'll ride bareback."

"How will we steer them?" Sabine's voice was shaking.

"I'll take the lead." Thalia turned to us with an expression of courage. "The other horses will follow. Choose the ones you rode to the Crag."

"Thank you, Thalia," I said, knowing she was now risking her life to save me. "You didn't have to do this."

"I know, and I will only ask one thing in return," she said, peeking out the door to see if it was clear.

"Anything. If we survive this, what do you want?"

She turned to me, her eyes boring into mine. "I want you to take me with you."

Before I could answer, she flew the door open. "Let's go." She ran over to the stall that housed her horse. She unhooked the latch, then climbed the railing and hopped onto his back. Sabine and I did the same.

"Hold on to the mane and don't fall off," Thalia instructed.

"Hey!" one of the stable hands hollered, rushing toward us.

Thalia kicked her horse and it galloped out. Sabine screamed and kicked her horse, and it followed, but she was bouncing all over. Instead of grabbing its mane, she reached down and threw her arms around the horse's neck and held on.

My horse automatically took off in a gallop, and because I'd frequently rode my horse Shadow bareback, I had no problem staying balanced.

Men were yelling, and I didn't dare look back. Instead, I focused on the sound of our horse's hooves, clacking down the cobbled path. People ducked and dove out of our way, yelling curses as we passed.

"Calla!" Thalia called, turning back to me.

We were nearing the gate that now had over a dozen guards who were blocking the exit with swords and spears drawn.

"They are Incendians," I said. "I can't hurt them."

"Then don't. Focus on the ground in front of them and the gate behind. Pave a way for us."

I steadied myself on my horse and raised my right hand, instantly feeling the power coursing through my veins.

A huge ball of fire appeared in my palm. I aimed it at the ground, five feet ahead of the guards, then set it free. The fire flew forward and slammed into the stones. Rocks and debris pelted the guards, the power of the fire's blast sent them flying backward.

Next, I sent another flame to the gate. It flew like an arrow, hitting its mark, exploding the gate into fragments and ash.

With a simple thought, a wall of fire shot up on either side of us, giving us a pathway out. Guards were screaming and scurried off, but none were severely injured.

They'd just witnessed the power of the true heir of Incendia.

Helia was right. The power had come easy. I could feel the connection, and with a thought, it did what I wanted. I could feel the power writhing under my skin, begging to be set free once again.

As Thalia rode past the wall, our horses followed close behind, heading toward the shore. In the distance, the ominous dark cloud grew closer, and with it, a heavy sense of dread lingered in the air.

"The shore is just ahead!" Thalia's finger aimed forward, toward the trees that lined the shoreline. As soon as we reached the sand, we slid off our horses. Thalia slapped her horse on the rear and it galloped away with the other horses in tow.

I glanced out at the sea and saw the dark cloud approaching. It was northwest, coming from Morbeth.

I remembered being told this was how Roehl transported his army of vampires who couldn't be in the sun, and because the sun was directly in its path, it was hidden, turning the island to dusk.

"What do we do? We don't have anywhere to go." Sabine

was panicking, pacing the shoreline, her hands tangled in her hair.

"I might have a way out of here," I said, making a fist with my left palm and closing my eyes. In my mind, I spoke. *"Kai, if you can hear me, I'm in Incendia and I desperately need your help."*

"How?" Thalia asked. "Looks like we'll have to fight. There is no help coming for us."

I held up my left palm that held the water tattoo, and it was glowing blue.

A cold wind whirled around us and there was a high-pitched ringing in my ear. It became so loud, it dropped me to my knees.

"Calla, this is Erro. It's important you listen to me."

Erro? My eyes scoured the shore, but there was no sign of him anywhere.

"What are you looking for?" Thalia questioned.

She didn't hear him. He was speaking in my mind, like he had the first time I'd met him in the Whisper Woods.

"We're coming, and the Prince will send me first. Use your magic and cast me back. I won't die, but I want you to run. Find a way off the island. He's coming for you, child. And he'll kill you all."

I fisted my palm again, this time yelling directly into it. "Kai. I could really use your help. If you don't come to Incendia soon, my friends and I are going to die!"

"Calla, look," Sabine said, pointing to the sky. There,

flying above us was a black crow. "Is that Trystan's?"

I saw a fire ignite in the bird's eye. "It's Flint. He was warning us," I told Sabine.

A gust of wind picked up from the south, blowing our hair, whipping the sand around us. All three of us turned to see a tornado out at sea, heading straight for us.

"We're going to die!" Sabine dropped to the ground and covered her head as the sand pelted us. I ran toward her, covering her with my body.

Thalia had also dropped to the ground, protecting herself. "Is that from Morbeth too?" Thalia asked, lifting her eyes to the huge funnel headed our way.

"I think it's a Wanderer," I said. After the conversation with Erro, it was the only explanation. Wanderers traveled through air.

"Oh gods. There is no way we can escape a Wanderer." Sabine was hyperventilating. Her deep sobs were making my heart ache.

I decided to meet the funnel head on. Standing on the shore, I faced the twister. I had one of two choices left. Fight or die. Or I could die fighting. Regardless, I was going to fight, no matter what. I wasn't Roehl's pet, and I sure as hell wasn't going to be tethered again to his magical leash.

I raised my hands and called to the power of Incendia. Called to the flame within me and summoned the surrounding water.

The ground beneath us began to quake, and I could feel the raw power of the island coursing through my veins. In my right hand, the flame appeared, bigger and brighter than ever before. It was ready and waiting for my command.

I held my left hand out toward the water and summoned it. Power pulsed through my legs, torso, arms, echoing through my palms.

Water shot out from the sea and began to spiral around the three of us like a shield.

"Goddess above," Sabine exhaled.

"Look at her eyes." Those words came from Thalia.

But I couldn't break my concentration. I had to keep my focus because the tornado was just off the shore.

I raised my arms, ready to thrust my power forward when the wind suddenly died. The tornado dissipated and there, through the spiral of water protecting us, I saw five figures standing on the shoreline.

CHAPTER ELEVEN

My arms fell to my sides, causing the water surrounding us to drop to the earth, and snuffing out the fire.

I blinked. And then blinked again, assuming I was seeing ghosts. But they were clear as day. There, standing on the shore, was Trystan and his cadre.

I froze, fearing this was just a wonderful dream. It had to be. He couldn't be here. *They* couldn't be here.

"Calla," an all too familiar voice lifted on the breeze. The sound of him calling my name was like the most exquisite melody.

Trystan ran toward me, ahead of his group. I watched, my feet fixed to my spot until he stood a few feet away from me. Both of us were frozen, gazing into each other's eyes.

Was this real?

But his perfect scent had caught the wind and embraced me, even before his hand reached out and his fingers gently feathered against my cheek.

"You're safe." Trystan sighed in relief, a grin curling on the edge of his sinful lips.

But it was his eyes. Those beautiful azure eyes that seized me and held me captive.

"Tell me this is real," I breathed, placing my hand over his.

His forehead leaned against mine. "It's real."

Uncontrollable tears spilled down my face. "You came for me."

"I did," he murmured, his thumbs gently wiping away my tears. "I told you before. . . in the end, I'll always know I tried to rescue the girl, even if she didn't want to be rescued."

My heart felt like it was going to burst. I flung my arms around Trystan's neck and his arms curled around me, his warmth embracing me.

"Thank you," I exhaled.

"Hey, Calla," Brone's rich voice spoke.

I glanced over Trystan's shoulder to see all four of his men with broad grins on their faces. Brone, Feng, Andrés, and Kylan stood in their fighting leathers with weapons gripped in their palms. They all looked dashingly handsome, especially with Trystan's crest on their chests.

"Hey, Brone. It's been a while," I sniffled.

"We see you've managed to escape the inescapable Red Wall," Andrés added. "And hot damn, you looked like you were about to unleash hell on us. What happened to you?"

"She's emerged from her cocoon," Feng spoke, plunging his long spear into the sand. "The caterpillar has now become a butterfly." He gave me a bright smile. "You are a magnificent creature, Calla Caldwell."

I could feel my face burn with heat. "How did you know I was here?"

"Trystan has his ways," Kylan said, striding forward, bowing his head. "It's nice to see you again, Calla."

"It's nice to see you too. All of you." My heart was nearly full having them here, but there was still one hole. One that could only be filled by Markus.

"They're coming," Thalia urged, seizing an arrow from her quiver.

I turned toward the black cloud, which was now only a mile off the coast. Thunder and lightning cracked within it, resounding through my chest.

I turned to Trystan. "Roehl is here. A Wanderer told me he's coming to kill me."

"He sent a Wanderer?" Brone growled, his eyes tightened and the muscles in his arms bulged.

Trystan grabbed hold of my hand and squeezed. "We are here to fight alongside you. You won't be alone."

I tried not to break down, realizing they'd come to my rescue. Again.

"I have to fight the Wanderer, alone," I announced. "And when I do, I need you and your men to take my friends off the island."

Trystan shook his head. His eyes narrowed as he steadied my face in his hands. "That's not going to happen, Calla. The only way I'm leaving this island is if you're with me."

"Trystan—"

Before I could speak, his lips crashed against mine and hands twisted in my hair. His kiss was wild and unyielding, taking me to a place far from the dark terror behind us.

When he drew away, my mind and body were numb and tingly.

"Trystan, you can't leave her like that right before a battle," Kylan scolded, slapping him on the shoulder.

"Gods-damned, that was intense," Andrés added, fanning himself.

But Trystan's eyes never left mine. "There wasn't a day that passed when I didn't think of your lips on mine."

My heart melted into a puddle on the shore, and even amidst the terror headed our way, I felt stronger, knowing he was here with me. Trystan Vladu, Prince of Carpathia, had come for me. He was my hero. My knight in shining armor. Or fighting leathers.

This wasn't a dream, or a connection to a bond. He was here and he'd arrived just in time.

"Calla!" Thalia hollered, an arrow shot from her bow.

Trystan's eyes tightened to whatever was behind me, his arms folded around my waist, swinging me around until I was behind him.

"Hold her," he instructed, and powerful arms wrapped

around me, holding me steady.

"Brone, let me go!" I growled, struggling to break free from his steel grip.

"I'm sorry, Calla. The prince gave me orders," he murmured in my ear.

Heat filled my veins. "You don't want to play with my fire, Brone. You'll get burned."

"Holy shit," Andrés cursed, pointing at my eyes, and backing away. "Dude, she's not kidding."

Trystan had drawn his sword and was running to meet the ominous cloud head on, which had just reached the shore. Kylan, Feng, and Andrés took off behind him.

Erro suddenly materialized in the area between them and the dark cloud. He was hovering about five feet off the ground, his eyes completely white. I could feel his power throbbing in the air.

Trystan threw his left hand forward, and a powerful wind burst in front of him, but Erro didn't move.

I knew Wanderers were magical, but how magical were they?

Closing my eyes, I invited the energy of the island to come to me. My body warmed and I could sense the magic flowing through my feet, felt it sing in my bones and simmer in my blood. The power flowing through me was so violent I wasn't sure if I could house it. But I had to. For him. For them.

And then . . . a shockwave of energy slammed into me, buckling my knees.

Brone cursed and his arms released me. When I glanced back, he was on the ground, twenty feet away. But he seemed fine.

Stopping in place, I called to my new allies—fire and water. They came, like serpents, weaving around me. Yin and yang—they formed a barricade between me and the approaching terror. But would they be enough?

A crow cawed above and when I looked, I saw Flint. I was positive it was him because his eyes were red with flames.

Flint dove from the sky, shooting toward me like an arrow, his body morphing from crow into the firebird I'd seen in the cave. Gods, he was fast, effortlessly weaving his way through the web of water and fire surrounding me, heading straight for my chest.

Then, Flint's body shot straight through mine.

I wailed in torment, plunging to my knees as a fire consumed me from within.

"Calla!" Sabine and Thalia screamed.

But I couldn't move. I couldn't breathe. The agony was searing and nearly unbearable, but just before my eyes went dim . . . the pain abated.

"Goddess above!" Sabine gasped.

When I spun to her, her eyes were wide, hands covering her mouth. So were Thalia's. Trystan's cadre turned and paused, staring at me with expressions I couldn't read.

What the hell was wrong with them?

It was then I felt something behind me. No, not behind

me. Something tugging against my back. I twisted my head to my side and choked, seeing a wing stretched out to the side of me. A wing formed of fire—burning bright crimson and orange and yellow and blue.

I swung my head to the other side to see a matching wing, extended and blazing.

Heavens above. The Fire Goddess had given me wings.

"Trystan!" Kylan's eyes tightened and my attention jerked back to him.

Erro had lifted his hands toward Trystan and at that moment, I felt an anger build in me I'd never felt before.

That anger roiled through my veins and reverberated in my bones and into my palms. I ordered the fire and water to come back to me, and they came effortlessly, swirling around me.

Then, the Fire Goddess's words resounded through my mind. *"Your gifts are part of you. You are one, connected through word and thought. They will be your greatest ally and will protect you from harm.*

"Fly," I charged, and my fire wings obeyed.

They were a bit awkward at first, unsteady, but I felt the connection between me and the wings as if they were just another limb.

With another thought, the wings flew skyward. Nearly a hundred feet off the ground, they banked and had me circling around Erro and Trystan.

Behind Erro, striding out of the cloud, was a shadowy

figure with crimson rimmed eyes. A man who turned my blood ice cold.

Roehl looked up at me and blinked, his eyes turning completely black. His lips curled into a vicious smile. A smile that sent a shudder down my spine and caused the hair on my body to stand erect, and then, I heard a terrifying whisper in the wind.

"You can't run from me, Pet. I will always find you. I will catch you. And then, you will pay."

Erro's eyes flashed to mine. As did Trystan's.

"Do it, princess," Erro spoke clearly in my mind. *"Do it and run. The Water Prince has arrived."*

My palms flew forward, shooting the water and fire toward my target. Together, they coiled around each other, bursting forward like a battering ram. The force of the two slammed into Erro, the blast so massive, it knocked everyone to their knees.

When the smoke cleared, Erro was gone.

Trystan sent another cyclone of wind forward, toward Roehl and the black cloud, revealing an army of hundreds of soldiers. They were clad in black armor with red dragons emblazoned on their chest plates.

"Hey, Sea Star!" a voice hollered. My attention swung to a wall of water on my left side, and at the top of the crest was Kai and four others. "Nice wings," he proclaimed with a devious smirk. "I heard you needed to be rescued."

Roehl was calling his power, a murky mist gathering

around him. But why hadn't he attacked yet?

His army rushed toward us. Arrows flew in the air, but I fired a burst of flame toward them, scorching them to ash.

"Run," I yelled to Thalia and Sabine, my finger aiming at Kai. "They're here to save us!"

Kai and his men lowered themselves and drove the water aside, forming a passage to them.

"Hurry!" he cried.

Thalia grabbed Sabine by the arm and together, they ran toward them.

Trystan raised his arms again and a cyclone of air appeared in front of him, so powerful, it sucked up soldiers and ejected them into the sky. I lifted my left palm, calling to the water nearest Roehl's army, and watched a massive wave rise into the air. With a flick of my wrist, I sent the wave crashing over a third of the men. The others were safeguarded by an unseen force.

Roehl.

"Move, Calla." Kai called.

As soon as my feet touched the ground, my wings disappeared, and behind me a bird screeched. When I spun, Flint was flying away toward another crow that circled in the sky. It was Nyx.

"Trystan, we need to leave," I implored. "Kai is going to take us someplace safe."

Trystan paused, glancing at Kai. "Do you want me to come?"

I threw him a narrowed glance. "Of course, I do. I thought you weren't leaving here without me."

"Tick-Tock, Sea Star!" Kai hollered. His men already had Sabine and Thalia.

Trystan turned toward his men. "Go."

"Underwater?" Brone growled. "I'd rather stand and fight."

The ground began to quake as Roehl again gathered his power. More arrows flew toward us.

Trystan swiped his hand in front of him, forming a barrier of wind between us and Roehl that arrows couldn't penetrate.

Roehl's black eyes concentrated on Trystan's wall. A massive fist, created of black mist, slammed against his barricade. Over and over.

"Brone, don't make me hurt you," I rumbled, holding a flame in my hand. He offered me a harsh expression but headed to the sea with the others.

I raced over to Trystan, who was still holding up the wind barrier, but Roehl's attacks were taking a toll. Rage now blazed in Trystan's blackened eyes.

"We have to go," I urged.

"I'm going to kill him," he thundered, then turned to move, but I clutched his arm, stopping him.

"Trystan, I don't want you to fight him."

"Why?" His black eyes snapped to mine. "He'll die for what he did to you."

Gods. He was risking his life for me, again.

"No, Trystan," I begged. "Please, we can fight him another day. Together."

But he wasn't giving.

"I need you, Trystan. Please," I breathed. His eyes softened at my words and with a blink, his eyes turned from black to azure.

Trystan sheathed his sword then grabbed my hand, holding the wind barrier in place.

As we turned to run, I heard Sabine.

"Wait!" she screamed, eyes wide, finger aimed behind us.

I stopped dead in my tracks, and when I turned around, Markus was sprinting toward us.

A dozen arrows were heading toward him, but before I could call a flame, wind ripped forward, sending the arrows off course.

"Thank you," I breathed.

Trystan nodded as Markus met us at the water's edge and bowed his head.

"I told you I'd catch up to you," Markus said with a narrowed glare.

"You did," I said, throwing my arms around his thick neck.

My heart was full now.

Trystan's barrier fell, so Roehl's army charged forward. Trystan grabbed hold of my hand and the three of us ran toward Kai and his men. When we reached them, Kai clapped his hands, and the walls of water fell, swallowing us whole.

Suddenly, a bubble of air surrounded us.

One of Kai's men had Talia and Sabine. His other three guards had Trystan's cadre. Leaving me with Kai, Trystan, and Markus.

"Kai, you came," I exhaled, trying to catch my breath. "Thank you."

"If I'd known you had more *friends*, I would have brought more men." Kai's eyes went to Markus and then to Trystan and he bowed his head. "How have you been, Prince Trystan?"

"I've been well," Trystan answered. "And you?"

Kai's luminous blue eyes found mine. "I was in the middle of a nap, when a deafening voice roared in my head, begging me to come and save her in Incendia or she and her friends would die."

Arrows littered the sea from above, and a bolt of lightning struck the water a few feet away. Kai's water dome acted like a shield, but it wouldn't hold for long. Not with Roehl's power.

"I say we get the hell out of here." Kai held out his hand to me. "So, Sea Star, would you like to ride me like you did the last time?"

Good gods.

My eyes nearly bulged from their sockets and my face felt like it was on fire.

"You what?" Markus growled and turned to me with an intent of murder in his eyes. I swear I heard a similar growl come from Trystan, but I didn't dare look. I wondered if it was too late to switch bubbles with Sabine.

"Look, it wasn't like that," I tried to explain.

Another bolt of lightning struck an inch away. I could feel the power surging through the water. Kai's water barrier was weakening. Roehl's next bolt would hit us.

More arrows littered the sea, bouncing off Kai's water dome.

In one swift move, Trystan grabbed my arms and fastened me to his back. "She's riding with me."

I couldn't object. "Please," I begged. "Let's just get the hell out of here."

Kai's eyes narrowed, a smirk lifted on his lips. He turned and motioned to his men, and they took off in a flash.

I was glad to see Sabine and Thalia safe, along with Trystan's men.

The surrounding bubble shrank until it covered only our heads. Kai grabbed Trystan and Markus by their forearms, then turned to me. "I need you to propel us forward, Sea Star."

"But—"

"Just put your left palm behind you and push the water away, like I showed you. You can do it."

"I'll do it," Trystan said.

"No, I've got this." Trystan had expended more of his power than I did, so I released my left arm and held it to my side. Trystan's hand grasped my right wrist, locking me onto him.

With a thought, water pushed from my palm, and we shot forward.

Kai let out a whoop. "Gods be damned, your power has grown since I last saw you."

He had no idea what I'd gone through to get this power. "Where are you taking us?" I asked.

Kai turned his head slightly to the side. "I thought it was a good time for you to see Aquaria . . . and meet my parents."

My heart jack hammered against my chest. I wasn't sure if I was ready to visit Aquaria. Especially knowing how grateful they were to my grandfather for saving the king's life. I wanted to go somewhere where people didn't know who I was. A place where I could rest in peace for a bit before Roehl came for me again.

Markus turned to me with a narrowed glare. I shook my head and mouthed the word . . . *"What?"*

I knew after the shoreline battle, Roehl would chase me to the ends of the earth.

"How did you two meet?" Trystan questioned, his hand pulling my wrist tighter around his neck.

"I'd like to know that too," Markus rumbled.

Dear gods. How did I get stuck with three Alpha males in a small bubble, in the middle of the sea? I was slowly being suffocated by testosterone.

Kai let out a boisterous laugh. "Ah, you're both wondering why I have a pet name for the princess?"

"Don't call me princess," I grumbled. "We met when we were sailing across the Sangerian Sea. After I killed the sea serpent, I fell into the water. I thought I was going to die but woke in a dome of water, somewhere at the bottom of the sea." I exhaled slowly. "Kai saved me, and when I was too weak to travel, he carried me back to the ship."

"It was luck, really," Kai added. "I just happened to be passing by and saw her fall like a shining star into my watery world. That's why I gave her the name Sea Star."

"You're the one who saved her?" Markus's voice lightened.

Kai grinned. "I am."

"Well, thank you, Kai," Trystan spoke. "For being there when I couldn't."

"I was there." Markus added. "I saw her fall but didn't make it to her in time. I swore to the king that I'd protect Calla, and when she fell, I thought she'd died and that my life was forfeit."

Heavens above. Now things were turning awkwardly mushy. Too mushy, and I wasn't sure how to respond.

"Thank you," I finally said. "All three of you saved my life, multiple times. I have truly been blessed by the gods and goddesses."

Trystan's thumb swept across my hand, making me smile.

I still couldn't believe he was here with Kai and Markus. If it weren't for Roehl's dark cloud covering the sky, Markus wouldn't have been able to come.

But what I really wanted to know was how Trystan knew I was in danger. Enough danger to carry his cadre in a freaking tornado to Incendia at the exact moment Roehl had arrived.

I rested my head on the back of his shoulder and felt him relax.

I'd asked him to come with me to Aquaria, but what if Trystan had other plans? What if he came to take me back to Carpathia?

Heavens above. He was only coming because I'd asked him.

My eyes were heavy and muscles aching, completely drained from the power I'd spent. Not to mention, Flint flying through my chest and becoming wings on my back. Even now, the power I was expending pushing us through the water.

Would there ever come a time when I could use my power without being drained? Could I get stronger?

"How much farther to Aquaria?" I asked.

"If you push a little harder, Sea Star, we could be there a lot sooner," Kai noted.

"I don't know if I can." My voice was weak, and sleep was quickly overpowering me.

"I've got you, Calla." Trystan reached down and grabbed my left hand, fastening it around his neck. It was aching from my palm to my shoulder.

"Rest," Trystan said softly. "Air can also push us."

I wrapped my legs around his hips for added grip and laid my head on his shoulder as darkness slid over my eyes. Then I felt us propel through the water, faster than ever.

"Now that's what I'm talking about," Kai cheered.

I was about to offer a snarky remark, but I was too tired and too comfortable. Instead, I gave in to the darkness, knowing the three alphas with me could work it out.

CHAPTER TWELVE
KINGDOM OF AQUARIA

My eyes drifted open, and I had no idea where I was. It was bright, and the air smelled different. My head lolled to the side, looking at a wide-open room with lavish furnishings in blue and silver. Sea shells in many sizes and shapes adorned a table, while the floor was a material that was the same color as sand.

Aquaria.

I shot up, my brain whirling.

"She's awake," a youthful female voice declared.

Blinking a few times, a pretty girl came into focus. She looked no older than ten with long, bluish-silver hair, and the same lambent ice-blue eyes as Kai.

"Princess Calla. You're awake," she chimed, stepping to the side of my bed and curtseying.

I smiled and stretched my achy arms over my head. "You must be Kai's sister."

"I am." A smile lit up on her dainty, pale face. "How did you know?"

"He told me all about you." My voice was gravelly, and my entire body throbbed. Why? How long had I been sleeping? I slid my legs to the side of the bed and tried to stand, but they were too weak and unsteady.

"Be careful," she stated. "You're probably weak because you've been asleep for five days."

What?

Sabine entered the room and quickly shuffled toward me, accompanied by Thalia.

"Praise the goddess," Sabine exhaled, taking my hands. "We thought you'd never wake up."

I rubbed my aching temples. "Was I really asleep for five days?"

Thalia plopped into an armchair nearby. "You were, but after that display of power, it doesn't surprise me." She shook her head. "Through tales, I have only learned of one Incendian royal who was given wings by the goddess. I never dreamed I would witness such an incredible sight. You were amazing," she said.

"You really were, Calla." Sabine patted my hand, an expression of wonder in her eyes.

I rubbed my temples. "I can't believe the queen. How could she hate me so much to call the freaking devil himself?"

"It's not hard to believe," Thalia said. "She hated you the moment you walked into the throne room and presented her your marks. Couldn't you see it?"

"I could," I sighed. "I just wanted to give her the benefit of the doubt."

Kai and Markus entered the room next.

My eyes instantly looked past them, but Trystan wasn't there. Maybe he decided to go back to Carpathia with his cadre.

"Don't worry. Prince Trystan is still here with his men." Kai said with a grin. "I've already sent someone to tell them you're up."

Kai made his way over to me and I almost didn't recognize him. His hair was drawn back at the nape of his neck. He was wearing long black slacks with a long white tunic embellished with blue and silver gems with Aquaria's crest on the front.

He held up both hands as he neared me. "I know what you're thinking. Don't judge me. My parents make it mandatory that I dress the part when I'm home."

I smirked. "You look . . . well, you look like a prince."

He crossed his arms over his chest and grunted.

The girl walked up to him and he lay his arm around her shoulder. "I see you've met my sister. I hope she didn't cause any trouble."

The girl elbowed him in the abdomen. "I didn't cause any trouble. Right, Princess Calla?"

I coughed and shook my head. "No, you didn't, and since we're friends now, you can just call me Calla." Kai snickered, but I ignored him. "What's your name?"

She skipped forward. "My name is Hali. It means sea."

"That's a lovely name," I said, slowly rising on my weak and unsteady legs, I tried to give my best curtsy. "Nice to meet you, Princess Hali."

Her perfect little nose scrunched. "You can call me Hali."

I giggled and glanced at Kai, who shrugged his shoulders.

I held out my hand, and she gripped it. "Hali it is."

Suddenly, I felt an overpowering presence and then detected that exquisite, perfect scent before he even entered the room. Glancing toward the door, the world seemed to pause as Trystan came into view. Gods, he was gorgeous. His dark hair was disheveled, and he was no longer in his fighting leathers. He was dressed informally, in black slacks and a black tunic, tied at the waistline with a black and gold belt. The outfit was simple, but on him . . . there was nothing simple about him.

As soon as his azure eyes found mine, I felt the need to sit back down on the bed.

Hali placed a hand over her mouth and giggled. "Calla, your face is red."

I threw my hands over my cheeks. "Is it? It must be hot in here," I exhaled, fanning myself.

Sabine and Thalia giggled in the armchairs. I twisted to them with narrowed eyes. They instantly halted and glanced at each other, before giggling again.

Markus stayed near the exit, while Trystan walked over and stood next to Kai, his eyes examining my face. "How are you feeling?"

"Fine," I responded, a little disturbed that everybody was in my room, dressed and looking beautiful. I, for goddess sake, was wearing a bedgown and had been asleep for five freaking days. For all I knew, I looked dreadful. I drew the sheet around me.

Trystan took another stride toward me. "You need to feed."

Kai nodded. "Yes, if you're up for it, my parents would love it if you could all join us for dinner tonight." He hesitated. "But if you're hungry now, I could bring you some food."

I shook my head and smiled. "No, thank you."

Kai didn't know I was part vampire and couldn't eat solid food. It was one of the things I'd neglected to mention. Would he and his parents still accept me even after they found out? I mean, they had to know Trystan was a vampire. And Markus too. But . . .

"Markus, how are you out in the daylight?"

"The light is not from the sun. It's produced from magic," Kai noted. "It's safe for their kind to be out and about at all hours in Aquaria."

I smiled, glad that Markus was finally able to join us. "It's good to see you, Markus."

"It's good to see you too, princess," he responded.

Kai cleared his throat. "Is everyone okay for dinner?" He glanced at me. "You don't have to if you aren't feeling up to it."

"We would love to join you for dinner," I answered. It would be impolite not to. I'd already been here for five days and had been asleep the entire time.

"Good," Kai replied. "Come, Hali. Why don't you run off and tell mother we will be having dinner guests, and I'll go tell the cooks?" He looked at me and bent his head. "It's great to see you awake and well. I'll catch you tonight." Kai grabbed his sister by the shoulders and herded her toward the exit.

Sabine shot up from her armchair and stood in front of Thalia. "Could you help me pick out a dress for tonight? If you do, I'll do your hair and makeup."

"Deal," Thalia said with a large smile. They both stood, but Sabine walked over to my bedside. She reached down and captured both of my hands in hers. "I'm so glad you're okay." Her eyes rolled to the side, to where Trystan stood behind her. But, so was Markus, watching us like a hawk. "I'll be back in a while to check on you and make sure you're fed." She winked, then bowed to Trystan as she made her way out of the room with Thalia.

When Markus didn't move, Sabine grabbed his hand and yanked him out. There was a struggle at first, but he eventually took off with them, leaving me and Trystan all alone.

I felt uncomfortable not seeing what condition I was in.

"It's great to see you're awake," he uttered, standing in place, his hands tucked into his slacks pockets. "How are you feeling?"

Trystan's presence was overwhelming and seemed to devour the space in the room.

"I'm fine," I replied, and tried to change the subject. "How is Brynna?"

"She's in excellent health and seems to be adjusting well. She and Melaina have become friends. Melaina comes to visit her from time to time."

I was glad she was taken care of, but inside, my gut twisted in knots. "Does she know? About her parents?" I inquired.

His eyes suddenly brimmed with emotion. A grief I felt in my core.

"She had many questions when she arrived and asked many times why she was in Carpathia. Melaina thought it best if she learned the truth, so she informed her."

"She must hate me."

"She doesn't hate you. She's just working on dealing with what happened. She lost her parents and her best friend in one day and is in a place she knows nothing about." He was trying to mask what she was really feeling. I knew Brynna. I realized it would take her a while to mend and come to terms with what had transpired.

"She'll come around. Just give her time."

His words had proved she was angry at me. She must have despised me, but I couldn't blame her.

"I cannot thank you enough for taking her in and taking care of her."

Those azure eyes glimmered. "She is special to you and

will continue to be well cared for."

I nodded, tears burning my eyes. At least my best friend was protected. I just hoped that one day she would find genuine happiness again.

His eyes carefully studied mine. "How are you feeling? The truth."

Shaking my head, I wiped the tears from my eyes. "To be honest, I feel like I was trampled by a thousand horses."

Trystan moved forward and sat on the bed next to me. His closeness made me squirm.

"Five days is too long, and you are still recuperating from the use of your power," he replied tenderly. "You'll heal much faster if you feed."

Trystan began to roll up his left sleeve, exposing a muscled and tattooed forearm. Tattoos that looked like runes. Then, he unsheathed a blade at his side.

"No." I seized his hand, halting him. "What are you doing?"

His head inclined to the side, his eyes softening. "I was going to ask you first, but . . . I'd like to feed you."

I shook my head. There had to be another way than for him to slit his arm right in front of me. The blade in his grasp was modern, the blade gleaming. It was then I remembered I needed to give him back his dagger. Maybe we could trade, since his was a relic.

He placed his blade down and grabbed hold of my hand. "My claiming bond was severed, so you don't have to worry about being stuck with me for the rest of your immortal life." A mischievous grin grew on his lips. "This is purely to sustain you so you can heal faster."

"How much faster?" I asked, raising my brow.

His eyes turned a deeper shade as he leaned in. His essence was intoxicating. "I am a pureblood. It will be instant."

I could use a quick fix, especially if I were going to meet the king and queen of Aquaria.

"But—" He hesitated. "There is a side-effect of feeding directly from a pureblood."

I crossed my arms over my chest and slanted my head to the side. "Like?"

A roguish grin grew on his tempting lips. "You might crave me."

"Crave you. Like, your blood?" I knew what his blood smelled like, and goddess above, my incisors nearly lengthened at the thought of it. Heat pooled in my center, my pulse raced. I hoped he couldn't tell that his closeness was affecting me.

A grin rose on one corner of his lips and gods be damned, he was so freaking sexy. But I was strong willed. I'd fought the temptation of his blood once. I could do it again.

"That's part of it," he purred, but his eyes, those beautiful eyes that seemed to be filled with stars, were studying my face.

Suddenly, Trystan sat up and began to roll his sleeve back down. "I'm not sure if you're ready for it."

Hell no. I was up for the challenge. I didn't want to spend

the rest of the night feeling like my body should be in a cast.

I grabbed his hand, stopping him from rolling his sleeve all the way down. His eyes met mine. "So, you're telling me that once I taste your blood, I'll never want any other?"

There was a sparkle in those beautiful eyes. "Probably not, but that remains to be seen. It depends on how strong you are."

"I'm very strong willed," I noted.

That sly grin was back. "Yes, I know you are, but this is much different from any other blood you've had. You will be feeding directly from a pureblood."

I leaned in closer to him. "I take it, that's a powerful thing?"

"Very," he breathed, so close his breath feathered against my face. "And just so you know, this is not something a pureblood would normally do."

"Then why are you offering it to me?"

"Because I told you before. I feel compelled to save you, but I'm not sure if you're ready for my blood."

He was challenging me. Or maybe he *was* warning me. But did he forget who I was?

I straightened my back and held up my chin. "Prince Trystan, I not only carry the blood of a vampire king but also Incendian royalty. I'm quite sure I can handle it."

"Are you?" he leaned in closer, and I found it extremely hard to breathe. "Because I'll compel one of the servants to come give you blood, right now."

I shook my head. "If you're recanting your offer, you should never have offered in the first place. I don't want a servant's blood. I want yours."

Trystan grabbed my arms and pushed me back on the bed, his face an inch from mine. I was frozen, breathless. Powerless with him being so close, his large frame pressing into me.

"I just want you to be aware of what could happen and make sure you're ready for it."

All words eluded me, so I nodded. Closing my eyes, I could taste his sweet breath on my lips. I was sure he was going to kiss me.

But he didn't. Instead, he pulled me back up to a sitting position. I let out the breath I'd been holding and opened my eyes to see him rolling his sleeve back up, his face serious, until he glanced up at me.

"Kai doesn't know about you, does he?" He must have meant that I was part vampire.

I shook my head, and a smile rose those perfect lips. It seemed as if he was happy Kai didn't know everything about me.

Trystan took his dagger in his hand. "Wait," I said, sliding off the bed. On the dresser were the clothes I'd come in. The ones Trystan had given me, cleaned and folded. Next to them, were the dagger and amulet. I grabbed the dagger and carried it back to the bed, sitting next to him. "This is yours, and I thought maybe you'd want to use it instead."

Trystan's fingers feathered against the white handle and

the runes began glowing bright red. I gasped and glanced up at him.

"Kylan told me what happened when you touched the dagger," he said, unsheathing it.

I nodded. "The runes glowed like they are now."

A beautiful smile widened on his lips. "Then, this is perfect."

Trystan sheathed his other blade in his boot, then he grabbed hold of my hand and turned his wrist upright. With the blade in his other hand, those gorgeous eyes met mine.

"Are you sure you want this?" he asked again.

I nodded and gave him a smile. "I am."

There was something oddly erotic about this entire ritual. I couldn't tear my eyes from his as he ran the magical dagger over his wrist, slitting it open. The scent of his blood made my body react. My head began spinning, my incisors lengthened and there was nothing I could do to stop them. Trystan's heavy eyes never left mine as he raised his wrist to my lips, freely offering me his blood. The blood of a pureblood prince.

There was something sensual about the smell of his blood and it drove me wild. Heat coursed through my body.

My eyes met his as I grasped hold of his arm and pulled his wrist to my lips. My eyes shut and back arched at the raw power of his blood.

Gods.

As soon as his blood touched my lips, I could no longer stop myself. It was a drug. A powerful drug that took me to a high I wasn't sure I could come down from. A high that surged through every molecule, every cell, every fiber of my being. A high sent me to the stars.

There was an inferno of heat in my core. A heat I couldn't squelch. Then, a need grew. A need so strong I found myself moaning as I fed.

Trystan.

I wanted him. Craved him. I needed to taste his lips, feel his bare skin against mine. His blood was erotic, sweet, and savory at the same time. It made my body tingle and feel things I'd never felt before. Crave things I'd never craved before.

My body began reacting without my approval.

My eyes opened, finding Trystan's locked-on mine. But they weren't the azure eyes I'd seen moments ago. These eyes were all-black and predatory. His incisors were lengthened, and even then, he was the most beautiful creature I'd ever seen.

I wanted him. Wanted him in every way. Trystan was mine. From the moment he claimed me, I was his. And right now, there was nothing more I wanted than to be bound to him forever.

Trystan ripped his wrist from my lips and pulled me to his lap, where I straddled him. My fingers wrapped around his neck, pulling his lips to mine. Mouths, teeth, tongues were fighting for dominance. Our breaths ragged, my heart hammering so loudly I knew he could hear it.

I moaned against his mouth, my body automatically

moving against his. Clothes. There were too many of them between us.

One of Trystan's arms wrapped against my back, the other tangled in my hair, deepening the kiss. A kiss so raw and filled with emotion.

"I want you," I breathed, my fingers fumbling to unbuckle the gods-damned belt from around his waist.

Trystan caught my wrists and with a twist, I was lying on my back with him on top of me. His lips were stained with his own blood and the sight of it drove me crazy.

"I need you," I breathed, my back arching. "I need you now."

Trystan blinked and then, his eyes turned back to the azure I'd grown to love.

"It's my blood, Calla. It's making you crave me." He had a pained look in those eyes. "You need to fight it."

"I can't," I moaned, moving my hips, trying to find friction against him, to find any kind of release to the overwhelming need that was growing inside. "I want you, Trystan. I want you to claim me."

Trystan's reaction was not what I was expecting. His eyes seemed sad, brow furrowed.

My mind was trying to process things, but my body wouldn't allow me to think. It ached. It burned. For him. For the first time in my life, I wanted something so badly, my entire body was yearning with need. A need was so strong I was willing to take him myself.

"I'm offering myself to you freely. Don't you want me?"

"Yes, I want you," he said, his face serious. "But not like this. I will not take you when you are under the influence of my blood," he said, his eyes still saddened. "You are only feeling and speaking this way because my blood is inside you. But once it wears off, you will think differently."

I shook my head. "You have to do something, Trystan." My insides felt as though they were about to combust. "I need you."

He paused a moment, then laid down next to me, pulling the sheet over my body.

"What are you doing?" I panted.

"I'm going to help you find release."

I had to touch him. Had to feel his lips on mine. I turned to him, tangling my fingers in his hair, pulling his lips back against mine. Then, I felt his hands on me, slowly lifting my bedgown. His leg came over mine, his knee pushing my legs apart, and then his fingers slid down, down, down.

Trystan kissed me again, a slow and sensual kiss, while his fingers—good gods. They were filled with magic. And those fingers sent me to the heavens before making me shatter, over and over again.

And each time, his lips crashed down on mine, dampening my cries.

Goddess above. I never wanted it to end.

The effects of his blood coursed through my body, my mind floating, my body still burning for him. Over the next few hours, Trystan's mouth and fingers did things I never thought possible. Made me feel things I'd never experienced before.

Finally, the burning subsided, but it left me exhausted.

"Sleep, Calla. You'll feel much better when you wake." Trystan gathered me in his arms, strong and sturdy arms that made me feel safe and secure. I nestled into his warmth and closed my eyes, savoring it.

Sabine was right. He was a pureblood prince who knew nothing about me except that he felt a connection through a portrait. But he came to Sartha to warn me, and in an attempt to save me, he claimed me, offering me a chance to live. On top of that, he sent his personal cadre to protect me and when I was captured, he came to Morbeth and offered Roehl part of his kingdom's riches to set me free. Even now, after the bond between us was severed, he still came to save me in Incendia.

Trystan was a pureblood vampire Prince of Carpathia, and he kept risking his life to save me. Why? Especially when I gave him nothing in return. I had refused his blood, and his offer to complete his bond, because I wasn't ready.

Looking back, I had done nothing but cause him trouble and put his life at risk. He even put his cadre's life on the line to protect me, and that made my heart ache. I wasn't worthy of him or his feelings toward me, and one day, he, or one of his men, would be injured or even killed because of me. I couldn't let that happen.

But at this very moment, my body was in no pain, my

mind was numb, and I felt safe in Trystan's arms. I snuggled closer and breathed in his perfect scent which wrapped around me like a warm blanket. Tears fell from my eyes thinking about how complicated my life had become. So much death and devastation. But with him around, it felt a little more peaceful. A little more . . . bearable.

"Thank you, Trystan," I breathed.

"For what?"

"For being my knight in shining armor."

He exhaled, his soft lips pressed against my forehead. "I'd do it all over again," he whispered, and those words made my heart swell.

"How did you know where I was?" I asked, my eyes so heavy I couldn't keep them open.

He rested his chin on the top of my head. "On the ship, when Nyx came to you, you were wearing an amulet."

"Mmm," I hummed. "It was a birthday gift from Brynna. She found it in an old shop in Sartha." He must have seen it through Nyx's eyes when she was pecking at it.

"That amulet is a family heirloom. It has been missing from my family for over one hundred years."

Wait. My heavy eyes popped open. "What?"

"It was my mother's." Trystan's eyes were gazing at the ceiling. "It was an anniversary gift from my father. Because she loved to travel and wander, he spelled it, so no matter where she went, as long as she wore the amulet, he would be able to find her."

"I'm so sorry," I said, hoping he didn't think I had anything to do with its disappearance. I couldn't have. I was only alive for eighteen of those one hundred years. "Please, take it back."

"No," he whispered, his fingers raising my chin so our eyes could meet. "The amulet is yours now. Fate saw fit to put it in your hands." He smiled, his fingers grazed my cheek. "Wear it, Calla. Because our bond was broken, the amulet is the only way I can find you. Promise me you won't take it off."

"I promise," I whispered.

"Good. Now rest," he said, kissing me gently.

"Will you stay with me?" I asked.

"I will," he said, hugging me tighter, pressing his lips against my forehead.

And that was the last thing I remembered.

CHAPTER THIRTEEN

I awoke to Sabine calling my name. "Wake up sleepyhead," she whispered tenderly.

When my eyes finally focused, she was standing at my bedside, onyx hair tumbling down her shoulders in big, beautiful curls. Her eyes were made up, and she was wearing a striking turquoise gown that was long and flowy.

"What the hell did Prince Trystan do to you?" Thalia giggled, appearing next to her.

My face and insides heated as my mind reflected back to the memory.

"Oh, it must have been good," Sabine laughed. "You will have to give us every single detail."

Gods no.

Thalia came and stood next to Sabine. She was wearing an aqua gown that was fitted at the top and was flowy on the bottom. Half of her golden hair was braided on the top of her head, the other half was down. Her face was glowing, perfectly done up.

The blue dresses were fitting for the water kingdom.

I lolled my head to the side to see an empty bed, even though I knew he wouldn't be here. An overwhelming sadness filled me, and my heart twinged.

"He had to meet with his men," Sabine said, taking my hand. "So, he asked us to come and wake you for dinner."

I yawned and stretched my arms over my head then slowly sat up. There was no more pain or weakness. "You look so much better. Your face is literally glowing, but your hair needs some work," Sabine noted, heading for the dresser. "Get up and wash your face, then have a seat."

Thalia shook her head and headed for a chair. "I'll be watching from over here. There is no way I could have pulled this off without her."

Sabine shook her head. "You immortals already have flawless skin so it's not hard to make you glow."

"How long was I asleep?" I stood and felt a bolt of energy surge through my body. It rattled me but I felt like I could breathe a little clearer.

"For a few hours. You realize you're going to spill every juicy detail about what went on here."

I let out a breathy giggle. "And what if there aren't any juicy details? I was drained."

"Yeah, sure." She threw me a sassy eye roll. "The most handsome *and* eligible prince is alone in your room and you go to sleep?" Her brow rose like she didn't believe me, then she spun to Thalia. "Is that even possible?"

Thalia shrugged and produced a wide grin. "I think Kai is pretty handsome too." Both Sabine and I glanced at her, her cheeks blushed bright pink. "What? It was just an opinion."

"Sounds like someone has a crush on the Aquarian prince," Sabine teased. "My Incendian sisters seem to be swiping up all the beautiful, eligible Princes."

"I didn't say anything about swiping a prince. I just said he was handsome. That's it," Thalia growled.

Before the attention shifted back to me, I hopped off the bed and rushed to the washroom. When I caught my reflection in the mirror, I gasped. Literally gasped.

Good. Gods. My hair was a rat's nest, and everyone was here to see me. I leaned closer, but my face was clean, not a spot of blood on it. How? When Trystan had blood smeared all over his lips.

I peered in a basket on the floor, and in it were washcloths stained with blood. Trystan must have cleaned my face while I was asleep. It had to have been him.

I splashed water on my face, brushed my teeth, and struggled to run a comb through the knotted wreckage. When I stepped out, Sabine was holding up a shimmery silver gown. It was simple but elegant, fitted at the top and flared out at the bottom, reminding me of a mermaid.

My eyes went wide. "Is that what I'm wearing?"

They both nodded.

"Why does it have to be a silver gown?" I grumbled. The last time I'd worn a silver gown was in Morbeth, during the Shadow Fest and I didn't care to wear another silver gown for as long as I lived.

"But this silver gown will have much better memories," Sabine said, knowingly.

"This also came with it," Thalia added, holding up a silver box. Tugging off the lid, she displayed a silver crown with a necklace and matching earrings.

I shook my head. "I'm not wearing a crown if you two aren't."

"Why not?" Sabine asked, slapping a palm to her hip.

Thalia placed the lid back on the box. "Calla, you can't deny that you are royalty. And royals wear crowns."

"But you are too," I noted.

Thalia shook her head. "I am not a direct heir. The only reason the guards call me princess is because the queen raised me. You, on the other hand, *are* the chosen one. You are the only female Incendian with royal lineage, and therefore . . . you are a princess." She gave me a smile that radiated like the sun.

"Not to mention, you are also a direct descendant of Morbeth's king," Sabine added.

"That's true. You're carrying two royalty cards, princess." Thalia waved her eyebrows, and I couldn't help but grin.

Thalia was different. Her entire demeanor had changed since we'd left Incendia. There, she was harsh and didn't show much emotion. Here, she was smiling and joking and even being nice to me. It was like she wasn't even the same person.

"Besides," Sabine chimed, a mischievous glint in her eyes. "The Princess of Aquaria chose the jewelry for you. You'll have to wear the crown, or you'll break Hali's little heart."

Gods be damned. "Then, cover most of it with a braid or wrap my hair around it or something," I groaned.

"Just let me do what I do best. Now sit," Sabine ordered, patting the chair in front of her.

Even she had changed since Morbeth. She was livelier and sassier. Total best friend material, which made me smile. It made me feel . . . normal.

My heart ached thinking of Brynna. From being tracked by Roehl and almost being killed, to Trystan's blood lust, I was glad she was being taken care of. She was my best friend from birth, and I missed her very much. I hoped she was happy in Carpathia.

I sat and closed my eyes as Sabine worked her magic, letting her and Thalia chatter away about how beautiful Aquaria was.

I wasn't awake when we'd reached Aquaria and hadn't been out of this room since.

In the five days I'd been asleep, they'd been to the markets, ate the food, met the people, and were even introduced to the king and queen. It all sounded so wonderful, but my mind was filled with one image.

Trystan.

Earlier, we were alone, and he didn't take advantage of me when he could have. I actually begged him to claim me, and he didn't. Gods, what was he thinking of me now?

Embarrassment heated my face.

But he'd warned me of what could transpire if I drank from his blood. Still, I agreed.

Instead of taking advantage of my lapse—or I should say lack—of judgment, Trystan helped me through it, in the most sensual, non-selfish way imaginable. Again, saving me, while he didn't get a thing out of it.

Was he being serviced by others in his kingdom? Maybe that's why he had extraordinary self-control. The thought caused my stomach to churn, but the truth was, Trystan was a prince. A gorgeous, too-good-to-be-freaking-true prince. I'd seen women nearly faint when he was in a room. He could have his choice of anyone he wanted.

I exhaled, squirming on my chair. Why was this affecting me? Why was I still having these powerful feelings for him? Maybe his blood was still causing me to feel this way. Just the thought of him caused my insides to melt.

"Would you sit still," Sabine scolded, immediately snapping the burn right out of me. "I'm almost done."

Goddess above, I loved her for that.

Gown on, and all made up, the looks Sabine and Thalia gave me were making me blush.

"You look stunning, princess," Sabine said, bowing.

Thalia curtseyed next. "Yes. You look like royalty."

"Stop," I moaned. "You both look like royalty too. No giving titles."

"Calla, sweetheart," Sabine spoke. "The difference between you and us, is that you *are* royalty. One day, you'll have to accept a title, whether it be princess or queen. You can't order an entire kingdom not to regard you as such. Especially when you are heir to two thrones."

"She's right," Thalia agreed.

"Well, if that day ever comes, I'll deal with it, but right now, I'm happy with Calla." I offered them both a melancholy grin. "I'd like to keep some normalcy in my life, as long as possible."

"I get it," Thalia said, her blue and green eyes were extra pretty and matched her aqua gown.

A loud bell tolled outside. Again, and again, for seven times.

"It's time to go." Thalia headed for the door.

"Is that the dinner bell?" I questioned.

Sabine nodded. "It is, and our sleeping beauty would've realized this except . . . you were slumbering."

"I've missed months of my life being asleep. But sleep has also saved me from my worst, tortured days."

Sabine stopped and folded her arms around my neck. "I'm sorry. I didn't think."

"It's nothing." I hugged her back. "During those darkest

times in my life, you were there for me."

"I was because you offered me hope and something to yearn for. A glimpse of this future. A future of freedom and true happiness."

"Hey, you two better stop before you ruin your makeup," Thalia huffed. "You can have a bawl-fest after dinner."

Sabine and I giggled. She checked my face and then took my hand. "Come on, Calla. We can't be late to dinner with the king and queen."

"Wait," I said, rushing back to the dresser. I snatched the amulet—Trystan's mother's amulet—and tucked it between my breasts. I needed to have it on me.

As soon as I stepped outside, I halted, my eyes drinking in the surrounding landscape.

We were clearly in another world. The sky, which wasn't the real sky but the sea, was all around us. We were enclosed in a dome, like the one Kai had created when he'd rescued me. Except this one was enormous, the extent of an entire city, and an entire city resided within it.

I was in awe, standing in an underwater fantasy world that seemed to be glowing with a magical ambient light. Its backdrop, the sea floor, was even more magnificent.

The buildings were composed of natural materials, particularly of sandstone with blue and gold tones. The ground was sand and landscaped with the most beautiful colored coral in all shapes and sizes, and sandstone pathways seemed to lead throughout the city.

The palace looked as if it were plucked right out of a fairytale. It was formed around a natural rock structure, and it was glorious. Tall white stone walls were uplit with blue lights. The palace itself had lofty towers and columns with many windows that were cut in the shape of seashells. It looked like a palace for the gods. Ancient, though stately and enchanting.

As we reached the marbled stairs that led up to the entrance, we slowed our gait. At the top of the stairs stood Trystan and his cadre. And standing on the opposite side of the stairs, was Markus.

Markus was just as tall as Trystan. He was dashing, his hair combed back, and he was dressed in black slacks and a black tunic with a turquoise belt tied at his waist. The same color as Sabine's dress.

When I glanced at him, his eyes weren't on me. They were aimed on Sabine, who must have known because she was blushing.

As my eyes caught Trystan, that burning need started to rekindle inside. I felt anxious, my stomach twisted in knots, and my heart thrummed loudly in my chest.

Heavens above, he was devilishly handsome, but . . . why were they all dressed in their fighting leathers?

As we neared the top of the stairs, Trystan offered me his hand. When I placed mine in his, he kissed the back of my fingers. "You're gorgeous, Calla," he said, his azure eyes glimmering.

Goddess above. I wanted to drag him back down the stairs and back into the bedroom.

Gods. Get your damn self under control.

"He's not lying," Brone said, standing behind Trystan with his hands folded in front of him. "You are stunning."

"You do look beautiful and . . . healthy," Kylan added.

I nodded and turned to Trystan. "I wouldn't be here if it weren't for his blood."

All four sets of eyes snapped to Trystan, who gave me a grimacing smile.

Shit. Was I not supposed to say anything?

"Trystan?" Kylan's eyes studied me. "Tell me you didn't."

"What's wrong?" I asked, seeing it was something they obviously didn't approve of.

It was even more imperative I deny the burning ache I had inside for Trystan and act normal.

Andrés laughed and shook his head. "You feed from a pureblood, Calla. You don't feel . . ." he leaned close to me and whispered, "horny?"

My freaking face felt like it was going to melt off. I cleared my throat and straightened my back, trying to appear as non-horny as possible. "You've all seen me control my thirst, even as a newborn. Do you think I can't use that same control over sexual urges?"

Kylan's eyes narrowed on Trystan. "I've never heard of anyone who could control the urges after they consumed the blood of a pureblood. Consuming from a pureblood is not something that is taken lightly. Purebloods are only to offer their blood to someone who is dying, or during consummation with their mate."

Consummation with their mate? But we weren't bonded. Nor had he claimed me.

Trystan came to my defense. "Calla hadn't fed in five days, maybe longer, and she'd expended a great deal of her power in Incendia. It would have taken her days to recover, and let me assure you, nothing happened," he said with a bite to his words. "As you've witnessed, Calla is like no other, and from this moment on, you will not speak of this matter again."

"But—" Andrés started.

Brone smacked him on the shoulder. "You heard the prince," he said in his low baritone voice.

They all placed their fists to their hearts and bowed their heads to Trystan.

Feng stepped forward and bowed his head to me.

"Calla, it is true. In all my years, I have never witnessed anyone like you. And I must say, you were magnificent on the Incendian shore."

When I'd first met Trystan's cadre, I didn't have any powers. They had been locked away under Leora's spell, so seeing me wield fire and water must have been a shock to them.

Andrés stepped forward looking a little embarrassed. "You did show incredible self-control for a newborn, and you don't seem to be showing any of the symptoms." He wiggled his brows and pumped his arms and hips a few times.

Kylan grabbed him by the shoulders and threw him behind him. "You're an embarrassment to the Carpathian throne," he scolded. Andrés shrugged and grinned at me.

Goddess, they had no idea what I was fighting inside. I inwardly let out a sigh of relief knowing I was somehow pulling it off but had to continue staying strong. Being so close to Trystan was making my body ache. In the most erotic way possible.

Brone stepped forward, took my hand, and placed a kiss on it. "From the moment I met you, I liked you, and I don't like many people." His eyes narrowed. "And even though you burned me, I still like you."

"Thank you, Brone. I'm so sorry about the blast. I had no control over it."

Brone shook his head. "I know, and don't worry. I've already healed."

"Thank you. All of you, for coming to my rescue," I said, my heart swelling as I looked at each of them.

Trystan stood off to the side with a broad smile while they all started asking questions.

There was a loud clapping behind us. "I'm sorry to interrupt," Sabine said. "But it would be rude if we miss dinner."

I nodded to her, but Trystan grabbed my hand and pulled me away from the others.

"I have to leave," he said sadly. "My father has ordered

me and my men to return to Carpathia. An urgent matter, but I doubt it has anything to do with Roehl. Carpathia is known for its strong wards and even stronger warriors."

I nodded, deeply saddened he wasn't going to be here. "Please be safe," I whispered. "There are no words to explain how grateful I am for everything you've done for me. One day, I will repay you."

Trystan stepped close—so close I could feel the heat of his body—and rested his forehead against mine. "You can repay me by staying alive," he said softly, his eyes swimming with emotion. "And by not riding anymore males."

I laughed and threw my arms around his neck. "Deal."

Trystan cradled my face in his hands before his lips crashed down on mine. This kiss was sweet yet sensual. The aching, the heat, the wanting, all flooded back at once. I knew everyone was watching, and hell if I'd let them see me succumb to my desires.

We pulled away, resting our foreheads against each other. "You really do have self-control," he breathed.

"You have no idea," I said, my brow crumpling. "Ninety-nine percent of my self-control is avoiding embarrassment."

Trystan chuckled, and the sound made my heart swell. "You're stronger than you think." He gave me a kiss on the nose then turned toward his cadre.

All of them were smiling ear to ear. Kylan threw a fist over his heart and bowed to me. "Until we meet again, Calla," he said. Andrés, Brone, and Feng did the same, then all waved goodbye. I waved back, saddened to see them leaving so soon.

"Will I see you again?" I asked.

A sly grin rose on Trystan's lips. "You will."

"Will it be soon?"

"That depends."

"On?"

"On what my father has for us to do."

I nodded. "Then, I guess I'll see you when I see you."

"I will see you again." He took my hand and pressed his lips to the back of it. "Don't forget me, Calla Caldwell," he said, his azure eyes glimmering.

"Never," I breathed, and he gave me a dashing smile.

"And wear the amulet. It's how I will find you."

"I have it on me right now," I said, patting my chest.

There was a hunger in his eyes as they moved down to my chest. "That's good." He then gave me a devilish grin, and one more soft kiss, then turned and followed his cadre down the stairs.

I watched until they were out of sight.

"Calla!" Sabine called from behind.

I turned and headed toward her, Thalia, and Markus. Markus was standing with his arms crossed over his chest and a narrowed glare in his eyes. I knew he'd seen and heard every word.

Sabine gave a little head motion, so I walked up to Markus and slipped my arm through his. "I'm really glad you're here, Markus. I hated the thought of leaving you behind."

His eyes softened as we walked toward the entrance. "I'm glad you listened to me. I know how stubborn you can be."

I turned and gave him a sparking grin. "Stubbornness is one of my better traits."

He groaned and shook his head.

"Have you been able to get out and see this place?"

His dark eyes shifted to Sabine. "She's dragged me to nearly every corner of this city."

"And?"

"And," his broad shoulders shrugged. "It's nice."

He looked like he was uncomfortable, but I guess that's how he'd been since I'd first met him. I thought back to the time he didn't want to walk me down the stairs at the Shadow Fest. But he did and since then, we've formed a bond.

"I'm sorry you had to follow me out of Morbeth, and I'm sorry the king made you take an oath to protect me. You really don't have to anymore. I can take care of myself, and I know the king will understand."

Markus halted, stopping me from moving forward. He then turned and faced me.

"Before I made the vow to the king, I saved you from the cell. It was my decision alone, and something I felt strongly I had to do." His brow furrowed. "Roehl should have never done what he did to you, and I'm sorry I didn't stop him sooner. But I will spend the rest of my life making up for it."

"Thank you, Markus," I said, feeling hot tears sting my

eyes. I hugged him again, and this time, he gently patted me on the back.

I dabbed away the tears with my fingers, changing the subject. "It must be nice to walk around during the daytime."

A low growl rumbled in his chest. "Not really. Now, I have too many waking hours on my hands."

Two men dressed in white greeted us at the door and requested we follow them.

As we entered, I was in awe. The inside of the palace was even more spectacular than the outside. We stood in the center of a large foyer where two grand staircases led to upper floors. In the center of the room, resting in a massive clamshell, was a massive circular aquarium filled with the most exotic fish.

Behind the aquarium was another tall rock formation with an actual waterfall that fell into a pool filled with more fish and aquatic plants.

The walls were made of sandstone, and there were statues of mermaids and mermen sporadically placed throughout the room. This place was amazing, and it made me wonder why Kai would want to run away from it.

"This way," one of the men said, leading us away from the foyer, into another room. As soon as I stepped in, Kai and his family were there to greet us.

Kai's smile widened when he saw me, and his ice-blue eyes sparkled. His silvery-blue hair was pulled back at the nape of his neck and he was dressed in white pants with a silvery jacket that looked exceptionally good on him.

Hali looked like a little princess in a flowy baby-blue dress. Her silvery-blue hair was braided on the top of her head to look like a crown.

Standing to the side of them were the king and queen. I don't know why I assumed the king would have looked old, but he didn't appear much older than Kai, and neither did the queen. They were both beautiful.

The queen had the same color eyes as Kai and Hali, with light blue hair that was made up on the top of her head, wearing a crown made of pearls.

The king's hair was silver, but his eyes were violet.

He stepped away from his family and headed toward us, his eyes pinned on me. When we reached our group, he held out his arms.

"Welcome to Aquaria. We are so glad you're all here."

He then motioned for everyone to enter the dining room, where the scents of spices and food wafted from. It hit my nose and my mouth started to water.

As the group moved into the dining room, the king extended his hands to me. "You must be Calla."

"I am," I said, curtseying before taking his hands. Instead of kissing my hand, he pulled me into a tight hug I wasn't expecting.

I glanced at the door to the dining room and saw that Markus had stopped.

"I'll be right in," I whispered.

Markus backed up into the room, watching me from a distance. I guess I'd have to get used to the fact that he would keep doing those creepy things, since he'd sworn to protect me. But I knew he probably had a gazillion better things to do than follow me around.

"We've been waiting to meet you," the king said. "We are so honored you've come. Please, I'd like you to meet my wife." He took my hand and led me over to his family.

CHAPTER FOURTEEN

"I know you've met my son and daughter, but this is my beautiful wife, Adira," the king said proudly.

"Gerard, please," Queen Adira exhaled, blushing.

Queen Adira was breathtakingly gorgeous, and her smile was tender and sweet. She promptly came over and wrapped her arms around me in a sincere hug.

This was a family of huggers. I appreciated that. My mother and father were huggers too.

Kai snickered from the side, and as our eyes met, he mouthed the words, "Sorry."

I smiled at him and closed my eyes, accepting the queen's warm embrace which reminded me of my mother. You could tell when a hug was a token hug, or when it was wrapped in affection. This one was filled with emotion.

"Isn't she lovely, mother?" Hali said. "I picked out her outfit, and all of her accessories."

When the queen drew back, her eyes were pooled with tears. "Yes, Hali. She is exceptionally lovely. You did beautifully, my dear." Hali smiled and sat down on a nearby chair.

"Mother," Kai spoke. "You're making this uncomfortable for Calla."

The queen stepped back a few steps and dabbed the tears sliding from her eyes. "I'm sorry, Calla. I am just so thankful." She reached down and took hold of my hand. "If your grandfather hadn't saved Gerard, I would have been lost all these years. My children would have been without a father, and the kingdom without a ruler."

I smiled at her. "I'm deeply thankful he was able to help. My grandfather was a respectable man. He led a simple way of life and was always there to help those in need."

She lay a hand over her heart. "I am sorry I wasn't able to meet him. Kai told us he passed."

I nodded. "He did, but before he died, he told me the tale of how he helped a man that lived under the sea. I think I was the only one who believed him, besides my grandmother."

Queen Adira patted my hand and smiled. "Well, at least you believed."

"I am also grieved to hear of Marius's death," King Gerard stated. "He was a caring and generous man, and will always remain, a hero in Aquaria."

"When our son came back and reported he had met Marius's granddaughter, we were astonished. We couldn't wait to meet you. Kai spoke so highly of you. He mentioned you were beautiful, but . . . you are gorgeous my dear." The queen's sweet words made me blush.

"He also mentioned that you are an Incendian royal who can also manipulate water and even killed the Sangerian Sea Serpent?" The king sounded like he was proud of those achievements.

I threw a sharp glance at Kai who offered me a devious grin and a shrug of his shoulders.

"Yes. I did, but my powers are still new, and I'm just learning how to use them."

The king slapped a hand on Kai's back. "Well, our son is greatly skilled in water manipulation. I'm confident he can teach you a thing or two."

Kai bowed his head. "Yes, father."

The king placed his palms on my shoulders. "Calla, you are an honored guest here in Aquaria. If you or your companions have any desire for anything, just ask."

"Thank you," I said, bowing my head.

"Has Kai shown you around the kingdom?" His violet eyes shifted back to his son.

"Father, she's been resting," he replied.

"Well, she looks well to me. Take her around tomorrow. Introduce her to the people. They've all been awaiting her arrival."

"Yes, father."

Heavens above. I wasn't ready to meet and greet an entire

kingdom. "I'm afraid I won't be able to stay long. Maybe a day or two at most," I said, afraid Roehl would come to this wonderful place and destroy it. Like they had with Incendia.

"I'm sorry to hear that. We must plan a ball, in your honor. Could you remain a few more days to allow us to prepare?" The king requested.

I'd already been here for five. That was pushing it, but the expressions in their eyes . . .

"I suppose I can," I answered.

"Excellent!" The king clapped his hands. "Then we must plan it," he declared, and his wife readily agreed.

Kai shot me a pained glance and shook his head. "Sorry." This was apparently why he left the palace a lot. His parents were wonderful and loving, but very pressing.

"Kai, please escort Calla," the king ordered.

Kai bowed his head and headed over to me, presenting his arm. The king gathered his wife on one arm, and his daughter on the other, and entered the dining hall. Kai and I followed.

"I'm sorry," he murmured.

"You don't have to keep apologizing," I said. "I know they are thankful, but I did nothing. My grandfather is the one who earned all of this."

"But you are his successor, and in Aquaria, if someone does something noble, the reward carries through the generations. So, the benefits generated by your grandfather's great deeds, have now passed down to you."

I sighed. There was no way out of this.

Kai halted and shifted his attention to me. "Your grandfather saved our kingdom, and we are grateful. You might as well grin and bear it."

"Easy for you to say."

"I know how to play my part."

"So, you *are* a player."

"The finest in Aquaria."

We both laughed as we entered the room, and then, my smile immediately died.

Heavens above, we weren't the only guests. There were at least a hundred bodies seated at long tables, and with my keen vampire hearing, I could hear the faint whispers of many voices.

"Who is she?"

"Has the prince finally chosen a mate?

"They look beautiful together?"

"Is she to be the next Aquarian queen?"

"Isn't she the Princess of Incendia?"

"She is the granddaughter of the mortal who saved our king."

The room started to whirl. Was it too late to turn around and go back to my room?

"Easy, Sea Star," Kai whispered, grasping my arm. "You look terrified. Just relax and take deep breaths."

I leaned over and whispered, "I thought this was going to be a simple dinner."

Kai chuckled. "Nothing is simple in Aquaria and for

your information, this *is* a simple dinner. Mostly leaders of our kingdom and their households. They gather and dine here once a week, and tonight happens to be one of those nights."

I clutched his arm, which was rock hard. "I don't know if I can do this."

Kai patted my hand lightly, his worried eyes gazed down on me. "First, relax your brow. It's deeply furrowed. Second, just paint on a smile and walk to your seat. Once you're there, you'll be safe."

I struggled to loosen my brow. "Where's my seat?"

"Up there," he said, his eyes drifting to the far end of the room, to a raised platform. The king and queen were already halfway there.

Kai peeled my arm from around his and stepped to my other side. "Relax, Sea Star. I'll be your shield tonight." I did as he said and inhaled in a deep breath.

As we passed by the people, Kai greeted them politely. He shook their hands, all while moving us as quick as he could toward our table. The head table.

Sabine and Thalia were already seated there, and I was so glad they would be near me, to offer support.

An older woman with short silver hair and deep blue eyes stepped in front of us and curtseyed. "Princess, it's so wonderful to meet you."

Kai stared at me and I didn't know what to do. Did I bow back?

"Thank you," I said kindly, smiling at her.

"Are you and the prince—?"

Kai let go of me and gently escorted the woman back to her seat. "I'm sorry, Laira. You will get to meet the princess tomorrow. I'll be giving her a tour of our grand city."

"That's wonderful," the woman said with a twinkling smile. She bowed as Kai took my arm and led me at a brisker pace toward the table. So fast, I felt like I was practically jogging, but fast enough that no one else stopped us.

Kai was still acknowledging them with smiles and head nods, and I painted on a smile that seemed to work.

As soon as we arrived at the table, Kai pulled out my seat which was right next to Thalia. Sabine was next to her and Markus was standing against a far wall, observing us, while acting like a guard. He wouldn't be able to eat the food, anyhow.

On my left, sat Kai, the king, queen, and Hali.

The king rose with his wine glass in hand. "In two days, we will have a ball to celebrate our guest, Princess Calla Caldwell. She is the daughter of Marinus Thorne, the mortal who saved my life. We've also come to discover she is likewise an Incendian royal. But!" he lifted his glass high. "She likewise has the power to manipulate water." The crowd whooped and cheered, then the whispers started again, but there were too many to make out what they were saying.

Sabine cleared her throat and when I turned, she threw me an impish smile and bowed her head. I felt like sliding under the table. I wasn't cut out for a life of royalty. I just wanted to be on my own.

Thalia patted my lap under the table. "Breathe," she whispered.

Kai had said the same thing, but they were born into this life. They knew the procedures and how to act. The only thing I knew was how to run.

"Please make our guests feel welcome and regard them as our own." The king turned to me and raised his glass. Kai nudged my knee and took his wine glass, so I took mine, raising it to the king. The king smiled, and all the people applauded, as we sipped. Then, with a wave of the king's hand, the servers filed out of the kitchen with trays of food.

This was dreadful. I was at the head table with at least a hundred pairs of eyes who would be watching me, and I couldn't eat their food.

I twisted to Sabine with a worried stare. Her eyes flashed behind me. "Tell him," she whispered.

She was right. I had to tell Kai.

I tapped his arm, and he turned to me.

"How are you holding up?" he asked.

Shrugging, I leaned closer to his ear. "Can I talk to you?"

"Anytime," he said, raising up his palm. "We have a connection, remember?"

Goddess. Why had I forgotten? I made a fist and closed

my eyes.

"You don't have to close your eyes," Kai said in my mind. I opened my eyes to meet his icy-blue eyes smiling at me. *"As long as you're directing your thoughts to me, I'll hear them."*

I nodded. *"I have to tell you something I should have told you before."*

"Are you sick?"

"No." How did I explain this? *"My great-grandfather is King Romulus. Of Morbeth."*

He went silent for a moment. *"Then why the hell is Prince Roehl trying to murder you?"*

"It's complicated and I'll explain it later, but he wants our entire bloodline dead—my grandfather, father, and me—because we are a threat to his throne."

"Holy shit. So—" he paused.

"I'm part vampire. I can't eat physical food, or else I'll get sick." I said with sorrowful eyes.

Kai started laughing.

"Why are you laughing?"

"Because we are immortals who live amongst the vampires. I've known Trystan for a long time, and there are a few vampires who reside in Aquaria."

"There are?" He nodded. *"What will your father think?"*

"Do you really want to know?"

I shrugged.

Kai tapped his father on the shoulder. The king leaned over, and Kai whispered into his ear. The king didn't even glance over at me but called to one of the servers. When the server came, he asked him for a goblet of ruby wine.

When the servant left, the king's eyes fell on mine. "My dear, don't be ashamed of what you are. You are a royal and will be treated as such, whether from Incendia or Morbeth.

"I'd rather not be associated with Morbeth," I said sadly.

"Yes, well, not too many people would. Morbeth has a dark history, but Romulus is a decent man. He rules with an iron fist, but it is necessary when the past only allows you to rule in such a manner."

I nodded. There was so much I still didn't know. I felt like an infant learning the ways of life.

The server came carrying a tray with a gold goblet sitting on it. He smiled as he set it down in front of me, then bowed and backed away. I could smell the coppery blood and immediately held my incisors in place.

Ruby wine. It must have been their code word for blood.

I really didn't need to feed. Trystan's blood was still more than enough, but I didn't want to be rude.

I turned to Sabine, and she gave me a nod. "Drink. Hopefully, it will settle your nerves."

Nodding, I picked up the goblet and took a sip. It was nothing compared to Trystan's blood. It tasted as if it were completely watered down.

It was then, I knew any blood would never be the same. Trystan had ruined the taste of all other blood for me. His blood was now my obsession.

"Why didn't you tell me?" Kai asked.

"I don't know. I guess I didn't want you to think less of me."

"How could I? Nothing can change who you truly are. But knowing you have blood ties to Incendia, and now Morbeth, puts you at even greater risk."

"Risk of what?"

"My parents. They have been trying to find a decent princess for me to wed."

Oh no. *"Kai, I'm not princess material, and, in all honesty, I have only been alive for eighteen years. I haven't lived yet."*

Kai laughed. *"You don't have to explain that to me. Why do you think I run away so often? I don't want to be bound to anyone either. Although, you are the only princess I've met who I can honestly say I admire."*

"Thank you. I don't know what you admire about me. Especially, when I have a dark curse following me."

Kai gave a warm smile. *"What makes you admirable is that you've overcome most of those struggles."*

"So far."

"You're in Aquaria now. You can rest for a few days. Roehl cannot break a ward he cannot find."

"What do you mean?"

"Our kingdom is heavily veiled and warded. For over a thousand years, our wards have never been breached."

"That's good to know."

I nodded, knowing I could relax for a few more days.

Platters of seafood and bread were set across the table. Sabine and Thalia dug in and I heard both moaning in delight. I was so jealous.

"Calla, I will eat and enjoy your share," Sabine said, gnawing on a crab leg.

I sucked in a deep breath. "And I will live my wildest eating fantasies through you."

Kai laughed and when I turned to him and smiled, I heard more whispers from the crowd. They thought Kai and I would make a perfect couple.

"Don't mind the people. They've all been waiting for me to choose a bride. I just haven't found one suitable enough."

"Do you think you'll ever find one?" I asked.

He shrugged and those luminous blue eyes landed on mine. "Perhaps."

I sighed, seeing that look in his eye. "Kai, I—"

"I know." He offered me a sad grin. "I see how you both look at each other, and how protective he is over you. As much as I'd love to hate him, Trystan is a good man."

"To be honest, I don't know what's going on between me and Trystan. I also don't want to give you false hope."

Even as I mentioned his name, my body and mind ached for Trystan, and I still wasn't sure if it was the effects of his blood . . . or me.

"Well, in case it doesn't work out between you two, I'll be here." He gave me a wink and a grin. "Besides, like I told you, I'm an immortal who is in no rush to settle."

Kai raised his wine glass to me, and I raised my goblet of ruby wine. "Cheers to friendship and freedom."

"Cheers," I said clanging my goblet against his glass.

CHAPTER FIFTEEN

The next day, I woke drenched in perspiration. I had dreamed of Trystan, who came back to Aquaria and did things to me. Wild and sensual things that . . .

Goddess above.

I required a cold shower.

The effects of Trystan's blood were potent, and I now understood why a pureblood would only allow blood to someone who was dying, or someone they were mating with. If I drank his blood while I was dying and had those thoughts and feelings, I would unquestionably fight to survive.

Dreaming of him had been a pleasant respite from the haunting nightmares of Roehl.

Roehl. The thought of the freaking bastard turned my blood ice cold. An unnerving shiver ran down my spine thinking back to his terrifying whispers in the winds in Incendia. Whispers of death. Because I knew he would never let this go. He would track me down until I was caught or killed.

I sat up and stretched, and for the first time in a long time, I was without any pain.

Kai was expected to meet me outside at noon to take me on a tour of his kingdom. As much as I didn't wish to go, I felt it was my obligation. The Aquarians had heard the tale of my grandfather—the mortal who saved their king—and they were grateful. I knew my grandfather would have loved to have come to Aquaria to meet them, but he was gone, and I was his only surviving heir, now that my mother was gone. I felt a responsibility to fulfill his dream.

Slipping out of bed, I wandered toward the dressing chamber. Aquaria's seamstress had delivered a few dresses, so I snatched the one that looked most comfortable. It was a lace, navy blue dress that fell to my knees. Simple, yet graceful. The lace was in a pattern that reminded me of waves, which, I presume, was proper for Aquaria.

Not long after, Sabine and Thalia arrived looking well rested and chipper. Sabine came in and made up my face, while Thalia sat and watched, plucking on a tray of fruit.

They both wore flowy cotton dresses. Sabine's was a coral hue, and Thalia's was a gradient of sand to white.

Sabine styled my auburn hair half up, half down, and fixed a modest silver crown with sapphires on it, which Hali had chosen.

"So, what did Prince Trystan have to say before he left?"

Thalia asked, her teeth sinking into a plump, juicy strawberry. I moaned, missing the taste of fresh, sweet berries.

"Trystan said his father ordered him and his men back to Carpathia and he doesn't know what for."

"Does he know about the ball?" Sabine rubbed some gloss on my lips.

"No, but I'm sure he has much better things to do than go to a ball. He does have a kingdom to run."

"Well, even with his kingdom, he decided you were a priority, and even stayed here, in Aquaria, while you slept. He didn't want to leave until he knew you were okay," Sabine said, pinching my cheeks.

"And how did he know you were in danger? I didn't see his crow until after."

I took the amulet in my fingers. "I received this as a birthday gift from my best friend, Brynna. She found it in a small shop in Sartha and said she had to purchase it for me. Evidently, it was stolen from Carpathia over a hundred years ago. Trystan said it was his mother's."

"Goddess! Are you serious?" Sabine squeaked and Thalia paused chewing.

I nodded. "He said his father had it spelled, so he would know where his wife was. Apparently, there are many dangers to ruling a kingdom."

"And that's how he found you," Sabine sighed, lifting a hand over her heart.

"Isn't it curious that this tiny piece of jewelry, missing for over a hundred years, ended up in my hands?"

"No, Calla. It's not curious. It's called fate." Sabine narrowed her eyes.

"Is it really?"

"Goddess above." Sabine let out a heavy, pathetic sigh. "Calla, honey. The universe has delivered a sign right around that lovely, little neck. How much more confirmation do you need?"

"I don't know," I exhaled. "I'm afraid of making any kind of commitment. I mean, I've only been alive on this earth for eighteen years. Everyone around me, except you, are immortals who have experienced countless lives. I feel—" I hesitated, trying to voice how I really felt. "I feel like I don't fit. Like, I was awarded a gift that should have passed to someone else."

Sabine grabbed my shoulders and stared straight into my eyes. "You have shown more bravery and more compassion than any immortal I have ever known. You may be inexperienced, but you have a heart. A heart that people are drawn to and will fight for. I mean, for goddess sake, you have the Captain of the king's guard, and not one, but two Princes fighting for you. If you can point out one immortal princess who can match that, I'll . . . well, I'll let you bite me and turn me into an immortal."

"Sabine," I shook my head. "I would never bite you." I grabbed her face and drew her closer. "But Markus might."

We both stared at each other for a moment and suddenly

erupted into laughter.

She straightened her back, crossing her arms over her chest. "Markus would never bite me."

"Why would you say that?"

"Because he treasures mortality. Even though we experience a brief life, it's usually a full life, and then . . . we sleep."

"Well, he's an immortal and does an awful lot of sleeping."

"That's true," she chortled.

A knock at the door had us turning. "Come in," I hollered.

The door swung wide, and Kai walked in looking dapper, and very princely. His hair was again drawn back, and on his head was a silver crown. He was wearing black slacks, a white-collar shirt, and a blue coat with tails that had the Aquarian insignia on the front.

"You look very dashing, your highness," I said teasingly, bowing.

He threw a smirk then bent at his waist. "And you look dazzling . . . princess."

"Okay. If we're to remain friends, first names only," I threatened.

His lips pouted. "Awe come on. You can't deprive me from Sea Star. You're stuck with that one."

"Fine, but only when we're alone, or with close friends."

"Deal," he declared, thrusting out his hand. I shook it and we both laughed.

"How long have you two known each other?" Thalia

asked from behind me.

Kai turned his eyes to her for the first time since entering my room and knowing she thought he was handsome, I thought I'd introduce them properly.

"Kai, have you met Thalia? She's a relative of mine from Incendia."

"A relative?" His brow lifted. "I have not had the pleasure." Kai walked up to Thalia and held out his hand. When she accepted it, he kissed the back of it. "It's nice to meet you, Thalia."

"You too," she replied, her cheeks turning a deeper shade of pink.

"Your eyes," Kai said, noticing them.

Thalia's eyes averted to the floor. "I know. It's a defect."

"No." He gently lifted her chin. "They're unique, but charming. I like them."

"Thank you," Thalia said.

"And you are also an elemental?" he inquired.

"I am, but my power is not as strong as Calla. I can summon fire and manipulate earth, but I am a lot more useful with my bow."

"A bow. Well, I would love to see that one day." Kai gave a crooked grin. He was dashing and had Thalia swooning. Then, he swung his attention back to me. "And to answer your question, Calla and I had only met once before she demanded I come to rescue you all in Incendia."

Thalia's eyes thinned. "You seem like you've known each

other for much longer."

Kai walked over to me and folded his arm around my shoulder. "There are some people you instantly connect with. Calla was shy but had a spark in her I couldn't resist. Plus, we spent hours, on our way back to her ship, discussing our lives. That's when I happened to find out her grandfather was the man who saved my father's life. So, she's a pretty big deal in Aquaria."

Sabine let out a heavy and exasperated sigh. "Well, Calla. It seems fate has provided you a few options."

I shrugged and offered her a troubled smile. *Why?* Why couldn't fate offer me one choice? Make it easy on me? But nothing was easy.

"How did you and Calla connect your elements?" Thalia questioned.

Kai raised his palm and presented them his symbol. "I am a manipulator of water, and because Calla is one too, it is easy to connect our elements. It allows us to contact each other, even over long distances.

Thalia seemed fascinated. "Can you hear her all the time?"

"No," he said. "Nor would I wish to. I think my head would burst hearing all the things you females discuss."

I sneered at him.

"Are you able to sever the connection to your elements?" Sabine questioned. "Say, if one or both of you became bound to anyone else?"

Kai's bright eyes settled on her. "It can be done but seeing the kind of trouble that is following Calla, leaving it connected at the moment might be advantageous."

"Yes," Thalia agreed. "If you hadn't come, who knows what would have happened to us."

Kai grinned, a sparkle gleamed in his eye. "I think Calla has yet to demonstrate her full power, and when she does . . . hell will burn."

"Speaking of power," I interrupted. "Do you have any place I can practice? Someplace secluded?"

"There is a place, and I can take you there after the tour, if that's what you want to do?" Kai offered me his arm then glanced at Sabine and Thalia. "Will you two be accompanying us for the tour as well?"

"Why not?" Sabine offered her arm to Thalia. "We have no plans, right?"

"No, we don't." Thalia linked her arm around Sabine's, and they strolled out the door.

"I like your friends," Kai murmured.

"I'm shocked you didn't introduce yourself sooner, being the top Aquarian player."

Kai laughed out loud. "Your guard, Markus, made it difficult to approach them. He seems very protective."

"He is. Especially over Sabine. She is the only mortal in our group."

"Ah, that does explain a lot." He escorted me out the door, and I spotted Thalia and Sabine about twenty-five yards ahead, both chatting and laughing. "How are you and Thalia related?" he queried.

"Her mother was Princess Leora's first cousin. I'd seen her before, when a witch performed a spell to locate my father, she was one of the faces I saw."

Kai's brow furrowed. "She's not a royal?"

"They call her princess in Incendia because she was raised by their current queen." I glanced over to him. "Are you interested in Thalia?"

Kai gave me a dashing smile. "I told you, Sea Star. I'm not ready to settle anytime soon."

I raised my brow. "Well, don't break anyone's heart, highness . . . especially a relative of mine."

"How about we get through this tour before worrying about anything else," he said.

"Sounds like a plan."

Kai led me down a pathway that took us left of the palace.

Aquaria was more than just an undersea city. It was as if it were plucked right from the pages of a fairytale. The homes along the path were dome shaped, each painted in earthy hues. Everything, the entire kingdom was . . . breathtaking.

Not long after we passed by the homes, we entered the center of the city. As we wandered along the path, I sucked in the pleasant scents of freshly baked breads and pastries wafting in the air. Vendors had set up their tables and wagons on the outside of a large square perimeter. There were flowers, clothes, fresh seafood, and vegetables. I even saw livestock.

"This place has everything," I exhaled in awe.

"We may live under the sea, but we lack nothing," Kai said. His eyes went upward, toward the top of the dome. "Sometimes, it does get lonely."

"Kai, I'm sure you could have your pick of anyone in this kingdom."

He gave me a sinful grin. "I could, but I don't. Everyone here knows everyone else. If I were to bed any of the females in Aquaria, my father would find out and have me castrated and my pearls hung in the center of the square."

I giggled at his facial expression. "So, that's why you escape up top?"

Kai's luminous blue eyes sparkled. "Sea Star, I'd rather you not discuss my sexual encounters. Especially while we are among many ears." He then swung me around to face him, and I instantly heard gasps and whispers. His mouth brushed my ear. "Since we're on the subject, how many lucky bastards have you bed?"

I narrowed my eyes on his. "None."

"None?" He burst out into laughter, and my cheeks blushed with embarrassment. His eyes studied my expression for a moment before his smile fell. "Gods, you're not kidding, are you."

"I'm not." I turned and walked toward a makeshift hut that had fresh bread on the sill.

"Hey," Kai said, catching up to me, grabbing my hand. I stopped and turned to him. "I'm sorry. I didn't know."

I shook my head. "How could you?"

"I thought you and Trystan—"

"Well, you thought wrong."

Sabine and Thalia suddenly appeared on the side of me with skewered shrimp kabobs, that looked amazing.

"You two sure know how to draw a crowd," Sabine whispered. Around us, people had stopped and gathered.

"Hey, let's go look at the pearl necklaces," Thalia said, pulling Sabine's arm.

Sabine glanced at me and waved her fingers. "Have fun!"

"I'm sorry if I embarrassed you," Kai said in my head. *"I promise to make it up to you. Shall we start again?"* He held out his arm to me, and I took it.

"I want some bread." I said, smiling sweetly.

Kai's brow furrowed. "I thought you couldn't—"

"Not to eat, silly," I whispered. "To smell."

Kai's face crumpled as he led me forward to the hut. "You are something, Sea Star."

I gave him a wide grin. "You have no idea."

CHAPTER SIXTEEN

We greeted about fifty people before we made it to the bread stand. The woman came out and personally addressed us, offering me a loaf for free. It was warm and soft and smelled like heaven.

"Thank you," I said, breaking off a chunk and inhaling it.

"Anytime, princess," she responded, bowing with a radiant smile.

Suddenly, Sabine popped up behind me and snatched the bread from my hands . . . with the sweetest smile.

"I'll hold on to this for you, princess," she said, patting the loaf. "Until you're finished with your tour." She said that last part so the bread woman wouldn't get offended.

"Thank you," I said through narrowed eyes, but was glad she came to my rescue.

"Thalia and I are going to meet Markus. We'll catch up to you guys later."

"That's fine," I sighed.

Kai and I strolled arm and arm through the circular square, and a few hours later, he had introduced me to practically every merchant. Random people were following us, waiting for their chance to speak, so I just put on a smile and addressed each one warmly.

Goddess above, was this what he had to go through daily?

I wasn't cut from the same cloth as the royals. This was exhausting.

I was a recluse and preferred to hide in the shadows but Kai, he was like Brynna. They both had a charisma that attracted people to them. People wanted to be around them and have conversations with them, and they did it, effortlessly.

Kai did most of the conversing, while I remained an accessory on his arm. I was fine with that.

A cute boy, maybe eight years of age, with sandy brown hair and brown eyes stepped up to me. "Are you going to be our princess?" he asked.

I swallowed the knot in my throat, trying to evade any direct answer. "I am just a guest here."

"But you and Prince Kai are wearing matching crowns. You look like you're courting."

I touched the top of my head. Shit. "This crown was a gift from Princess Hali," I said.

The boy smiled widely. "I think you are pretty and would make a suitable princess in Aquaria."

"Thank you." I grinned and bowed my head.

Kai unlatched his arm from mine and seized the boy by the shoulders, steering him toward a group of boys his age. "Run along, Brooks."

The boy took off and gave a high-five to the others. He must have been dared to come and talk to me.

Suddenly, an old woman with silver hair and milky white eyes bumped into me.

"I'm sorry," I said, but she grabbed hold of my arm. I felt a coldness seep into me as her cataract eyes met mine.

"Death lingers around you, heir of blood and fire," she spoke. "And because of this, your blood prince will die. The prince to whom you share a bond."

Kai grabbed our hands and ripped them apart, then tugged me aside.

What the hell just happened?

"I'm so sorry," he apologized. "Don't listen to her. She's a blind, old woman who thinks she can see the future."

I jerked him to a stop. "Can she?"

"What?" Kai's brow crumpled.

"Can she see the future?"

"She can. She's a Seer," a young woman with short black hair and hazel eyes spoke. "I'm sorry if my Gram scared you. She can't help the visions that come to her."

"So, her visions . . . do they come true?"

The young woman nodded. "They do."

I spun to Kai and spoke to him in my mind. *"I have to find out more."*

"Calla, don't. It'll only bring despair."

I didn't care. I had to find out.

I strode back over to the old woman, who was standing still in the crowd and grabbed hold of her hand. Her opaque eyes snapped back to mine.

"Tell me what you see," I breathed.

"He is tied to you—this Blood Prince. And you will watch him die." She inhaled a heavy, wheezy breath. "Die by the hand of the dark prince with red-rimmed eyes."

Goddess. That had to be Roehl. He was the only blood prince with red eyes.

"What is the name of the blood prince tied to me? What does he look like?" I pleaded. "Please, tell me."

The old woman began convulsing. Her granddaughter ran over and tugged our hands apart. "She doesn't have details. She only sees flashes."

My entire body was shaking. The only blood prince I was tied to or shared a bond with was Trystan. Was it true? Was Roehl going to kill him?

Kai wrapped his arm around my shoulder. "I think we've had enough of the square."

I let him lead me away toward the outer dome. My mind reeling, struggling to process what the old woman had said.

"Don't let it get to you. Seers see things, but it isn't invariably true."

"I've never seen her before, but she called me heir of blood and fire. She also saw death around me and the dark prince with red eyes."

"You don't know if it's Trystan."

"Then who else could it be?" My voice was shaky. "We are somehow tied together and had a partial bond. There is no other blood prince I know that qualifies."

"You don't know when it will happen." He tried to settle me. "And if it hasn't happened, there must be a way to change it."

"Has a foretelling ever been changed?"

"I don't know," he said. "We still don't know when this takes place. Sometimes, it's years ahead." He stopped and spun me to face him. "But if anyone can change the course of the future, it's you, Sea Star." He offered me a sad smile. "I'll inquire around and see if there is anyone who can help us."

"You'd do that?"

"Of course. Because I believe that we are tied together. Maybe not the way I'd like to be," he grinned, holding up his palm. "But we do have a connection, nonetheless."

"Thank you, Kai."

I felt some of that gnawing pressure lift off my shoulders. Like Kai said, I would find a way to change the future.

We stopped at a large steel gate with the Aquaria symbol on the center post. Two guards stationed outside, and both bowed to Kai.

Kai gave them a nod before leading me down a long sandstone pathway, toward a private, circular tower. He brought me up a staircase, and when we arrived at the top, Kai opened the door and led me inside.

Goddess above, would I ever not be in complete wonder of what Aquaria had to offer? Around the perimeter of the circular room was an enormous aquarium that encompassed the entire room. The floor was made of a blue sea glass that illuminated a soft light. The décor was grand, in hues of silvers and blues, along with more sculptures of a sea god, mermen, and merwomen.

At the center of the suite was a circular bed, and a magnificent chandelier with thousands of blue and white crystals dangling from above. There was also a couch, a few armchairs, and a table. Kai walked up to one of the aquariums and held his hand up to the glass. All the fish gathered in front of him, as if they were drawn to him.

"What is this place?" I breathed. It was a dream.

"Welcome to my chamber, Sea Star."

I choked and twisted to him with wide eyes. "*This* is yours?"

He nodded, and I shook myself from the wonder. "You don't live in the palace?"

"I haven't stayed in the palace for a long time." His eyes were assessing me. "What do you think?"

"I think, if I had a place like this, I would never leave."

Kai laughed and ambled toward me. "It could be yours, and you would never have to leave. I would never leave Aquaria again either."

Gods, he was inviting. So unbelievably daring, but I

couldn't. Not while I had such deep feelings for Trystan.

"I—" How did I respond to that.

"You don't have to answer, Sea Star," Kai said with a smirk. "It wasn't a question, but a statement."

"I just want you to know—" he placed a finger to my lips.

"I already know." He strolled over to a table that housed liquor and poured himself a glass. "How long have you known Trystan?"

I casually walked the outer part of the room, my eyes on the aquarium and all the multicolored fish I'd never seen before. "I don't know. We met in person once and after that, I met him in my dreams, through the partial blood bond we had."

"So, he rescued you, but also turned you into a vampire." His tone wasn't pleasant.

I shook my head. "He didn't turn me. It was already in my blood, but Leora had placed a spell on our bloodline to hide all magic. Trystan just unlocked that part of it." I turned to Kai with a sad smile. "If he hadn't bitten me, drew out the monster," I hesitated, tears pooling in my eyes. "The things Roehl did to me in that cell in Morbeth . . . I would have died as a mortal."

Kai was suddenly behind me, enclosing me in his arms. "I'm sorry, Calla. I don't know what happened, but I can only imagine it was a nightmare."

I dried the tears from my eyes and turned to see those luminous eyes brimmed with worry. "It was worse than a nightmare, and he still haunts my dreams."

Kai stepped back, his eyes searching mine. "That bastard. How could he do that to his own flesh and blood?"

"Because he's a wicked asshole who wants Morbeth's throne all too himself. Little did he know, we never wanted any throne. My family and I would have been happy to live a simple and quiet life in Sartha." Hot tears pooled in my eyes. "I hate him. So much my bones ache."

"I wish there was something I could do."

"Does your father know about Roehl?"

"He received the death decree from Morbeth back then, but didn't think anything of it," he said, brow furrowed. "I haven't told him anything else. I wasn't sure if you wanted to share that information."

I was glad they didn't know. The tension would have been too much knowing Roehl was searching for me. "Thank you, Kai. You and your family have done more than enough for me and my friends, and you came when I called for you. You rescued us from Roehl and his army."

"That was nothing. I would have been a fugitive if I didn't come and save Marinus's granddaughter." Kai's eyes softened. "If you want, you can stay here for the rest of your stay."

"No," I answered.

Kai held up his hands. "Don't worry, I'll stay in the palace. My sister will be thrilled."

"I can't stay in your room, Kai."

He shook his head, eyes tightened into slits. "Why not?"

"What will people think?"

"Sea Star, you already know I don't give a damn what people think, and you shouldn't either." He walked over and poured himself another glass of amber liquid and swallowed it down. "Invite your friends to stay too. Hopefully, you'll make memories, instead of nightmares while you're here."

Kai strode over to one of the walls and pulled out a drawer hidden under the aquarium. Pulling out a few pieces of clothing, he crammed them into a pack, then sauntered back over to me. "I'll have your things sent here and will make sure your friends know."

"Thanks, Kai. For everything. I never really had a chance to thank you for coming to Incendia and saving us."

He shook his head. "I'm sure Trystan would have whisked you away, one way or another." He started to head out but hesitated. "I'm glad you called. And I'm glad you're here. My parents wouldn't have left me alone until you came."

"Oh, and about this ball—"

Kai laughed again, heaving his pack over his shoulder. "Be prepared, Sea Star. It's been a while since they've thrown a ball. The entire kingdom is invited, and my mother has been working everyone round-the-clock."

Gods be damned. An immediate surge of panic filled me.

"Don't worry. I'll try to deflect for you as much as I can. But your strongest ally will be the dance floor. People won't disturb you there."

"I'm not a dancer," I said, grimacing.

"It's easy when you have someone experienced leading."

I nodded, grateful he was here, and happy to help me. "Thanks, again."

He nodded and gave a sad smile. "Remember, if you ever need me—"

I held my fisted palm to my chest. "I'll call."

He gave a dashing grin then headed out the door.

Gods. Why was my life so complicated? I liked Kai, but never had those overwhelming feelings with him, like I did with Trystan. Trystan's closeness made my body ignite, and my mind go numb. With a glance, he could melt me into a puddle. He was the first to save me. The first to claim me, without his father's consent, even when I had no title or power. And his touch. Gods. His touch was magic.

Walking over to Kai's bed, I plunked down on my back. It moved. The freaking bed was moving.

I rolled off the bed and flung back the linen to reveal that his bed was made of water. *Water!* I guess it was fitting for a water prince, but I wasn't sure if I could get used to being on a bed that moved all night. I closed my fist. *"You sleep on a bed of water?"*

Laughter. *"It's soothing. It lulls me to sleep, Sea Star."*

"I get horrible sea sickness."

"Then push the button on the right side of the bed."

I stood and checked the bed, and right on the side of the frame was a silvery button with a blue gem in the center. I pushed it, and the bed flipped, displaying an entirely new set of bedding. This set was black and dark blue.

I shoved my hand on the bed, and this time, it didn't move. Plopping my body down on, the mattress melded around me. It was so comfortable.

"Is that better?" Kai asked.

"It's so soft. I seriously wouldn't want to leave this room if it were mine."

"Be careful what you wish for."

"I'm just going to close my eyes and reboot for the next wave of meetings."

"I'll tell the servants to wait awhile to bring your things."

"Are we having dinner again?"

"If you like, we can dine with my parents. Or . . . I can take you and your friends somewhere else a little more secluded."

"I would love that."

"I'll let them know. I'll be by in a few hours to collect you."

"Where is your washroom?"

"Stand in front of the statue of the God of the Sea and pull his trident."

"You're kidding, right?"

"Not this time."

I sat up off the bed and shuffled over to the sculpture of the God of Sea and stopped in front of it. Whoever had sculpted it was glorious. He had a short beard and a handsome face with remarkably muscular abs that disappeared into a wave of water. In his right hand, he held a large trident.

"Don't fondle it, Sea Star. Just give it a firm yank."

"Easy for you to say." I gripped the trident with both hands and tugged. It was a lever, and as soon as I let go, the floor moved.

"Kai."

More laughter. *"The washroom is under the chamber. Enjoy the ride . . . and the view."*

When the floor stopped moving, lights suddenly illuminated another large, circular room. This was the largest washroom I'd ever encountered in my life, with the same stained-glass floor, but in various hues of blue. An entire section was windows, that looked out on the sea and all the creatures that swam within it. On the opposite side of the room was the wash basin and towels and all kinds of ointments and soaps.

In the center of the room was an enormous circular tub, already filled with steaming water.

Heavens above.

I went over to the tub and ran my fingers across the water's surface, and it was the perfect temperature. Next, I moved to the glass wall and peered out at the sea. It was boundless and breathtaking. A masterpiece of colors and shapes and movements. I could lose countless hours standing here, gawking into this magical watery world.

My eyes caught on a long, dark creature, slowly gliding on the seafloor, weaving through coral and rocks. Its head and body were snakelike, but it had wings on its back and horns on its head. Was it another sea serpent? It didn't look like the one I'd slain. My eyes were affixed to this creature as it drew closer to the exterior dome.

What the hell was it?

It suddenly outstretched its wings and shot through the water, striking its snout against the barrier, causing me to stumble back a few feet.

Gods!

It was enormous, at least twenty feet long with pointed fangs and red eyes that reminded me of — What if Roehl was using this creature to look for me—to spy on me before his next attack?

I ran and dove behind Kai's tub.

"Kai!" I yelled into my palm. *"There's something outside. A creature. Snake. Sharp teeth."*

"Does it have a white patch on its snout?"

"What? I am not going to look." My body was quivering, my back pushed against Kai's tub.

"You're safe, Sea Star. Nothing can break the barrier. Look for the white patch on the creature's snout."

I gathered enough courage to inch the top of my head out. The creature's red eye was there, searching the washroom. Then, it swung when it spotted me move.

That's when I noticed it. On its snout was a small patch of white.

"It has a patch," I confirmed into my palm, sliding back into hiding.

Kai laughed. "That's Spot."

"Spot? What the hell is that?"

"He's harmless. He probably wants to play."

I snorted. *"You play with that thing?"*

"Occasionally." He paused for a moment. *"Do you want me to come back to the room?"*

"No, I'm fine. But your pet is looking at me like he wants to devour me for lunch."

"Mmm."

"What does mmm mean?"

"I was going to say something inappropriate, then decided against it."

"Mmm." My eyes rolled. *"Bye, Kai."*

"See you, Sea Star."

I inhaled in a breath and calmly stood. The creature, Spot, looked me dead in the eyes, then opened his mouth, exposing rows of razor-sharp teeth. Heavens above. It did want to eat me.

I scurried backwards until I reached the wall and punched the button. The floor began to rise, and I finally exhaled when I made it back to the top.

That was it. I was staying in the bedroom where the fish were small and there were no windows to the outside world.

My body still felt strong, thanks to Trystan's blood, but my mind was overwhelmed and exhausted. Not to mention my cheek muscles were still sore from smiling and greeting hundreds of Aquarians. I'd never smiled so much in my entire life.

The Aquarians were kind and wonderful, nothing like the Incendians, but after meeting the Seer—my mind and heart throbbed. If she was a true Seer, like her granddaughter said, then Roehl was going to kill Trystan. I had to find a way to stop it.

"*Kai, are you there?*"

There was a pause before . . . "*See any more sea monsters?*"

"*No. I wanted to know if you could take me to that remote spot you spoke about. I need to practice and release some steam.*"

"*I can definitely help you release steam.*"

Goddess help me. "*I need you to teach me how to manipulate water.*"

"*That's not what I was thinking.*"

"*I know, but I have to practice if I have any chance of defeating Roehl.*"

"*Of course.*"

"*Can you let Sabine know?*"

"*I can. When did you want to leave?*"

"*As soon as possible, and I'll need the clothes I arrived in.*"

"*I'll send a servant shortly.*"

"*Thank you, Kai. You're the best.*"

"*You're welcome, Sea Star.*"

CHAPTER SEVENTEEN

Me, along with Markus, Sabine, Thalia, and Kai stood in a small area concealed behind a large rock structure. It was veiled with magic, so it appeared as part of that wall, but we walked right through it.

"What is this place?" I questioned.

"A secret exit, only admissible to Aquarian Royals," Kai replied. "It's warded with magic, so no one else would be able to access it, let alone find it."

Kai lifted his hand, then pressed his palm to a pad that looked like the surrounding stone. I never would have known it was there if I weren't looking for it.

"It is accessed through our marks. Only royalty can enter here."

A door slid open, and we entered another small room. When we were all inside, it slid shut. "You should be able to access it too, Sea Star. Since I connected our elements."

That was good to know.

Against the far wall was a clear door, and on the other side . . . the sea.

Before we left, Kai instructed me, step-by-step, on how to make a water bubble so I could travel. I wasn't sure how it was decided, but I was taking Markus, and Kai would take Sabine and Thalia.

I leaned over to Kai. "If this water bubble fails, we're going to drown."

"I'll stay behind," Markus announced. His acute vampire hearing caught my apprehension.

I threw him a narrowed glare. "Thanks for your confidence, Captain."

Markus crossed his muscled arms over his broad chest. "First of all, I detest the water. Second, drowning is my greatest fear."

My brow raised. "After all these countless years, you've never learned to swim?"

He returned a particularly sullen expression. "No, it's not something I find enjoyable."

"It's up to you, Captain. Just know, if I die out there alone, I will come back and haunt your ass."

Markus growled. "I don't care."

"How about I take Markus and Sabine and you take Thalia," Kai suggested.

Thalia's head jerked to Kai with wide eyes. "I don't feel like dying today."

Kai chucked, and I growled, throwing my arms over my chest. "So, that's how it is. You all lack confidence in my abilities."

Sabine hopped over and clutched my arms. "I believe in you, Calla. I'll ride or die with you."

Thalia and Markus rolled their eyes, while I folded my arms around her.

"Thank you, Sabine."

Kai was leaning against the wall, one leg crossed over the other. "Are we ready yet?"

I held up my left palm and wiggled my fingers. "Ready."

We all stood at the glass door while Kai pressed his palm against another pad. It slid open and Kai pushed the water away, forming a small air dome just outside. Once we exited, gathering in that small dome, the glass door shut behind us and my heart kicked up.

Kai peered over to me. "When I count to three, I'll release the dome. That's when you'll put up your own around you and Sabine."

I swallowed hard. "Could you please count to ten? Three seems a bit too soon."

He cocked a brow and grinned. "Sure."

I held up my palm, my heart hammering against my chest as Sabine stood behind me. We agreed her being on my back would be the easiest and safest way to transport her. I had to do this. This was part of learning what my gift could do. If I could master traveling through water, that would open an entirely new world. A world Roehl wasn't acquainted with. At least, I didn't think he was.

Kai started the countdown, and I winked at Sabine as she clutched my shoulders tight.

His eyes shifted to me as he spoke in my head. *"You've got this, Sea Star. Just stay close and follow me."*

I nodded, determined.

As soon as he hit ten, I shoved the water away, encasing me and Sabine in our own little bubble.

"I did it!" I squealed.

"I'm so proud of you," Sabine exhaled. She must have been relieved we weren't going to drown. "We've got this."

"We do," I replied.

Thalia was on Kai's back, while Markus held his arm. Suddenly, they shot forward.

"What are you waiting for?" Sabine smirked.

I twisted my head backward slightly and gave her a grin before pushing my water power.

Sabine and I shot through the water. She screamed and then started laughing. "Goddess, this is amazing. And to think, just a few months ago, you were chained in a cell and practically lifeless. Now look at you."

"I would have died if it weren't for you. You were the one who brought Summer to unbind my powers."

"I had faith. I knew you were the one the Seer spoke of. I just didn't know I'd be part of it."

"I met another Seer today," I said. "In the square."

"What did she say?"

I shook my head. "I'll tell you all about it when we get back."

"Now that you've told me, I'll make sure you do." Sabine squeezed my shoulders. "As long as I have a front-row seat to see Roehl's destruction, I'm good."

"When Roehl's destruction comes, I don't want you anywhere near."

"Why?"

"Because you're mortal and fragile."

"Sometimes, I wish I were immortal like the rest of you. Maybe not a vampire, because then I'd have to hide during the day."

"Well, you and Markus could hide out together." I peered back and smiled.

Sabine laughed. "I like Markus, but he's so uptight."

"Oh, he was a lot more uptight in Morbeth. The night of the Shadow Fest, when I'd met him for the first time, I asked him to escort me down the stairs. It was like I was asking him for a limb, and you should have seen his face when I asked him to unzip my dress when we were back at the room."

Sabine gasped. "You asked him to unzip your dress?"

"He was searching for the witch from Carpathia who had come to set me free. They said she was in my room, so Markus was looking for her. I asked him to unzip my dress to throw him off."

"And?"

"It worked. He zipped it halfway down and left."

Sabine burst out into laughter. "That does sound like something Markus would do." There was an abrupt pause. "It seems like Prince Kai really likes you. Do you have any feelings for him?"

I let out a breathy sigh. "Honestly, Kai feels more like the best friend I've been missing all my life. I know I could be romantic with him, but . . . it would be nothing like Trystan. When I'm with Trystan, well . . . the world around me fails to exist, and when he touches me." I shook my head and sealed my lips. I didn't want to get too personal.

"It seems your heart has already made its choice. Anyone, who is not blind, can see the way you and Trystan affect each other. Especially when you're in the same room. Goddess, even I have a hard time breathing."

"Sabine!"

"It's true, and it makes me sad for Kai."

"Well, I can't afford to get involved with anyone right now. My life is too complicated."

"But if you did get involved with someone like Trystan, who—goddess above—kissed you like he was taking his last breath of air on that shore in Incendia, I know he would fight heaven and hell at your side. He's already proven it and I believe Kai would too."

"And that's the issue," I sighed. "I'm fighting a war of my own bloodline, and I don't want anyone getting injured or killed by getting involved."

Sabine hugged my neck. "Sweetie, it's too late for that. They are involved. Everyone around you is involved because we choose to be. You need to accept that, and as for being in a relationship, you need to do what your heart feels. It's okay to love, Calla. Goddess knows, sometimes the only gift we get in this terrible life is to find love. True love. An unexplainable love that will hold on to you even after you've let go."

She adjusted herself on my back and whispered in my ear. "And I expect you've already found it."

"Let's just see how it all plays out." My heart was still aching about what the Seer said.

"Fine. But I know where I'm placing my bet."

I laughed when suddenly, Sabine screamed as something enormous from the side swam at us. It was that snake creature I'd seen in Kai's washroom. The one with the rows of pointed teeth.

"Goddess above. What is that?" Sabine bellowed, her nails biting onto my shoulder.

"Sea monster," I exhaled.

Kai was about twenty yards ahead, so I pushed my power to quickly catch up.

"Sabine, when I count to three, grab onto Markus's shoulder," I commanded, but she didn't respond. "Sabine!"

"Yes. I will," she said, her body quivering.

I caught up to Kai, and he looked over to me with a worried expression on his face.

"Take Sabine," I said.

"What's going on?"

"The sea monster is back."

I nearly crashed into them, allowing Sabine to grab hold of Markus. She flung her arms around his neck and legs around his waist. Once she was secured, I shot away from them, hoping to draw the monster away.

It worked. The slithering creature with wings shot out from behind a rock.

"Don't run, Sea Star," Kai said, almost in a laugh. *"He's faster than you think."*

I didn't have time to answer when the creature swam around me, wrapping its slimy body around mine.

I let out a blood-curdling scream, waiting for it to crush me.

But it didn't.

"Don't move," Kai said, from who knows where.

But I couldn't move and could hardly breathe. I was going to die and couldn't do anything because my arms were fastened at my sides. The creature's horned, snakelike head came face to face with mine. Then, it opened its mouth, filled with razor-sharp teeth.

This was it. It was going to eat me.

I closed my eyes waiting for the pain, only to feel a nasty, slimy substance on my cheek. I popped my eyes open to see the creature had its lengthy tongue out. It had broken through my air bubble and . . . it was licking me.

Ugh. I nearly gagged as slime dripped down my face and

neck. The creature suddenly unraveled its body from mine and swam away, slipping behind a cluster of coral.

"Sea Star," Kai said, grasping my shoulders. His worried expression suddenly shifted to a wide smile, followed by raucous laughter. "He likes you."

"What the hell just happened?" I exhaled, my body stiff.

"Spot is playing hide and seek, and now, it's your turn to find him."

"Spot?" I shook my head, wiping the slimy substance from my face.

Kai made a gesture to the cluster of coral where *Spot* peeked his red eye out.

Gods. What was becoming of my life?

"Where are the others?" I asked.

He pointed behind me, a hundred yards away, to a large dome. Safely inside, I could see my three friends.

"Wait here. I'll be right back." Kai shot over to the cluster of coral and threw his arms around Spot's neck. "Got you!" he hollered. The two of them wrestled, but the creature didn't look like he wanted to hurt him. They were . . . playing. They were gods-damned playing, and it was a sight to see.

After a few minutes, Kai and Spot faced each other. "Go on now. We have work to do. We can't play today."

And then, it almost looked as if the creature looked sad. It shifted its gaze to me, then dropped its snakelike head, making me feel awful.

"I'm sorry, Spot," I blurted. "We'll play another day,

okay?"

The creature reared its head like it understood, then twisted and shot away.

Kai returned to me and took my hand. "I'm sorry he scared you. I had no idea he was following us." He gave me an impish smirk. "It seems even the creatures of the sea are enthralled with you."

I shivered, still thinking my life almost ended.

When we arrived at the dome, I saw it was much taller than the one Kai had created when he'd rescued me. This one was almost a hundred feet high, and it pushed out about one hundred yards.

When we pushed through, Sabine ran over and put her arms over me. "Goddess. I thought you were going to die. What was that thing?"

I thumbed back to Kai. "His pet."

Markus stood behind with a look of murder in his eyes, arms folded across his broad chest. "Your pet nearly ate Calla," he growled.

Kai smiled and crossed his arms over his own chest. "He wouldn't have eaten her. He was playing."

"Playing? He almost crushed her," Markus growled.

"Actually, he didn't," I said, in defense of Spot, and Kai, because Markus seemed like he was in a foul mood. "The creature wrapped himself around me so it could . . . lick me. It was its way of telling me it had found me, and it was my turn to find it."

They all turned their attention to Kai. "It's true. The creature is quite taken with her. Besides, I wouldn't have hesitated if I knew Calla was in real danger." Kai looked at me and smiled. He was handsome and dashing in a devilish way. His personality was so different from Trystan.

"Calla wanted to come here to practice," Kai said. "Shall we get started?"

With a snap of his fingers, water came into the dome and circled around him, gathering into a large ball in his palm. Kai then manipulated it into many shapes—a dragon, a wolf, a ship, and then . . . the water took on my likeness.

Thalia looked at him with complete awe. "Goddess. You're amazing," she breathed.

"It's not me. It is a gift I was born with." He looked at Thalia. "You can manipulate earth, right?"

"A little," she said, glancing down at her palms.

"Well, let's see it," Kai urged.

Thalia threw her hands behind her back. "No, I couldn't." Her eyes slid to mine. "We're here for Calla, anyway."

I knew how she felt. I hated attention, so I flipped the conversation. "Kai, how do you keep the water from crashing in on us?"

Kai tapped the side of his head with his finger. "It's as easy as a thought. Almost like telling the water to hold until you are ready to release."

"That's it?" I squeaked.

Kai nodded. "Are you ready for your first lesson, Sea

Star?"

"I—don't know." Kai gave me a sly grin, and I groaned. "Why are you looking at me like that?"

Kai stepped forward, folding his hands behind his back. "Because I'm going to drop the water barrier and I want you to create one in its place."

"No!" I gasped. "I don't know how. I can't. I barely figured out how to make a small bubble around me and Sabine."

Kai shrugged. "Like I said, it's as easy as a thought. You'll need to focus. Look at the area you want encased and tell your gift what needs to be done."

I could see the fear on Markus, Sabine, and Thalia's faces, which was probably mimicking the terror on my own.

"If I do this, promise me that if I fail, you'll put the dome back up, immediately."

Kai slowly stepped around me. "I will not," he replied, narrowing his eyes. "Because knowing I will be there to save you already puts you at a disadvantage. It gives you weakness."

I didn't like where this was going. "What if I weren't here to save you? Would you let your friends drown?"

"That's not even a question," I exhaled. "I would never let anything bad happen to them."

Kai raised his hands slowly. "Then, save them, Sea Star."

I started to panic as Kai raised his hands higher.

"Kai, please don't," I begged.

His luminous eyes narrowed on mine. "Focus."

I focused on my friend's faces, filled with the fear of death.

Knowing their lives were in my hands, raised my anxiety to an entirely new level. Especially after Markus's confession of his fear of drowning.

I would have to put up a water barrier. Strong and unbreakable that would keep them safe. I couldn't fail them. I couldn't let them drown.

Kai suddenly dropped his hands and smiled.

I shook my head. "What are you doing?"

"What's happening?" Sabine asked, her hands over her heart.

Kai walked over and stood next to me, then turned toward the others. "I've released my barrier, but it appears, Calla had already put one up."

My head snapped to him. "What?"

He nodded a grin lifted on his lips. "Easier than you thought, right?"

"I—" I had no idea what to say. Did I really put up a barrier, or was he pretending like I did?

Kai threw an arm around my shoulder. "You passed test one, Sea Star," he said, then walked away.

Oh gods. If this was test one, I was terrified of whatever else he had in mind.

CHAPTER EIGHTEEN

I trotted after Kai. "How do I keep the boundary up while we're practicing?"

"It'll hold until you release," Kai replied, glancing backward. "And for the record. I wouldn't have let any of you drown."

"I know," I exhaled. My hands were shaking. The stress alone was going to kill me.

"Are you really doing that?" Thalia asked, her eyes directed at the top of the dome, a hundred feet up.

Looking up, I swept my hand from right to left, and the water above rippled, like I was touching it. "I suppose I am."

Markus had an indecipherable expression on his face. A blend of worry, dread, and maybe relief. He gave me a sharp nod before turning his back and strolling away, checking the boundary.

"So, what's next?" I inquired.

Kai gave a roguish smirk. "Next, you'll learn how to

throw water daggers."

"Oh." My eyes expanded, while Sabine and Thalia looked delighted.

"We have nothing to sit on," Sabine noted, her eyes sweeping the dome.

The ground began to quake and suddenly, rocks pushed through the sand. Thalia's palms were faced down, her eyes focusing.

Manipulator of earth.

She was calling forth rocks, and they rose through the sand, five of them. A couple were smooth and long, perfect to sit on.

Sabine ran her hand over one of the flatter ones, dusting off the sand. "This is amazing, Thalia!"

"Next time, you'll have to show me how you do that," I said.

"Manipulate earth?" Thalia asked, brow furrowed.

Sabine patted her on the back. "I presume you guys haven't heard the news." Sabine looked at me and winked. "The Fire Goddess told Calla that because she is the only chosen Incendian royal, she has a connection to all the elements. Fire, water, earth, *and* air. Our girl has got it all."

Thalia, Markus, and Kai's attention jerked to me, waiting for affirmation.

I shrugged my shoulders. "It's true. She did tell me I could wield all four elements, but up until now, I've only been able to call fire and manipulate water."

"Why didn't you tell us?" Markus asked.

I threw a hand on my hip. "Because we were with other individuals and I didn't know who I could trust."

"Have you tried to summon earth or air?" Kai asked.

"I have. I tried to make a plant move . . . but it didn't."

"It's because that poor plant was dead," Sabine blurted.

"Or maybe you still have to awaken those gifts, since they haven't ever been used," Thalia added. Maybe she was right. But how would I awaken them? Helia said I was connected to them all.

"Will you help me?" I asked Thalia.

She offered me a pleasant smile. "Like I said, I can't do much, but I'll try."

Sabine wrapped her arm around Thalia's shoulder. "You helped me. I would have had to dig for a full month to have a seat that you made rise in less than a minute."

"It was impressive, Thalia," Kai said. She blushed as he shifted his attention to me. "Now it's Calla's turn."

Goddess help me.

Kai held out his palm and a ball of water rushed into his palm from outside the dome.

His ball suddenly transformed into a dagger. A water dagger!

"Your turn Sea Star."

I held out my left palm and summoned water. A ball came and hovered in my palm. "Isn't a water dagger the same as a water ball? If they struck a target, they'll both do the same thing, right?"

Kai turned to Thalia and pointed to the ground about ten feet in front of us. "Could you produce a stone over here, please?"

Thalia nodded then came and stood by us. In seconds, a long rock, around seven feet high, emerged from the ground.

Kai stood to the side and cocked a brow. "Okay, Sea Star. Let's see what you've got. Throw your water ball against the stone."

I peered over to Markus who remained behind Sabine, arms crossed over his chest. With a nod of his head and a glint in his eye, he was telling me to go for it.

I drew my arm back and punched the water ball forward. It sailed toward the stone, striking it dead center. I gave Kai a toothy grin.

Kai ambled toward me, his back to the stone. As soon as he reached me, in one smooth movement, he whirled around and hurled the water dagger in his hand. It flew so fast I could scarcely see it. As the dagger struck the rock, it exploded. The top third of the stone split in two and crashed with the impact.

Kai turned and threw me a smirk. "That's the difference, Sea Star."

"There is no way I can throw that fast," I mumbled.

Kai raised his brow. "Isn't that why you requested to come here. To practice?"

I groaned and nodded. Even Helia said the more I practice, the stronger I'd become.

"Then, pull up your royal britches, Sea Star, and let's get started."

For the next few hours, Kai had me making water daggers and throwing them. I couldn't open the rock like he had, but I did chip at it, and I was proud of that.

Kai then proceeded to create a sword made from water. He showed me how, if used properly, it could cleave a man in two. I wasn't sure if I'd ever want to hack a man. Sending a giant wave to wipe them away was simpler, and I wouldn't have to know how many had perished.

But he made me practice, over and over, until I could call a water sword and wield it accurately. By the end of our practice session, my arms were like mush and my back was throbbing. I was completely exhausted. Markus had taken a spot on the ground and looked like he was comatose, while Thalia and Sabine were chatting and laughing amongst themselves.

When it was time to go, Sabine came over to me.

"You did great today," she said. "I'm so proud of you."

"Thank you," I said.

"Let's go get ready for dinner. I'm starving."

Sabine was much more relaxed as she grasped my shoulders and rode back to Aquaria, and that made me happy. However, Markus had the same grumpy scowl on his face the entire time. But I appreciated him that much more for showing up and making sure I was safe.

Safely back in Aquaria, Kai escorted us to his quarters. One of the guards at the front pulled him aside. Because

Sabine and Thalia were chattering noisily, I couldn't make out what they were saying.

Kai turned with a clap of his hands. "It appears my parents are requesting your presence for dinner tonight. All of you." His brow crumpled as he looked at me. "I know you wanted to go someplace private."

"It's okay. We would love to join them for dinner." I addressed my friends. "Right?"

"Right," Thalia agreed right away.

"Of course," Sabine added with a smile.

And as usual, Markus didn't respond, but we all knew he would come, willing or not.

Kai nodded and grinned, then bowed his head to me. "You did well today, Sea Star."

"Thank you. I guess a shove and motivation can make things happen."

"It's how my father taught me. I'm sorry if I seemed a little brash. I felt the need to push you, provided your present circumstances."

"I know. I appreciate it. And I can't wait to throw a water dagger at Roehl's face."

Everyone laughed. Even the guards, who presumably didn't know what the hell I was talking about. Or maybe they did.

"Ladies, we'll leave you to get ready. When you hear the bell toll, in a few hours' time, the guards will accompany you to the palace."

"Thank you, Kai." I looked at Markus. "And thank you for coming, despite your fear of water."

Markus cracked a smile, then bowed his head. Then he and Kai strode away.

"Follow me, ladies," I said, striding past the guards. "Wait until you see our room."

"You mean, Kai's room," Thalia corrected.

"Yes. And it is . . . well, you'll have to see it for yourself."

As soon as we stepped inside the door, they were as dumbstruck as I was when I first entered. Thalia slowly roamed the entire fringe of the room, taking in the aquarium and every living thing in it. Sabine immediately raced to the center of the room and claimed the bed.

"Where's the washroom?" Sabine questioned, gazing up at the magnificent chandelier.

I dragged myself over and stopped in front of the God of the Sea. "Come here. I'll show you."

They both looked at me like I was crazy. "I'm serious. Come and stand over here with me. I'll take you to the washroom."

"Do you have to use water magic?" Thalia asked.

"No. Just some brawn," I laughed. As soon as they both stood next to me, I yanked the trident, and the floor began to move.

Sabine screamed and clutched onto me, while Thalia's eyes still held that expression of awe.

When we stopped at the bottom and the lights magically

flickered on, they both gasped.

"Goddess. If I had a washroom like this, I would live in Aquaria," Sabine breathed, heading straight for the huge, circular tub at the center of the room. "At least ten people can fit in here." She leaned over and dipped her hand in the water. "It's warm."

"I need a bath," I said. "My muscles ache."

"I need one too," she said. "We can all take one together." She stripped down to her undergarments. "We can all soak and then get ready for dinner."

I was game. As soon as I began stripping down to my undergarments, Thalia did the same. Soon, all three of us were in the tub and it felt amazing. Magical even, soothing my sore muscles.

"Kai is pretty cute, right Thalia?" Sabine prompted.

"Yes," she said. "He's unlike any guy I've ever known."

"Well, you've been on an island all your life. It's understandable." Sabine laughed. "I think any male outside of Incendia would be unlike any guy you've ever known."

Thalia flicked water at her and laughed. "You're right."

"I think you and Kai would make a great couple," I said. I wasn't lying. I could see she was infatuated with him, but I also noted how Kai regarded her. He included her whenever he could.

Thalia shook her head. "No, Kai only has eyes for you, Calla."

"No, he doesn't," I said. "He's definitely noticed you."

OF FIRE AND WATER

"Besides, our Calla only has eyes for one prince," Sabine said, with a mischievous grin.

"Everyone knows that." Thalia laughed. "Trystan is dangerously handsome."

"He is, isn't he," I sighed, my thoughts running to Trystan.

Sabine let out a loud snort. "There she goes again. To that faraway place where only Trystan is."

"I am not," I lied.

But I was. Even after spending the day with Kai, I still couldn't get the thought of Trystan out of my mind. His kiss. His touch. The taste of his blood. Gods. Even now, my body craved it. Craved him.

I wondered how he was doing, and what was so urgent that his father had called him home. In the back of my mind, I hoped it wasn't anything to do with Roehl. But Trystan had assured me that Carpathia had strong enough wards. I wished so because my best friend was still there. Somewhere in his palace, and the thought made me happy, and a little envious because she was living there.

But there was that ominous veil of sorrow that seemed to hang over me from the Seer's prophecy.

"There she goes again. I think we should get out of the tub, Thalia. Calla looks like she's going to combust," Sabine laughed.

"Do you ever think of Kai in a romantic way?" Thalia asked. I knew it was because she didn't want to overstep any boundary. To be honest, there was none.

"I really like Kai," I said, and her expression dropped. "But Kai is a good friend, and nothing more. We're close because he saved my life and took care of me, and I will always be indebted to him for that. He might want something more, but what he wants, I can't give." I turned to Sabine with a smile. "Because my entire being feels strongly toward another."

"Get some Carpathian ass!" Sabine laughed, and Thalia giggled too.

I crossed my arms over my chest. "Excuse me, mortal who wants the Captain of the Guard's ass."

Sabine gasped and laughed even louder. "Touché. And since we're pointing fingers," she aimed her finger at Thalia. "We all know you want the water boy's ass."

Thalia's eyes nearly popped out of her head. "I—"

"Let's just enjoy whatever time we have left here," I said, changing the subject, seeing Thalia's cheeks turn bright red. "Tomorrow night is the ball, and then, I have to leave." I looked at them. "Aquaria is a beautiful place, and it's safe. If both of you choose to stay here—"

"No," Sabine snapped. "I've already told you. Wherever you go, I'm going."

"Sabine," I exhaled. "You're—"

"I know. I'm mortal . . . but I'm still useful. You are the only friend I have, and besides, the Captain of the Guard's fine ass will be with you. I'm not staying back."

I laughed, then swam over to her and wrapped my arms around her. "Thank you."

"I'm not staying either," Thalia added.

"But what about Kai?" Sabine asked.

"There are greater things at play here. Calla is a chosen Incendian royal. As an Incendian female, I am bound to fight alongside her."

I smiled, tears welling in my eyes. I was overcome with love and loyalty by these two strong women who had become my closest allies.

Sabine splashed water in my face, making me gasp.

"No tears!" She hollered.

And soon, all three of us were screaming and laughing and splashing water all over Kai's beautiful washroom floor. Hopefully, I'd be able to manipulate it back into the tub.

CHAPTER NINTEEN

After we'd dressed in our gowns, one of the guard's, posted outside of Kai's tower, accompanied the three of us to the palace. Along the way, people stopped and bowed, making me feel uncomfortable.

"Get used to it," Sabine said through clenched teeth.

"Never," I growled back, making her cackle.

Kai was at the palace entrance with Markus. The two, again, looking well-manicured and remarkably handsome. This time, Kai was wearing a white button-up shirt with a blue coat which made his ice-blue eyes stand out even more.

Markus was in all-black. Again. I guess it was his signature color.

"This way," Kai said, allowing us to walk in first. A servant in white greeted us, then led us to the dining room. This time, we were taken to a different room. When we walked in, I felt much more relaxed. The dining room was much smaller and more private.

The king, queen, and Princess Hali were all sitting at the table, but as soon as we entered, they rose and greeted us.

"Please, sit down. Make yourselves comfortable," the king said.

Kai sat next to his father, directly across from his mother. I sat next to him, across from Hali, and next to Hali was Thalia. Sabine and Markus sat on the side of me.

"Thank you for having us," I said, bowing my head.

"It's our pleasure. I heard Kai took you somewhere to practice."

I smiled and nodded. "He did, and I learned a lot. He's truly gifted."

"He is," the queen said with a tender smile.

With a raise of the king's hand, servants began bringing out trays of food. Gods. I was still struggling to deal with my food cravings.

"So, Calla," the king said, taking a sip from his goblet. "Tell us about your upbringing."

"I'm sorry, Sea Star." Kai said in my mind.

I glanced over to him. *"It's okay. I don't mind."*

Sabine bumped her knee against mine, because of the lengthy pause.

"Well," I said, taking a sip of water. "I lived a comfortable life as a mortal. I grew up in Sartha, and you already know one set of my grandparents lived in Aquaris. My father's parents are ministers who still live in Sartha. My dad owns a few mines in Sartha and used to travel with my mother to

Merchant Port to trade. I never liked being on the water, so most times I'd stay home while they traveled."

The table was now laden with meat and vegetables and freshly baked bread. It was hard to focus while everyone was stabbing and plating their food.

"Did you have servants, or a nanny?" the queen inquired.

"I had a nanny until I was old enough to be on my own."

"How old were you when you were able to stay alone?" Hali questioned.

"I was ten when they agreed I was old enough."

"Ten? I'll be ten in two months," she chimed.

"Yes, but because I am king of Aquaria, you will require supervision until you are much older," the king declared, his eyes narrowing on his daughter.

Hali sighed, her bottom lip pouting as she began slicing a piece of meat on her plate.

A servant walked over to the king with an envelope on a tray. The envelope was black and had a red wax stamp on it. One I recognized.

It was the same stamp used on the envelope Trystan left me right after I'd transformed.

I was impatient to know what it was about and was wondering if the king would share with us.

The king gingerly picked up the envelope and slowly cracked the seal. He then opened it and read it . . . silently. His brow lifted in surprise.

"What is it, father?" Kai asked.

"It seems there is to be a wedding."

My heart twisted.

"Who?" Kai pressed.

"It says that Prince Trystan of Carpathia is to be married to Princess Ivy of Northfall, in one months' time," the king replied.

My heart dropped out of my chest and hit the floor with a thud.

Trystan was engaged.

When did this happen? Why was I only hearing about this girl now? Did his cadre know? Was he already engaged when he offered me his blood?

Gods. The thought turned my stomach.

Sabine grabbed hold of my hand under the table and squeezed.

"Are you alright dear?" the queen asked. "You're looking rather pale."

"I'm sorry," I said. "I need to use the washroom."

Kai pushed out his chair and stood. He held out his hand to me and I took it. "I'll show you where it is."

We walked out of the dining room, back to the grand foyer. I stumbled over to the great aquarium and stood in front of it, staring at the hundreds of multicolored fish inside.

But my mind was numb, and my heart shattered.

Why would Trystan give me hope and then rip it away? Why would he tell me he felt a connection between us and claim me?

He kissed me. Passionately. He offered me his blood, and came to my rescue, time and time again. Why? Why would he do that when he was engaged?

What I felt for him was raw and real, and I had believed he felt the same way.

"Calla," Kai whispered, his hand resting on my back.

I turned to him, tears rolling down my face. I flung my arms around his neck and he drew me into a hug. "It'll be okay."

"He lied to me," I sobbed.

"Maybe he has a good explanation."

"He's engaged. There are no explanations."

I'd never worn my heart on my sleeve, and I shouldn't be doing it now. I had to be strong. For my friends. Leora had a heart-crushing relationship. She loved Romulus, and then, his father ended her life and destroyed her kingdom.

I'd never met the king of Carpathia, but I was certain he wanted his son to marry another pureblood. Someone who could join two kingdoms together.

But it still didn't take away the grief.

I let go of Kai and dried my face.

"Do you want to leave? I can escort you back to my room."

"No," I said. "I won't let this spoil our dinner. Or the ball. Your parents have been gracious enough to host us, and I will not act like a weak, lovesick child." I glanced into his narrowed eyes, brimmed with concern. "I'll be fine. This is just another hardship for me to survive."

Kai gave me an unreadable expression.

"What is that look?" I asked.

"I see strength and courage in you," he breathed. "I see a future ruler in you."

"I don't want to rule," I said honestly. "I want to live."

Kai nodded, knowingly. "But sometimes we are born without that choice, Sea Star. Royals are appointed to lead." He let out a heavy sigh. "I know I say a lot of negative things about ruling and I'm constantly running away and rebelling. But I also know that there will come a day when I must stop and become the man I was destined to become. I will have to become the strength and hope my people need and expect me to be."

I peered up into those luminous icy-blue eyes and smiled. "You will make a wonderful king, Kai. Your parents and your people already respect you. I saw it in the square. They genuinely love you, and I can see you love them."

"Occasionally," he said, shrugging.

"You're still teaching me," I said. "Now, please. Lead me to the washroom. I need to fix my face and get back to dinner."

He hesitated, giving me that furrowed brow of concern. "Are you sure? They will understand if you want to turn in early."

"I'm sure. It would be impolite of me to leave, especially over a matter that is out of my hands."

After I collected myself in the washroom, I exited to find Kai standing outside, waiting. He held out his arm, and I took it as he led me back into the dining room.

When we entered, it was disturbingly silent, and all eyes were on us. Most of them furrowed with concern.

"I'm sorry," I said with a smile. Trying to be brave and strong.

"You don't have to be sorry, dear child," the king said. "Have a seat. The servants have brought you some ruby wine."

"Thank you."

Kai pulled out my chair and then sat next to me, while Sabine grabbed my hand again.

I turned to her. "I'm fine. I truly am," I whispered, even though my heart was crushed. "We'll talk after dinner."

She smiled and patted my hand, and I composed a smile and pledged to get through the rest of the dinner. I was glad the queen talked mostly about the ball preparations. It seemed like the event was going to be much grander than I imagined.

I just had to get through one more day, and I was actually looking forward to the ball.

CHAPTER TWENTY

Back in Kai's room, Sabine pulled me to the bed and made me sit while she snatched a chair and dragged it in front of me. Thalia chose to circle the walled aquarium, probably feeling a bit uncomfortable. I didn't blame her. I realized I'd have to spill my feelings, even though I would much rather keep them bottled inside.

Sabine leaned forward and seized both of my hands, her eyes full and already brimming with tears. "I'm so sorry, Calla."

"Don't be," I said, fresh tears stinging my eyes. "I suppose fate sent me a curve."

She rose and folded her arms around me. "How are you feeling? Honestly."

"I'm crushed but not broken."

"Yes, and I will make certain you don't break." She sat back down and wiped away her tears. "I know how much you opened your heart to him. Did you have any idea he was engaged?"

Tears were rolling down my face, my stomach coiled. "If I'd known, I wouldn't have let him kiss me in Incendia. Or here, for goddess sake." I also wouldn't have let him give me his blood, which made me horny as hell, and the thought embarrassed the hell out of me. Gods, I practically begged him to claim me. No wonder he showed restraint. He was freaking engaged.

I buried my face in my hands. "I can't believe I let myself fall so deeply for him. I set myself up for this heartache."

Sabine took my hands in hers. "How could you not have felt that way, especially when he was the one who pursued you first?"

I dropped back onto the bed and stared up at the chandelier, flickering with beautiful sapphires and transparent crystals.

"Maybe it was a sudden arrangement," Thalia noted, her finger lightly tapping a starfish suctioned on the side of the aquarium glass.

"Sudden?" Sabine bit. "How can someone get married to someone in a month and not know who their fiancé is?"

"Arranged marriages are still a thing," Thalia said. "I haven't heard of one in a long time, but it used to be very popular with the royals. It kept kingdoms united."

She was right. King Romulus had an arranged marriage, which is why he couldn't be with Princess Leora, his true love.

"But Trystan had to have known, right?" I glanced at

Thalia and back at Sabine. "He must know this Princess of Northfall to agree to the arrangement and a wedding."

"I suppose," Sabine sighed. "I must say, I am absolutely shocked that Trystan didn't mention anything. Neither did his cadre."

"Maybe his cadre swore an oath not to tell," I moaned, rolling over and hugging the pillow.

"That's it. I'm done. I will die a virgin."

"What?" Sabine grabbed my shoulder and rolled me back to her. "You aren't."

"I am," I sighed. "Thanks to my grandparents, the ones who took in my father when he was left on their doorstep. They are ministers, and when I turned eight, they gave me a purity ring. I made a promise to remain a virgin until I married. However, I almost broke that vow with Trystan on the night of my eighteenth birthday."

"Thank the goddess you didn't," Sabine said. "I really like Trystan, but this was too much. It was a slap in the face, to all of us."

"Have either of you met Trystan's father?"

"No," they both answered.

"I heard he is very handsome, just like his son," Sabine replied. "I haven't heard too much about his mother though."

I grasped the amulet around my neck. "I'll send this back to him. He can return it to his mother or his fiancé."

"Maybe it's best," Sabine agreed.

His new wife.

I never imagined Trystan with anyone else. Not after the things he did and said to me. He claimed me and gave me a flask of his blood to seal the blood bond between us. Did he have a fiancé back then?

He made me promise not to take the amulet off, but it was no longer rightfully mine. Not when I knew who the owner was, and he was about to be married. We weren't intended for each other after all. We were star-crossed lovers, like Romulus and Leora. Trystan was engaged to be married, and while he would be off courting his soon to be bride, I'd continue to fight for my life.

I kept myself from outwardly breaking down, but inside my heart was about to explode. These feelings I had for him weren't going to leave overnight. I knew I would get through this, but it would take some time. Because truth was, as much as I tried to talk myself out of being sad, I was. Trystan had been there for me from the beginning. He rescued me in Sartha, and continued to do so in Morbeth, Incendia, and he had even come to Aquaria at my request. He sent his inner circle of men to protect me, and he was even in my dreams, thanks to the partial bond, helping me survive.

And he was taking care of Brynna.

I was more hurt than anything that he didn't tell me.

I needed to shut off my mind. I didn't want to think anymore.

"I need to sleep. Do you guys have anything to help me?" I begged.

"I do," Sabine said. She stood and moved to her bag, rummaging through it. Then, she drew out a short clear vial.

"Remember the vial I gave to you in the cell to help with the pain?" I nodded, recalling that it also put me to sleep. "This is the only vial I have."

I held out my hands. "Then, I won't take it."

"No," Sabine came and placed the vial in my palm. "You need to sleep, and this will hopefully help shut your mind off."

My bottled emotions suddenly erupted, and I began weeping uncontrollably.

Sabine dropped to her knees and hugged me. Thalia stayed away, but I could tell she felt bad.

"I'm sorry," I bawled. "I've never had these feelings before." I peered up into her concerned eyes. "I don't think he knew. I never told him how I felt. Maybe that's why he moved on."

"No, Calla," she loosed a long breath. "He knew. We all knew."

I shook my head, recalling what he said to me after I drank his blood. I told him I needed him and even offered myself to him . . . but he resisted.

"I will not take you when you are under the influence of my blood. You are only feeling and speaking this way because my blood is inside you, but once it wears off, you will think differently."

Gods. Did he really think that I only felt that way under the influence of his blood? He didn't know of the countless times I'd thought or dreamed about him. I didn't tell him, and now . . . I'd lost him.

"I know it hurts like hell, but you'll get through it. Thalia and I will make sure of it." She popped open the vial and held it to my lips, and I drank. Then she fluffed the pillows and tucked me into bed.

I wiped the tears from my eyes. "There is one thing I'm sure of," I sniffled.

Sabine brushed the hair away that was matted to my teary cheek. "What's that?"

"That the gods gave you to me."

"I feel the same way," she said, smiling. "Now sleep. You need your rest. The ball is tomorrow night."

The ball. It was another distraction I was looking forward to. A distraction from Trystan's engagement and the fact that Roehl was still out there, planning to kill me.

Whatever Sabine had given me was strong and already numbing my brain.

Thank the gods. It was exactly what I needed.

CHAPTER TWENTY-ONE

My legs were heavy as I ran from a dark cloud thundering behind me. I was in a desert, with sand stretching as far as my eyes could see. There was nowhere to hide and all I could do was keep pushing forward.

Suddenly, the sky turned black and long arms of mist reached out from the cloud, wrapping around my ankles and wrists yanking me down. I struck the ground, desperately clawing at the sand, trying to grasp onto anything.

My fingers hooked onto something solid. I grasped on to it as the mist pulled me back, unearthing a long bone. I caught something else, shrieking as I tore a skull from the ground. Suddenly, I was no longer being dragged through sand, but the remains of the dead. A grave of countless bones.

The black cloud was all around me, absorbing the air from my lungs. I clawed at my throat, trying to draw air. Then, a pair of crimson rimmed eyes appeared in front of me.

"You can't run from me, pet," a terrifying voice hissed. *"Soon, you will be a nameless corpse in the midst of Dead Man's Land."*

I called my flame and thrust it forward . . .

"Calla!" Sabine screamed. "Get up!"

I opened my eyes to see Sabine and Thalia trying to put out an armchair that was on fire near the front door. Sabine was scooping water from the aquarium with a whisky glass, but it wasn't working. I lifted my left hand, calling water from the aquarium, and sent it to the fire. It splashed down, instantly extinguishing it. Sabine and Thalia gasped, swinging toward me with wide eyes, mouths hanging open, clothes soaked, and hair dripping wet.

"I'm sorry," I apologized, sliding off the bed.

I recalled how Kai pulled the water from my wet clothes on the ship, so I held out my hands and, in my mind, called the water I used to douse the fire.

To my utter surprise, and the surprise of Sabine and Thalia, water began to bead off the floor, their bodies, hair, the chair, and floated all around them.

Their faces went from soaking confusion to expressions of shock and wonder.

"Goddess, this is unbelievable," Sabine gasped, pushing water droplets across the room with her fingers.

"Open the door," I said, not wanting to put the water back into the aquarium.

Thalia opened the door, and I sent the water beads out.

Sabine glanced back at me when the last of the water beads went out the door. "Your eyes. Whenever you're using your power, they change color."

I blinked, now that the water was gone, and everything was dry.

"They change color?"

Sabine nodded. "When you're using your gifts, your eyes turn brilliant gold. But in Incendia, they looked like they were on fire."

"That's because she was on Incendian soil. Her powers are much greater there," Thalia added, then walked back toward the couch where she chose to sleep. "Why'd you throw the fire ball? Did you have a bad dream?"

"I've had them for a while now." I was still a little groggy from the potion Sabine had given me. "What time is it?"

"I don't know. Probably a little after midnight," Sabine said.

"Gods, I'm so sorry I woke you both."

"It was Roehl again, wasn't it?" Sabine asked, and I nodded.

"He enters into my dreams, and I can never run fast enough from him. Then, I hear his voice, whispering, telling me I can't hide, and that he'll find and kill me. This time, he said he'll throw my bones in Dead Man's Land."

"Dead Man's Land is in Morbeth right? Just outside the Red Wall," Thalia asked.

"It is," Sabine said. "The ground is cursed and desolate.

There is nothing but sand and bones from those who fought at the Red Wall in the Great War.

Thalia laid down and pulled her blanket over herself. "If Roehl is coming into your dreams, he is probably using dream telepathy. Witches or those with powerful magic, can enter the dreams of others and manipulate or control whatever goes on."

"Bastard," Sabine spit. "We have to find a way to stop it." She walked over to the sculpture of the God of the Sea and clutched hold of his trident. "I'll be right back." With a smirk she tugged it and lowered into the ground, fluttering her fingers until she disappeared.

I laughed and settled back into bed.

"You two are close," Thalia said out of the blue.

"We are. We went through a lot in Morbeth, and she was instrumental in helping me escape. She's like a sister to me."

"She's a good person."

"She truly is. Sabine has a heart of gold," I said. "I hope she'll find a good man and a safe place to settle one day. I don't like that she feels the need to be with me. My life is too dangerous for a mortal. I'm afraid for my own life, but even more afraid for hers. Roehl knows Sabine. She was one of his personal servants, and I can't ever let him find or take her." I glanced into Thalia's eyes. "I may be running now, but there will come a day when I have to stand and fight, and I don't want her near."

"I understand," Thalia said. "I give you my word. I'll also

do what I can to ensure her safety."

Tears of thankfulness filled my eyes. "Thank you, cousin."

"Cousin," Thalia breathed, a smile stretched on her lips. "I am glad you came to Incendia and I'm sorry for the way the queen treated you. You are an Incendian Royal and should have been treated as such."

"I wasn't looking for a royal welcome. I wasn't even sure what I'd find there. I'd already expected that if I found anyone on the island, that I'd have to gain their trust. I just wanted some answers and hoped that in the process, maybe they would accept me."

"All Incendians have, are the words of their queen. They know nothing else and have been told to never trust outsiders. I'm sure if given some time, they would gain your trust."

I laughed inwardly. "Not while your queen is there."

Thalia sat up and gave me an expression I couldn't read. "I'm sorry, Calla. I have something to tell you. I should have told you sooner, but so many things have been happening all at once."

"I understand," I said. "We've all been occupied."

Thalia tugged at her golden hair. "I never knew what Roehl looked like until that day we were on Incendia's shore," she started. "But I've seen him before, in the palace in Incendia. I thought it strange that the guards never informed me of his arrival, but now I know it was because they never saw him. One night, I saw the queen and Roehl together. They are lovers, Calla. That's why she turned you over to him."

"Gods." I rubbed my temples. "Well, that explains a lot. Now I know why she despised me, and why she wanted to keep me inside the wall."

"Don't worry about it," Thalia said.

"How can I not worry? She's already proven her allegiance is to Roehl. If she decides to help him capture me . . ."

"She won't," Thalia said forcefully. "She knows what Morbeth did to Incendia, and so does every other Incendian. They would revolt if they knew she was bedding Morbeth's Prince. The guards would never follow Roehl."

I inhaled deeply and exhaled noisily. "You mentioned she has mages, right? The ones who contacted Roehl?"

Thalia nodded. "There are two she works with. Only her handmaidens and I know of them. They are kept away from the public eye, but she rewards them with whatever they desire— rooms, food, clothing. That day she left the dining room and said she had a meeting . . . that's when she summoned her mages."

"Did I miss anything?" Sabine said, rising from below.

"A lot," I sighed. "I'll tell you all about it in the morning,"

Sabine frowned. "Wait. Does it have anything to do with handsome princes?"

"No. It's about Roehl." Thalia replied, drawing her blanket back up.

Sabine held up her hand. "No thanks. I'll wait until tomorrow."

I slept soundly until morning, and we all groaned as we tumbled out of bed. Tonight was the ball in my honor because my grandfather saved the King's life. I still didn't think I should be receiving any recognition. I mean, we were related, but I certainly had nothing to do with it.

For the first time in my life, I was looking forward to music and dancing and the company of people who would take my mind off Roehl and Trystan. I hated adding Trystan's name to the list, but . . . shit, he was freaking *engaged* and getting married. My mind shouldn't be on him anymore.

But . . . I wondered what this princess from Northfall was like. Was she beautiful? She must have been if she was a vampire. What color hair did she have? Eyes? If she was a pureblood, what was her power?

"Are you thinking about Trystan?" Sabine scolded. My head jerked to her.

"Gods no."

Her hands were on her hips, head inclined to the side. "Then who were you thinking about? I know it was something serious because your eyes were slightly glowing."

"No, they weren't." I replied, quickly heading toward the God of the Sea, planning my escape. "It was probably the lighting." I quickly yanked the trident, but before I even lowered a foot into the floor, Sabine ran and hopped on. Thalia noticed Sabine, so she ran over and jumped on too.

Gods. I couldn't catch a break.

"Whooo is it?" Sabine sang. "Whooo are you thinking about?"

I growled. "I was wondering what the Princess of Northfall was like."

"I was wondering when you'd ask." Sabine looked at Thalia. "Dammit, I owe you a gold skrag."

I gasped, throwing a hand over my heart. "You guys were actually betting against me?"

Sabine grabbed my shoulders. "Yes, and I lost, because you didn't ask about her last night."

I grabbed her arms and shook her back. "You drugged me and put me to sleep. How could I?"

Sabine laughed and then her dark eyes turned to me. "The Princess of Northfall came to Morbeth once, with her parents. It was when the Queen of Morbeth was still alive. They tried to arrange a marriage between her and Roehl, but . . .

I interjected. "Roehl was a jackass and the King and Queen of Northfall declined."

Sabine shot me a sassy look. "Actually, it was quite the opposite. King Romulus and his wife thought the Princess of Northfall was a stuck-up bitch. She is pretty, but she has a permanent scowl etched on her face, and she is known to abuse her servants. I was young at the time but saw one of her servants bring her coat. Because she wasn't fast enough, the princess slapped her in the face. Hard. In front of everyone.

Even Roehl shook his head and walked away. If it were me, goddess help her, I would have smothered her in her sleep."

"Then why would Prince Trystan be engaged to her?" Thalia asked.

I think that was the question on everyone's mind.

I stared into Sabine's dark eyes. "You said she was pretty?"

Sabine rolled her eyes to the back of her head. She clutched my shoulders and shook me. "Calla. She is pretty, but you are ten . . . no, one hundred times prettier than she is. And you are kind and considerate. So, you beat her in every way."

"I will have to agree, based on what Sabine said. I've never met the Princess of Northfall, but I think you are amazing, and when you and Trystan are together, even a blind person could see how perfect you are for each other."

"But none of that matters anymore." I walked away, toward the window that looked out into the sea. "We'll have to leave here tomorrow morning." I leaned against the window and looked at Sabine and Thalia. "Where do you guys want to go?"

"Not to Carpathia or Northfall," Sabine hissed.

"I was thinking, since we're close, how about we go to Sartha? I'd like to show you both where I grew up." I also wanted to check in on my horse Shadow.

"I'd like that," Thalia said.

"I would too." Sabine smiled. "Let's go get something to eat. They have the best brunches here, and since this is our last full day, I don't want to miss it."

"Go ahead," I said, not wanting to see anyone just yet. "I'm probably going to soak in this nice warm tub for a while."

"Since you can't eat, I won't push. Are you sure you don't want company?"

"As much as I love you both, I am looking forward to some alone time."

"Ah," Thalia laughed. "In other words, you want us to get the hell out."

"We understand . . . but no crying while we're gone." Sabine pressed the button, and they began to rise.

"I won't cry. Not today."

"Good. See you soon."

I nodded and turned back to look out the window. I was glad we'd be returning to a place I knew. First, I wanted to find a witch who would be willing to travel with us. I needed someone to veil us, to keep Roehl from finding out where we were. Just until I could come up with a plan that would put me ahead of the game.

Maybe I could ask Kai. He seemed to know a lot of the people here. There had to be a few witches in Aquaria, and I wanted someone I could trust.

CHAPTER TWENTY-TWO

Alone, I discarded my clothes and stepped into the tub. The warmth caressed me and soothed the muscles that had tensed after the nightmare. This tub was one thing I would miss about Aquaria.

Leaning back, I rested my head against the back of the tub and closed my eyes, thinking about the new plan to head to Sartha. I wondered if there was any chance I'd find my father there. Would he come back home after what happened to my mother?

I knew Roehl hadn't captured my father because I had no doubt, he'd use him against me. He must have remained in hiding. My father was a clever man who had a lot of acquaintances in high places. There was a reason he hadn't been captured. Or Nicolae for that matter. I prayed they were safe and would stay out of Roehl's deathly clutches.

At least in Sartha we would be heading to a place I could

navigate with ease. I had everything in Sartha—unless Roehl had destroyed it—including the few thousand skrag I'd saved up over the years. It would help us survive until we could find a place to settle and start a new life. A life far away from all the death and pain Talbrinth had housed.

Talbrinth wasn't the only continent. There were six others we could choose from. We'd just have to pick one and find a way to get there. Captain Sebastian Salloway would take us, I had no doubt, but there was no way of reaching him, and I sure as hell wasn't going anywhere near Crimson Cove.

The sound of the floor lowering from above had me sinking lower in the tub. "Returning so soon? Or did you forget something?" I called out.

"Calla."

That voice. It wasn't Sabine. Or Thalia.

Even surrounded by warm water, my skin turned ice cold.

My body shivered, heart hammered against my chest, and the air in the room became heavy.

I slowly twisted to see a figure standing behind me.

My heart stopped, and everything else in the room disintegrated away.

Was this real? Was he here? Or had I fallen asleep?

"Trystan?" I exhaled.

In a split second, Trystan was inches away, one hand tangling in my hair, the other wrapping around my bare back. His lips crashed down on mine with a hunger and fierceness that left me breathless and limp in his arms. He kissed me like his life—our lives—depended on it. A kiss that had my mind drowning in the moment.

And I kissed him back.

Before I realized what was happening.

"What are you doing?" I pushed him away, covering my breasts with my arms. "You shouldn't be here."

"I had to see you." His eyes were brimmed with so much grief and emotion. Gods. I hated that I still wanted him so badly. His scent, his voice, his presence . . . it affected me more than it should have. I had to stand strong.

"You don't get to be engaged and barge in here and kiss me," I said trembling. "I'm not going to be your side-whore, Trystan. I am worth way more than that."

The sorrow in his eyes intensified, as if my words wounded him. "I, of all people, recognize you are worth so much more," he said, his chest heavily rising and falling. "I came here to set the story straight."

"What's to set straight?" I asked. "Last night, I saw an invitation to a wedding written in ink and secured with Carpathia's seal. I think that's straight forward enough. I get it. You're off limits . . . and so am I." I wanted to exit the tub, but my clothes were too far and so were the towels.

Trystan took notice and went over to the wall and grabbed a towel. He handed it to me, then strode toward the window, gazing out at the sea.

I wrapped the towel around me, clutching it tight as I stepped out of the tub.

"How did you get in here without being seen?"

"I know the guards outside. When I was younger, I used to sneak out of my palace and come and stay here with Kai. He used to do the same. When he ran away, he'd come to stay with me in Carpathia." Trystan paused, his hands tucked deep in his pockets. "I told the guards I'd be quick."

"You didn't have to come all this way to apologize." I tightened the towel around me, hoping the trembling in my voice wouldn't give away how much my heart was still hurting. "I'll be fine."

"But I won't." Trystan turned, and I felt the sadness radiating in those eyes and the agony in each of his ragged breaths. With a few long strides he closed the distance between us, reigniting the flame inside me. "My father arranged the marriage before I returned from Aquaria," he said softly. "That's why me and my cadre were ordered back. He said I've been reckless. My choices are unfit of a Prince of Carpathia. So, he thought it necessary to tie me down. I had nothing to do with it."

I understood, but his apology didn't repair my broken heart. "Do you know her? The Princess of Northfall?"

He nodded and a thousand questions battered my mind. But the one I needed answered was, "Do you love her?"

He growled, thrusting his hands up in the air in frustration. "What do you think, Calla? Why would I travel here alone, against my father's wishes, to come and see you?"

"I don't know, Trystan," I replied a little too firmly.

Taking in deep, steadying breaths, I composed myself. "Since we met in Sartha, we've danced on that delicate thread of what our relationship is truly based on. I still question why you came that night to my party. You offered me a choice—to secure the blood bond with you or run. When I chose to run, you still sent your cadre to protect me. Then, you came for me in Morbeth, and even when I had the partial bond removed, you still came for me in Incendia.

"I don't know what we are to each other. Are you just a hero who is always there? A knight in shining armor? A Friend? Because we both know from this point on, we can never be lovers. Not when you are about to be wed in a month." I attempted, but failed, to hold back the tears that threatened to reveal how I sincerely felt. Because the fact remained . . . he was engaged.

"After all this time," Trystan said hoarsely, "you still question my feelings for you? Have I not revealed to you how I truly feel?" He stepped away, raking those long fingers through thick hair. When he turned back to me, those beautiful azure eyes pierced straight through my soul. "That first night I saw you at your birthday party, standing alone in a shadowy corner, I realized, from that moment on, my life would never be the same.

"I knew Roehl was coming for you. I knew what he was going to do to you, and every molecule inside me begged that I help you. At first, I wasn't sure how because I'd come to Sartha on an impulse.

"But then I saw you—this beautiful, frail thing, hiding in the shadows. So breakable. So young and innocent. I knew right then what I had to do. I had to claim you, and marking you was the only way I knew I could save you.

"I realized you wouldn't understand, and would react the way you did, but I had to protect you. I had to keep you alive. There was no other way, and the moment I pushed my teeth into your fragile shoulder and tasted your blood—" He shook his head and loosed a long breath he'd just taken. "I knew you'd be frightened and alone in your cottage. So, I stayed with you for those three days while you transformed. I despised myself for putting you through the suffering, but I knew when it was complete, you would be stronger.

"I held your hand. I made you a promise it would end soon, and when the shift was complete, I left. It was cowardice of me, but I couldn't face you after all the pain I'd put you through. I didn't want to see the look of hate in your eyes when you woke and found me there.

"Calla, ever since that day, I can't sleep until I know you're safe. When I'm not with you, I constantly wonder where you are and how you're faring.

"That night, when you showed up in Carpathia through the partial bond and stood on my balcony, I swore you were an angel. Even if it were a dream . . .that moment, I caught a glimpse of what my future could be like. Not with anyone else, Calla." He tenderly caressed my face in the palms of his hands. "The answer to your question is no. I do not love the

Princess of Northfall. Nor will I ever. The reason I came here was so you would know how I truly feel.

"You, Calla, are the golden sunrise on my darkened shores. The warm breeze that embraces my cold and desolate soul. I claimed you back then, not merely because I wished to save you. I claimed you because I knew there would never be anyone else for me. I claimed you because even before I knew you, I ached for you. I claimed you because I selfishly wanted you for myself."

My heart.

How could it be so gods-damned full but so broken at the same time?

Tears fell in torrents after hearing his words. But those beautiful words were also like daggers, piercing straight through my chest.

"You can't say these things to me, Trystan," I cried. "You can't tell me how you truly feel and then walk away to your fiancé and leave me here to suffer with a foolish heart that is broken and bleeding."

Trystan stepped back, an expression of pain swirling in those now darkened eyes. His fingers gently raised my chin to meet his gaze. A gaze that held the weight of the world in one question.

"How *do* you feel about me, Calla?"

And there it was. The question that would lay bare my broken soul and raw emotions.

I shook my head. All words caught in my throat as his

eyes searched my face for an answer.

And then, before my mind could process everything I'd kept bottled inside, my lips whispered what my heart screamed out.

"I love you, Trystan."

His eyes went wide, a moment of shock, then . . . a smile bloomed on his beautiful face. Trystan's eyes brightened as tears rolled down his face, and his lips, those beautiful lips pressed against mine. But this kiss was different from any other. It was raw and tender, laden with desire and passion and knowing. It was a kiss that had me drifting on a cloud.

Love. I never dreamed I'd speak that word out loud, at least not for a very long time. But it had happened, and I didn't even have to think about it. The word came naturally. As natural as one would breathe air, and it was the one emotion my heart wouldn't lie about.

This man, standing before me, a man whose life was interwoven with mine, was just as lost and broken as I was. Bound to a marriage he had no say in. To a woman he didn't love.

"Say it again, Calla," he begged, in a tone just above a whisper.

But I couldn't.

The words wouldn't exit my lips. They were caught in my throat.

A coldness wrapped its tendrils around my chest and my heart. A heart, that a moment ago, had been filled with so much light and warmth.

My head shook, and a tear trailed down my face as I took a step away from him. That coldness seeping between us like a frigid wintry wind.

Trystan was the Prince of Carpathia. Engaged to the Princess of Northfall. Two pureblood royals who would unite two vampire kingdoms with their union.

And here I was, a mishmash mess—not even a half-blood. A mortal, vampire, and Incendian mut. If Trystan and I ever joined, I had nothing to offer him. No kingdom. No crown. No throne.

I was a walking curse. Followed by a wicked darkness that had vowed to kill me. A darkness that had found a way to enter my dreams and torment me. A darkness that would kill everyone I loved.

Death lingers around you, heir of blood and fire. Because of this, your blood prince will die. The prince to whom you share a bond.

Those were the words spoken by the Seer. Words that would follow me into my dreams and haunt me. Trystan was the only blood prince I'd had a partial bond with, besides Roehl, but her prophecy also confirmed that Roehl was the one who would kill him.

Die by the hand of the dark prince with red-rimmed eyes.

"I can't, Trystan. We can't."

I took another step back, but he caught my arm and pulled my body flush to his.

"Why? Why can't we?" His breath was ragged again, and the anguish flickered back in his eyes.

"Trystan, you have a kingdom and a people who need you, who depend on you. You will be married soon to a pureblood who your father approved of." Tears were pouring down my face again. The pain in my chest was now radiating through my body, knowing that once he married, I would never see him again. "Since the moment I met you, you've suffered because of me. Even your cadre told me they didn't understand why you chose to save me. I have given you nothing and I have nothing to offer you."

Trystan blinked, and a tear escaped his eye, rolling down his cheek. "You have given me a reason to live, Calla. Something to fight for." Trystan grabbed my shoulders and stepped back so he could see my face clearly. "I will leave Carpathia. I will leave my kingdom, right now, if you choose me. I will take your hand and will never let go. I will stand and fight alongside you, and I will hold you and love you, until the very end of our days."

A deep sob ripped from my chest.

Gods, how I wanted to say yes. To take hold of his hand and run away. To see his face every waking day and fall asleep in his arms every night.

But that would be the most selfish thing I had ever done. Selfish to every single Carpathian who depended on the future of their Prince. Trystan was the only heir to the Carpathian throne. The only son of the King. Yet, he would risk it all—everything—to run away with me.

I couldn't let that happen. I wouldn't. My heart and conscience wouldn't allow me to. Because it knew what I had to do.

Trystan felt so strongly that he needed to save me, and he did so by coming to Sartha and claiming me.

Now, my entire being was crying out for me to save him, and the only way I could do so, was to let him go.

And walk away.

CHAPTER TWENTY-THREE

"Trystan? What are you doing here?" Kai's voice sounded behind us. I hadn't even heard him come down.

Trystan's eyes slid to Kai then back to mine, waiting for my response. To take his hand and run away with him . . .

Or—When I held his hand, a spark of hope ignited, but it quelled as he glanced down and realized what I had placed in his palm. His mother's amulet.

"I'm sorry, Trystan," I wept. My heart was split open and bleeding out from the multiple wounds I'd just inflicted on myself. "I'm so sorry. I can't."

I closed my eyes and took a step back, trying to block out the look of sheer misery and grief etched on his face. Then, I took another shuddering step backward.

"Calla," Sabine called out. Soon, her arms folded around me. Around the towel I was still clutching on to like a lifeline.

"Trystan, can I speak to you?" Kai asked in a calm tone.

Trystan hadn't known that I had called Kai through our connection. To come to his washroom. Immediately.

I could hear Trystan's strides as he crossed the floor, heading away from me. Then, I heard the floor rising. When it stopped, my swollen eyes slid open, and my trembling legs gave way. I dropped to the ground in a sobbing heap. Sabine wrapped her arms securely around me and held me in her arms.

"It'll be okay," she whispered. "It'll be okay."

One thing was for sure. I would never forget the look on his face. It was scorched into my memory. I had wounded him. Deeply. And it was something I would carry with me for the rest of my life.

Thalia was standing against the back wall, her face set with worry . . . because of me.

Even though I'd torn Trystan's heart out and trampled on it, I had to get up. I had to stand and not buckle, for the sake of my friends. Right now, I wasn't strong or stable. I was pathetic. A sobbing mess on a washroom floor.

I wiped my face and tried to stand, and Sabine helped me to my feet.

Still clinging to the towel, I made my way to the window and peered outside. At the bottom of the tower, Kai and Trystan stood. Kai was talking to him, a hand resting on his shoulder, but Trystan's head was bent, a hand clasping the back of his neck, his shoulders drooped forward.

Seeing him in this condition crushed me all over again. I had to look, realizing it would perhaps be the last time I saw him.

Kai hugged his friend and whispered something into his ear. Trystan shook his head and walked away.

Kai followed him, and I watched, my heart draining out with every step he took, further and further away from me.

And then Trystan paused, his head wrenched back, his eyes filled with a deep and guttural anguish, glanced up to me.

Goodbye, Calla. They spoke so heart shatteringly clear.

I placed my hand on the window, new tears staining my face. My chest heaved as he turned and walked away.

Goodbye, Trystan.

CHAPTER TWENTY-FOUR

I roused to Sabine and Thalia's low laughter. Opening my swollen, blurry eyes, I saw them with gowns folded over their arms, heading toward the God of the Sea.

"What time is it?" I inquired, wondering how I'd gotten tucked into bed.

"A few hours before the ball," Thalia replied. "We were going to get ready and wake you when we were done. We wanted to let you sleep in."

"How did I get here?" I said, rubbing my temples that throbbed like hell.

"You passed out after Trystan left," Sabine said sadly. "Thank God Kai came back to check on you. He carried you up to bed, and Thalia and I slipped on your bedgown after he left." Her eyes swept over my face, disclosing a sadness I hated seeing. "How are you?"

"I'll be fine." I knew I would. I'd never encountered a

broken heart before especially one caused by me.

"That's good to hear." Sabine placed her hand on the trident. "Take your time getting up and come down when you're ready. Your gown is in the washroom."

"Thank you," I said, forcing a smile.

Sabine yanked the trident and as they descended, I fell backward onto the pillow, gazing upward at the sparkling chandelier.

My heart was cold and distant, and I wondered if it would ever find warmth again.

Tonight was our last night in Aquaria. I had to make sure it was memorable, not only for me, but for Sabine and Thalia. I knew they were looking forward to it.

I slid out of bed and slowly shuffled over to the fish aquarium and stared inside. Hundreds of tiny fish swam around with no cares in the world. They had everything the sea had, in a smaller world, but they didn't seem to mind. They were zigzagging through coral and live sea plants, darting in and out of little rock caves, some sucking gods knew what off the sand at the bottom and spewed it out.

I lay my hand on the glass and smiled. Suddenly, all the fish came, swimming around the one spot my left palm rested. It's the same thing that happened when Kai raised his hand to the glass, and the fish came, as if they were attracted to him.

I was in awe, and as soon as I put my hand down, the cluster of fish broke away and went back to whatever they were doing.

Maybe that's why the sea creature Spot came to me. Maybe he could feel the same connection I had with Kai, and it made me wonder if all Aquarians shared this gift. Or if it was because of the link Kai placed on our elements.

I slowly maneuvered the circular chamber, taking in the life in the aquarium.

"Oh, to be a fish," I breathed. "Do you have hearts that can be easily broken?" I hoped not, because there was literally no place to escape to, unless they relocated to another part of the aquarium.

After my round, I decided to head down to the washroom, but a glimmer caught my eye. There, lying on a short side table, was the amulet I had returned to Trystan. I strode over, picked it up, and it warmed against my fingers. He had left it.

Before I was wrenched back into a gloomy sadness, I set the amulet down and headed toward the God of the Sea. Trying to change my focus, I wondered what gown they'd chosen for me. After all, this was a ball in my honor—and of my grandfather, Marinus. I hoped the gown was simple and not over the top. I wanted to be comfortable, I thought, as I tugged the trident and the floor lowered.

Down at the bottom, I could hear Sabine and Thalia laughing heartily, and it was a welcomed sound.

"Calla!" Sabine's eyes were sparkling as she called me over. "Wait until you see your dress."

"Oh, no," I groaned.

"No," Thalia said, with a lively glint in her eyes. "Look."

CAMEO RENAE

They stepped aside to reveal an elegant, one shoulder, sea blue gown. The bodice was fitted, trimmed with pearls and with sparking teardrop shapes that overlapped each other, creating the appearance of scales. From below the waistline was a luxurious fabric that billowed and shimmered.

"A gown fit for . . . you." Sabine bowed her head with a broad grin.

I knew she was going to say *a princess*, so I gave her a genuine smile for not using the word.

"It's beautiful." I agreed, gliding my fingers over the soft fabric. "You guys get ready, I'm going to soak in the tub until you're done.

"Okay." Sabine rested a tender hand on my shoulder and gave me a knowing look. A look that said I'd be okay and that she'd be there for me. I knew I would be.

"Sit," Sabine ordered, patting a chair, and Thalia obliged. While Sabine gathered her devices to make her beautiful, I slipped out of my bedgown and slid into the warm tub. I wasn't as reserved as I normally was. They'd obviously seen me naked to put on my bedgown.

While Sabine and Thalia discussed their meals and sightings in the background, I slipped into the water.

Opening and closing my fist, I observed the water stir—pushing and pulling with rhythmic ease—echoing my movement. It was easy now to manipulate this element that had been born long before I was. Such a simple yet complex thing that sustained living things—the source of all life.

OF FIRE AND WATER

Since my new journey began, I'd feared the water, and that fear kept me from traveling with my parents on the Argent Sea. It kept time and new memories away. Memories I would never make.

But now, water was a part of me. A companion who came when I beckoned.

I sank under the glassy water and settled there. So calm. So tranquil. Running out of air, I fixed a bubble around my head and breathed.

Hands suddenly seized my shoulders and jerked me up.

"Calla!" Sabine gasped. "What the hell are you doing?"

"Relaxing."

"We thought you . . ." her eyes drifted to Thalia who was standing right next to her, eyes wide. "We thought you were trying to drown yourself."

"Gods no. I had a bubble over my face."

Relief washed over their faces.

Thalia crossed her hands over her chest before blowing out an unsteady breath. "Thank the goddess." She wiggled her fingers over the water. "Okay, go back to . . . relaxing. We'll be over here if you need us."

I smiled as they linked arms and walked away. My sisters. My allies.

An hour after being primped and prodded and my hair curled and braided, I was finally ready for the ball. Hali had chosen a simple gold and pearl crown to sit atop my head.

Sabine and Thalia looked stunning in their gowns. Each in a different shade of blue. Sabine's gown was a rich navy, with a fitted top and billowy bottom, and a deep neck with soft fabric shoulders. While Thalia's was a sleeveless powdery blue that molded to her shapely body.

Before we exited the door, I paused and peered back into the chamber. "Go ahead. I'll meet you at the bottom of the stairs," I said, and they agreed.

I made my course to the amulet and picked it up. Yes, it was Trystan's mothers, but it was also a birthday gift from my best friend. A double gift.

Carefully, I placed the amulet around my neck, and as soon as I did, I felt a warmth where it lay on my chest. It felt right. Like a piece of me had been returned.

Kai and Markus were at the gate, as handsome as ever in their suits, to escort us to the ball. Their faces instantly brightened as we headed their way.

Kai was in all white this time, his silvery-blue hair let down. His smile beamed like the sun.

Markus was donning a pure-black suit—his signature color—tailored perfectly to fit his muscular frame and broad shoulders. His dark eyes were fastened on Sabine, who was already blushing.

As we approached them, Kai bowed at the waist. "You all

look exquisite."

"Thank you," I said, bowing back. "And you look dashingly handsome, *highness*." Of course, I said the highness part in my head.

"Shall we," Kai said, extending both of his arms toward me and Thalia. Thalia paused, like she wasn't sure what she should do, so I nudged her.

"Go on," I whispered. A smile bloomed on her red lips as she linked her arm with Kai's. Then, I did the same, while Markus already had Sabine on his arm.

The sandstone pathways were empty and as soon as we reached the palace, I realized why. Hundreds of individuals, all dressed in their finest, dotted the front and the stairs.

"Gods," I breathed, my heart picking up pace.

Then, I heard Kai chuckle. "Be brave, Sea Star. That's just a small part."

"A small part of what?"

As Kai steered us through the crowd, anybody in our path stopped and bowed, their faces smiling and showing respect.

I swallowed hard, my heart now racing. I glanced over to Thalia who was smiling pleasantly, looking so cool and collected.

How the hell could she do that?

"Unfurl that brow," Kai said smoothly in my mind. *"The people will think you are angry with them."*

I loosened my face and put on a smile.

"Much better." I glanced at him and he gave me a wink.

Yes, this was just what I needed. A distraction. Even though it made my anxiety shoot through the roof, I was thankful for it.

The bodies, the bows and smiles and greetings were never ending as we maneuvered up the stairs and into the palace, where even more bodies congregated.

But the atmosphere was light and happy, and everyone was friendly. They were welcoming me.

It was a far cry from the Incendians, who sneered and called me a witch and a fake.

"Here we are," Kai said, as we made our way toward two massive doors that swung open and closed with bodies pushing both in and out, pausing and bowing as they passed us.

Kai ushered us express and as we entered the doors, we were swept away into an entirely different world. An underwater fantasy world that captured my breath.

The walls weren't walls, but seascapes decorated with coral and rocks stacked to look like ancient ruins. There were sculptures and fountains that spewed out colored water. Mist from the fountains fell out and slid across the floor and over our feet.

Above us, floating across the entire ceiling, were transparent glass lights that looked like bubbles. Up lights in blues and greens completed the underwater ambience.

People were still bowing while my eyes swept the room.

"This is incredible," I said, taking it all in. There was a

band on a raised platform who played music. A harp, a few violins, flutes, and a mandolin. The music was soft and smooth and ebbed like the sea on a windless day.

"Would you ladies like anything to drink?" Kai asked.

I shook my head, thinking about hiking this dress up to relieve myself, but Thalia replied, "I would love a drink."

He led us to an empty stone bench that sat between two mermaid statues. "Stay here. I'll be right back," he said, disappearing into the crowd.

Markus and Sabine were walking in a different direction, arms still linked, laugher on their lips. They were beautiful together. A perfect match. Sabine was the sweet to his salty. The light to his dark. My heart felt lighter seeing them happy . . . together.

"Do you think you'll ever open your heart again?" Thalia asked, her eyes also on Markus and Sabine.

I shook my head. "Not anytime soon." I not only couldn't. I wouldn't. The shards of my heart would take a lot of time to piece back together. If ever.

She put her head down, her hands twisting nervously around each other.

A few couples made their way over and bowed to me. I stood and greeted them with a smile and sat as they left.

"You should dance with Kai tonight," I said. "He'll need a good partner and I'm not really in the mood."

"No, I couldn't," she said. But I knew there was a reason

behind it.

"Look, it's our last night here." I took hold of her hand. "You should be happy. Dance. Open your heart."

"I haven't been with anyone in a very long time," she said nervously.

"How old are you?" If she was taken in by the Queen after Morbeth attacked. Gods. She must have been old.

"I'm still young for an immortal . . . but ancient, in mortal years." She laughed. I swore she was no older than twenty.

"You don't look much older than me," I admitted.

"The benefits of an immortal life."

Kai returned with two drinks in his hand. He handed one to Thalia and held up the other to me. "Are you sure you don't want one?"

I shook my head, and he gulped it down.

"My parents are at the other end of the room, and I'll never hear the end of it if I don't bring you over there to see them."

I stood and held my arm out and then glanced at Thalia. "Come on, cousin. We must meet the king and queen."

Thalia stood and linked her arm in Kai's other arm.

"You seem a bit more relaxed," Kai said.

I hadn't noticed, but I was unconsciously smiling and nodding my head to people as they passed by.

The king and queen were dressed in the most gorgeous finery, seated on thrones fit for underwater royalty. Thrones that were made of coral and pearl. The king was also in white, like Kai, and the queen in a white gown with gold trim and blue gems shaped like teardrops.

They stood and greeted me with warm hugs.

Thalia stood back with Kai and bowed.

"Where's Hali?" I asked.

The queen's eyes rolled. "Running around here somewhere with a few of her friends."

I laughed, remembering I did the same at her age every time my parents attended a formal event.

"This place is beyond beautiful," I said. "I feel as if I've stepped into one of my fantasy books."

The queen gave a proud smile. "Thank you. It's been a while since we've had a reason to throw a celebration like this. It kept us busy. I'm so glad you love it."

"I will never forget this night," I said.

"Good!" the king clapped, laughing heartily. "Maybe it will bring you back to us soon. Kai seems a lot more settled now that you're here."

"I think he's settled because he has to be here, looking in on three girls who have invaded his space." I glanced back and Kai nodded. "But I do look forward to returning. Aquaria is an incredibly beautiful place."

"We're happy to hear that," Queen Adira replied.

The king held out his arms. "Have fun. Dance. Drink. And be merry."

"I will," I said, bowing my head.

Kai held out his arm, and I took it as he quickly led us away.

"You did good," he said.

"Your parents are sweet. I like them."

Those words made him smile.

The music shifted into something a little faster but beautiful. The crowd cheered and cleared the center of the floor. Kai paused, his luminous blue eyes on mine, while Thalia unlinked her arm and stepped back with the crowd. My anxiety built as I watched her leave.

Kai bowed deeply at his waist and when he came up, he offered me his hand and a sinister grin. "May I have this dance, Sea Star?"

CHAPTER TWENTY-FIVE

"Kai," I growled in my head.

"Just relax and let me lead," he said. *"And please. Hurry and take my hand. Everyone is watching and I'm starting to feel like a fool."*

I let out another soft growl before taking his hand. Kai pulled me against him, his other hand resting on the small of my back, and as soon as he did, the crowd clapped.

"Why didn't you warn me."

"If I had, you would've been anxious the entire time. Maybe you would have even disappeared or tried to get out of it."

"That's not a lie."

"I did it so you wouldn't stress out about it." He threw me a sarcastic look. *"I know you better than you think."*

"Prove it."

"I know that distracting you can make you loosen up and

dance like you've been doing it all your life."

I popped out of the conversation to realize Kai was right. We were dancing. Moving effortlessly across the floor. Round and round as the people watched with wide eyes and smiles. Then, I heard the whispers.

"They're perfect together."

"A charming couple. Beautiful dance."

"Did you see the way they were looking at each other? My heart."

"I hope she marries Prince Kai."

I caught the king and queen holding hands with gleaming smiles on their faces. The queen had a hand over her heart and a look of pride twinkling in her eyes as she watched Kai led me around the dance floor.

"Don't lose focus." Kai spoke. *"Keep your eyes on me."*

"When is this song going to end?"

"Soon. Why? Am I that horrible that you would leave me after the first dance?"

"I'm leaving because I hate being the center of attention. And to be honest, you're a wonderful dancer. I'm extremely impressed."

"Then I shall count all those boring years of dance practice as a triumph."

"You should. Your mother looks so proud."

He glanced at her, then turned back to me with a mischievous smirk. *"Oh, my mother is outright giddy because her son has a beautiful princess in his arms and is whisking her around the dance floor like a champion."*

The melody died and Kai ended the dance by dipping me backward. Then he paused, my back arched, head hanging.

"Let me up."

"Why?"

"Because everyone is looking!"

"Let them look." Kai laughed, then lifted me up and placed a gentle kiss on my cheek.

The crowd went wild with gasps and whistles and my face went hot, turning a deep shade of red. Before I could say anything, he linked his arm around mine and hauled me off the floor.

The next song started, and couples began dancing. It was a sight to see. Gentlemen and women in long gowns seemed to be floating across the floor.

"Why did you do that? Now people are going to think we're courting."

"And that would be bad because—"

"Because we aren't, and I don't want to get your parent's hopes high."

"My parent's hopes were high the moment I mentioned I'd met you. Meeting you in person sealed those hopes."

I inwardly groaned.

"What is the world without hopes and dreams, Sea Star," he whispered in my ear.

I smirked, knowing I couldn't argue with that.

Glancing across the dance floor, I spotted Thalia standing alone, looking a bit out of place.

"Can you do me a huge favor?" I asked Kai.

A brow cocked, interest aroused. "Depends on what is."

"Would you dance with my cousin, Thalia? She looks dreadfully bored, and I really wanted her to have a wonderful time tonight." I gave him a toothy grin. "Please. And please don't tell her I told you. She is rather taken with your handsome face and dashing charms."

Kai's eyes grew bright. "Is she now?"

"She is."

"And what about her *cousin*? Does she think I'm handsome and dashing as well?"

Gods. He wasn't going to stop.

"She does. Very handsome. Very dashing," I said, which raised a sly grin. "She's coming this way. Please dance with her."

"And what will you be doing?"

I shrugged. "It's my ball isn't it? I'll be mingling with the people and drinking punch."

I waved at him and walked away, heading toward the drinks, which was a fountain all its own. People were dipping their cups in and walking away. How convenient.

Out of the corner of my eye, I spotted the old woman

I'd run into the other day. The Seer. She was sitting on a bench at the back of the room with her granddaughter. I headed their way, wanting to ask them the one question that had been burning on my mind.

When I finally reached them, the young woman stood and curtseyed. "Princess."

I gave her a warm smile. "How are you both doing?"

"Fine," she said.

I figured I would get just to the point, since it was evident, she was a one-word answer kind of girl.

"Could I ask you a question?"

"Sure," she said, a little uneasy.

"Your Gram's visions. Can they be altered?"

Before she could respond, the old woman began moaning, then reached out and grabbed my hand, her opaque eyes on mine.

"He will die," she said, her voice sounding more like an old hag. "The blood prince will die by the hand of the dark one with red-rimmed eyes." Her body began trembling, a tear rolled down her wrinkled face. "He will die," she repeated. "And you will watch."

"Gram," the girl bellowed, struggling to yank our hands apart, but I held on and kneeled in front of the Seer.

"When is he going to die?" I begged her for an answer. "Please, tell me."

The girl yanked harder, tearing us apart, severing the connection.

"She can't tell you," she said. "Like I said before, she can only see glimpses."

The Seer was now swaying back and forth, moaning softly, tears streaking down her face.

"I'm sorry," I breathed. I didn't mean to upset her.

The girl quickly curtseyed, then grabbed hold of her Gram and escorted her away.

I was left numb and trembling . . . again.

She'd repeated those same words she said in the square. *The blood prince would die by the hand of the dark one with red-rimmed eyes. And I would watch.*

The girl didn't even answer my question. Could the visions be altered? I had to know.

Glancing around, the room had filled with more bodies, and I couldn't see where the girl had taken the old woman. But on the dance floor I spotted Kai and Thalia and Markus and Sabine. They all looked so happy and carefree.

I had a feeling the girl wouldn't stay here. Her Gram was shaken, so the only logical thing would be to take her outside to get some fresh air. Or take her home.

If she did the latter, I'd have to catch up to them quickly. I was desperate to get the answer tonight. Because tomorrow, we would be leaving this beautiful place.

Quickly weaving my way through the crowd, I didn't give the passing people time to bow or greet me. I kept my eyes skimming just in case I caught sight of them.

Moving out of the ballroom, I finally headed to the foyer and caught a glimpse of the young woman leading her Gram outside.

"Princess Calla," Hali called out, rushing toward me. She was all dolled up in a coral-colored gown. "Oops, I mean . . . Calla.

I smiled and threw my arms out, and she ran and gave me a hug.

"You look so beautiful," she chimed. "I knew you'd look lovely in that gown, and with that crown.

I took her hands in mine. "Everything you have chosen for me has been absolutely perfect. You are also looking beautiful tonight. You're the prettiest princess that ever walked the earth."

"Thank you," she said, blushing. She glanced behind her. "I have to go find my friend. I think she's gotten lost on her way to the washroom."

"Oh no. Then you better go find her. Ask one of the guards to keep an eye out for her too."

"I'll do that," she said swiftly walking away. She turned and waved. "See you later, Calla."

I waved back. "See you later, Hali."

When she disappeared into the sea of bodies, I hurried toward the exit, bowing my head to those who made eye contact with me.

Once outside, I scanned the stairs and beyond.

In the distance, my eyes caught on a man who looked out of place. Someone who wasn't wearing a suit and was . . . limping. My eyes fixed on his black hair, watching as he pressed through the crowd, undoubtedly injured. As he got closer, I recognized his garb. Fighting leathers.

I started moving toward him, my pulse racing, heart hammering inside my chest, echoing through my ears.

And then, the man appeared at the foot of the stairs, blood smeared on his face and soaking his side. His legs wobbled, threatening to give, so I ran down the stairs toward him.

"Kylan," I cried, as his legs finally gave, and he fell to the ground.

The people around backed away, their eyes wide with a mix of horror and fear.

"Kylan," I bellowed, as his weary, bloodstained arm stretched out to me.

Reaching him, I dropped to his side and grabbed hold of his hand. His face was coated in blood. His right shoulder had a stick protruding from it—an arrow that had been broken in half.

"Kylan," I wailed, looking into his bloodshot, tear-filled eyes. "What happened?"

He gazed at me, brow furrowed, and uttered one word.

"Roehl." He then heaved forward, coughing up blood.

But that one word. That one name, sent fear wrapping

its dark tendrils around me, squeezing until I could scarcely breathe.

I moved behind Kylan, resting his head on my lap.

"What happened?" I asked, brushing some hair that had matted to his face with blood.

"Roehl," he wheezed again, his eyes rolling back.

Gods no. He can't pass out.

I gently lifted his head, the back slippery with blood.

"Where is Trystan?" I asked. He moaned, his eyes closing.

I shook him, waking him, desperate for an answer.

"Kylan, where is Trystan?" I said firmly, my face inches from his.

He shook his head, and I felt that void in my heart grow deeper, colder.

Kylan took in a shuddering breath.

"Roehl found your father," he exhaled.

No. My heart stopped beating and the world went dark.

Kylan moaned again. "Trystan found out and went to try and save him. We were outnumbered."

He winced in pain, blood seeping from the wound.

"I'm a healer," a man with black hair and eyes said, kneeling beside Kylan, his eyes tight as they assessed his wounds. "The arrow must come out immediately, or he'll die," he said in an urgent tone.

I needed answers. "Kylan, where are they now?" I begged.

Kylan swallowed. His mouth dry. "Roehl has them. In Aquaris."

Aquaris. I had a feeling my father would have hid there.

His blood-soaked hand rose and touched my face, his eyes filled with anguish.

Kylan blinked and tears rolled down his face. "I'm so sorry, Calla," he said, his words barely audible. "If you don't go to him, they'll both die."

Kylan's eyes rolled back and closed.

He was alive, but barely. His breath shallow.

"Someone carry him to my office. Now," the healer ordered.

Three men stepped forward, lifting Kylan and quickly carried him away.

I was alone. Blood soaked through my gown and stained my arms and was now smeared on my cheek. The world around me turned dark and cold as ice.

"Death lingers around you," the Seer had said.

My greatest fear had come to pass.

Roehl had captured the two men I loved most in this gods-damned world.

He knew he had me. He knew I would come, and there

was nothing that would stop me.

I kicked off my sandals and ran towards Kai's tower. Ran as fast as my feet could carry me.

Inside his chamber, I ripped off the dress and crown, quickly throwing on the black pants, tunic, and boots from Trystan, and the cloak from Sabine.

I sprinted to the secret exit Kai had showed us earlier—the one only accessed by royals.

I quickly searched for and found the hidden pad and held my breath as I pressed my palm against it.

The door slid open, and I hurried into the adjacent room, letting it slide shut behind me.

Thank the gods. It worked.

I walked toward the glass door and pressed my back against the wall, trying to catch my breath. My mind a cobweb of emotions.

Trystan had gone to Aquaris to save my father, endangering his life and the life of his cadre.

Even after I turned him down, he still went. For me.

An unexplainable love that will hold on to you even after you've let go.

I sucked in a shuddering breath.

I would never forgive myself for the pain I caused him. My stomach hadn't stopped aching and my chest had a gaping oozing hole in it since he'd left.

Truth was, I loved Trystan. Much more than I was able to admit. But I was a coward.

I was afraid of Trystan's father, who had told Trystan he'd been reckless, and that his choices had been unfit for a Prince of Carpathia. I was afraid because I knew he was referring to me. I was the unfit choice for his son. I was the reason he made reckless moves. So, he chose to arrange a marriage that his son didn't agree with.

Yet, despite his father's wishes, Trystan held out his hand to me. He was willing to give up his kingdom, his crown, and his birthright. But I wouldn't allow him to do that. I wouldn't allow him to give up everything . . . for me.

I was a coward, who would never forget the pain etched on his face.

I was a coward, who failed to take the hand he held out to me.

I was a coward, who stepped back from him.

I stepped back . . . and watched him crumble.

I was no longer going to stand back or stand down. I was going to stand up and fight for him. It was my turn to give back to Trystan, this man who had given everything for me—risked everything for me. I would fight for him, not only because I loved him. I would fight for him because he had fought for me from the very beginning. I would fight for him, even if it meant giving up my life.

Heat began to writhe under my skin and burn in my palms. I felt that power inside, raw and ready to heed my call. It surged through my veins, burning away the fear. Burning it to ash.

I glanced down to see my entire body encased in fire.

"Kai, I'm leaving." I had to say goodbye.

"Calla?" His voice sounded worried. *"The guards just told me about Kylan. Where are you?"*

"I have to go. Please take care of Sabine and Thalia."

"Calla, you have to tell me what's going on. Where are you?"

My heart ached and stomach knotted, knowing I couldn't tell him. Because I knew if I did, he'd follow me.

"I can't tell you, but you'll find out soon." I swallowed hard, saying a prayer to the gods that they would save Kylan so he could tell Kai. *"Tell Markus not to worry. He knows I have a mind of my own. And thank you, Kai. For everything. Your family is amazing, and you've been a wonderful friend."*

"Why are you saying these things to me? Where are you, Calla?" Kai was yelling now, his voice panicked. *"Calla! Tell me where you are!"*

"Goodbye, Kai," I said, closing my eyes, which were burning with tears.

"Calla!" Kai pleaded. *"Please."*

I couldn't tell him. Sabine and Thalia were safe here in Aquaria with him. Markus would be too. I didn't want Markus anywhere near Roehl because I knew he would make Markus pay too great a price for defying him.

Kai was still yelling through our connection, begging me to tell him where I was.

But Roehl wanted me.

And me alone.

I held Trystan's amulet in the palm of my hand and made a fist. "Bring me luck," I whispered.

No more crowns. No more gowns. I wasn't going to meet Roehl as a princess.

I was going to rain down hell and fire.

Yes, I was going to save my father.

But I was ready to burn the entire world to save Trystan.

I pressed my palm against the pad on the wall, and the glass door slid open to my watery exit. Stepping out into the small dome I'd created, the door slid shut behind me, sealing my friends safely inside.

I inhaled a deep breath, and quickly said a prayer.

Then held up my palm.

And jumped.

NOTE FROM THE AUTHOR

Hi Friends!

I hope you're enjoying Calla's journey. I'm so sorry for leaving you on a cliffhanger but I am working hard to get you book three.

Thank you so much for reading my stories.

You don't know how much it means to me.

xoxo,

ACKNOWLEDGEMENTS

I have to give a shoutout to my girls.

My betas who keep me on my toes and tell it like it is.

Thank you for being the extra pairs of eyes that spot all the plot holes and errors, and all the crazy memes and threatening messages you send as you're reading.

Also, for all the amazing feedback you gave that brought this book to where it is.

I couldn't have done it without you.

Love you ladies.

Amber Garcia
Kimberly Belden
Jaci Chaney
Cheree Castellanos

Karla Mathis Bostic

Emily Piland

Ewelina Rutyna

And of course, to my husband Vance, who kept me well stocked with peppermints and caffeine.

I couldn't have done it without you, either.

You rock, babe.

ABOUT THE AUTHOR

Cameo was born in San Francisco, raised in Maui, Hawaii, and now resides with her husband in Las Vegas. She is a dreamer and caffeine addict who loves to laugh and loves to read to escape reality.

One of her greatest satisfactions is creating fantasy worlds filled with adventure and romance. It is the love and incredible support of her family and fans that keeps her going. One day she hopes to uncover a magic wardrobe and ride away on a unicorn. Until then . . . she'll keep writing!

For updates on Cameo, visit:

Website: http://cameorenae.com

Made in the USA
Middletown, DE
05 April 2023